THE Rocker's MUSE

THE Rocker's MUSE

NEW YORK TIMES BESTSELLING AUTHOR
PENELOPE WARD

Editing: Jessica Royer Ocken
Proofreading and Formatting: Elaine York, Allusion Publishing
www.allusionpublishing.com
Proofreading: Julia Griffis
Cover Design: Letitia Hasser, RBA Designs, rbadesigns.com

Chapter 1

EMILY

Maybe I should just leave.

In the middle of the California desert, this lone building seemed so out of place. Even so, the one-level, earth-toned structure almost blended in with the natural surroundings. This was definitely a place you went when you didn't want anyone to find you. There was a small lot behind the building with several high-priced cars parked, but literally nothing else in the vicinity for what seemed like miles.

I felt the pressure of knowing I was about to be kicked off the premises as I wandered around, attempting to peek into windows. Then out of nowhere, a door opened. A man wearing all black came out.

Trying my best to seem casual, I cleared my throat. "Oh, hello."

"Are you here for the interview?" he asked.

Interview? "Uh..." Clearing my throat, I straightened and lied, "Yes." *What are you doing, Emily?*

"Well, then you're late."

1

"I'm...so sorry. Traffic."

"Well, that's typical of L.A., isn't it?" He chuckled. "I instructed the agency to have you call me when you got here. I was just coming out for a smoke, but since you're here, we can get started." He turned back toward the door. "Come with me."

Letting out a shaky breath, I followed him inside. We passed a door that said *Control Room*, and I could hear the distant sound of drumming and cymbals coming from somewhere in the building.

"I'm sorry for having to drag you out to the desert for this," he said as I scurried behind him. "But I needed to be here while the band is recording their new album, and figured I'd kill two birds with one stone by having the candidates come out here. We don't have a ton of time to fill this position."

He wore a T-shirt with the name of the band on it: Delirious Jones. They were popular these days after some of their songs had gone viral. They'd been around for a while but had only seen real success in the past couple of years. Their music was definitely rock, but usually described as modern, post-grunge.

I continued my ruse. "The ride out here was no problem," I assured him. "Once I got off the highway, it was quite scenic."

The man brought me into a kitchen with a vending machine. He pulled out a chair for me, and then sat on the other side of the table. He held out his hand. "Doug Elias, by the way."

I took it. "Nice to meet you."

"Did you bring a resume?"

Uh. No, considering I'm not supposed to be interviewing for a job today. I rubbed my palms on my thighs. "No, I'm sorry."

"Let me check my email. Maybe the agency sent it over."

I cleared my throat. "Yeah. They said they would." Gazing out at the desert through the window behind him, I prayed I didn't get myself into deep shit.

"What's your name again?" he asked.

I could barely remember it. "Emily Applewood."

He scrolled through his phone and shook his head. "No. I don't see anything."

I straightened and lied again. "That was a misunderstanding, then. I would've brought it if I'd known you didn't already have it."

"No worries." He crossed his arms and settled into his seat. "Well, I guess start with your background. What experience do you have?" He opened the notes app on his phone.

"I'm...in between jobs at the moment. I recently graduated from Nevada State University with a degree in communications, but I haven't really figured out what I want to do with it yet."

All of that was true, at least.

For the next several minutes, I rambled about my experience interning for a TV station in Las Vegas. I didn't even know what the hell I was interviewing for. But at least I had hands-on experience with *something* I could talk about.

"What makes you want to work for the band?" he asked.

What have I gotten myself into? I had nothing. I'd barely heard their music—other than one song on You-Tube I didn't remember the name of.

When I didn't say anything, he tried again. "What's your favorite of their songs?"

Shit. My face felt hot. I couldn't name a single one. "Honestly, I'm not a fan," I confessed. "Unfortunately, I can't name one of their songs. I just thought this would be a good job opportunity for my own personal growth, a chance to experience something new." My face had to be red right now.

He grimaced. "How do you not know even *one* of their songs?"

"Just not my personal taste."

The man scratched his chin. "Well, usually my biggest issue is having to weed through the groupies for these types of positions, but this is sort of the opposite problem. Can't say I've ever encountered it before. Could be a point in your favor, but I'm not sure I should be hiring someone who isn't familiar with them *at all.*"

Scrambling for something, I shrugged. "Does anyone really *know* them? They just *think* they know them, right?"

"I suppose you have a point." He typed something into his phone. "Anyway, what questions do you have about the position?"

"I'd love to know more about the specific responsibilities of the job."

Like...please tell me what the job even is.

"Well, you'd basically be a lackey for *lack* of a better word. You'd be fetching whatever the band and crew needs,

4

assisting with loading and unloading stuff at each location. Anything and everything, really. This is definitely not for someone with a big ego. You can't be afraid to get your hands dirty. And it would be a lot of work and a true commitment since you'd be on the road for several months."

I gulped. "On the road?"

"Yes." He narrowed his eyes. "What did you think? You'd be going on tour with us. Didn't you read the job description?"

"Of course I did," I said, attempting to save my ass. "It just took a minute for 'on the road' to register. I was thinking they *flew* to events. *Road* implies...bus, yes?"

"We travel on tour buses for the North American leg. They'll be hitting Europe later this year, which will be mostly air travel on a private jet from city to city. But that wouldn't involve you. This position is for the US tour only."

"I see..." My mind wandered a bit as he spoke for several more minutes—I think about some of the logistics of the job.

After I gave him my phone number, he suddenly stood. "Anyway, while I like the fact that you don't seem starstruck, I have to be honest. You're giving me the impression that you might not be ready for this. But I'll hang onto your information, and depending on how the other interviews go, you may or may not be hearing from me."

"Okay," I said, standing as well. "Thank you for your time and consideration." *Why not ask?* "Would I have an opportunity to meet the band while I'm here?"

He shook his head immediately. "I'm sorry. That won't be possible. They're busy recording and can't be interrupted."

I swallowed. *Worth a shot.* "I understand. Thank you again for your time."

He nodded. "Safe drive home."

My heart pounded as I headed down the hall toward the exit. I decided to stop in the bathroom to splash some water on my face.

Inside the lavatory, I looked at myself in the mirror. My cheeks flamed as I processed the last twenty minutes and pondered whether to stick around here in the desert or just head back to Nevada. *What now?*

Then I caught movement behind me and jumped. Through the mirror, I spotted a man's bare ass at the urinal on the opposite wall.

Before I could do anything else, he turned, spotting me as he zipped his fly. "Whoa. What the fuck?"

Chapter 2

EMILY

I shook my head. "I'm sorry. I didn't realize I'd walked into the men's room."

He had a long beard and wore a hood. His blue eyes were piercing, and he seemed to have high cheekbones and a handsome face through all that facial hair.

He looked at me skeptically. "Why are you here?"

"I thought it was the ladies' room. I—"

"Yeah, I got that. I don't mean why you're in the bathroom. I meant the building. No one's allowed in this place."

"I was let in by...Dan Elias for a job interview."

"*Doug* Elias, you mean?"

"Uh, yeah."

"Interview for what?" The man turned to the sink and proceeded to wash his hands as I explained.

"To assist on Delirious Jones's upcoming tour. But I don't think that's going to be happening. Pretty sure I flubbed the interview, because I was unprepared." *As in, I had no idea I was applying for a job today.*

And why am I still standing here talking to this guy?

"I see."

"Do you work here?" I asked.

He stared at me like I had ten heads. "Yeah. I work with the band."

"Can you tell me what it's like working for them? Would I be getting myself into some deep shit by taking this position? I don't think I'm gonna get it, but in the event they call me back, I'd like to know if I'm getting in over my head."

"What do you consider deep shit?"

"I've just never been part of a scene like this."

He chuckled. "You mean like...sex, drugs, and rock and roll?"

"Right."

"Well..." He crossed his arms. "There are a few things I should warn you about."

"Okay."

"You should know, there are orgies almost every night."

My eyes widened. "There are?"

He nodded. "Then there's the BDSM bus."

"BDSM...bus?"

"Yup. Whatever you do, make sure they don't assign you to that. Unless you like your nipples clamped and your ass whipped on the regular."

I chewed my lip. "Um..."

"And do you do magic mushrooms?" He pointed at me. "If so, you'll fit right in." The smirk on his face finally gave him away.

"You're bullshitting me?"

"I am." He chuckled. "There are no orgies, and as much as a BDSM bus sounds kind of fun, it doesn't exist."

"What about the drugs?"

"There are always some drugs around. But the guys in the band don't do them. Just a little weed here and there. Why are you so concerned? No one would force you to do anything you didn't want to. If you see something you don't like, just look the other way. In any case, if you're working the tour, trust me, you'll be too busy to notice."

"I guess that's a good thing." I swallowed.

"Why did you apply for the position?" He cocked his head. "You seem apprehensive about it. You shouldn't do anything you don't really want to do."

That's a great question. "Things have been tough in my personal life the past few years, and I need a change."

That was my second truthful statement of the day.

"I'm sorry to hear that," he said. "You want to talk about it?"

"Not in a men's room with a complete stranger. That would be a bit weird."

He shrugged. "You weren't the one with your ass hanging out a second ago. Talk about weird."

"Well, that's one point in my corner today." I looked away as a few seconds of awkward silence passed. "Is the band nice?"

After a moment, he nodded. "They're okay. The lead singer, Tristan, has good days and bad. He's not as talented as people give him credit for. He mainly got lucky to be where he is. He's struggling with some stuff this year, actually, and it's showing."

Hmm... "That's too bad."

"What do you think of their music?" he asked.

I shrugged. "I've heard of them, of course. But I'm not a fan or anything. I don't really know their music."

He grinned. "Seriously? Why the hell would you want this job, then?"

"I sort of...fell into the opportunity. I'll go home tonight and google more of their stuff so I can be prepared if by some miracle I get the position."

"Well, if you want to check out their songs, look at their earlier stuff—from five or six years ago. Between you and me, the more recent material sucks in comparison, even if it's the most popular."

"I'll do that. Thanks for the tip."

"You're welcome."

I pointed over my shoulder at the door. "Well, I'd better get out of here and find the right bathroom."

"What's your name?" he asked.

"Emily."

Then the door opened, and another man entered. He looked between us. "What the fuck are you up to in here, Tristan? We're waiting on you."

Tristan?

He'd said he *worked* for the band.

Oh gosh.

I suppose being the *freaking lead singer* qualified as work. I hadn't recognized him. My cheeks burned all over again, and a rush of adrenaline shot through me.

Tristan winked at me. "Nice talking to you, Emily. Good luck with the job."

Both men left together, leaving me with my jaw hanging open.

That evening, I'd barely gotten back to my home in Henderson, Nevada, when my cell phone rang. It was a number I didn't recognize. "Hello?"

"Is this Emily?"

"Yes."

"This is Doug Elias from the interview today."

"Oh..." My heart skipped a beat. "Hi."

"I'd like to offer you the position, if you want it."

What? "Wow. Um...okay. I wasn't expecting that. You gave me the impression it was a long shot."

"Yeah, well, apparently, you ran into Tristan in the bathroom, I'm told? God knows how that happened. But am I right?"

"Yes." I licked my lips.

"He liked your...trepidation. Said it proved you cared. He also liked the fact that you didn't know who the hell he was. He said that was refreshing. So, even though I personally wouldn't have chosen you—no offense—it's his preference that I offer you the job."

Holy shit. My throat felt ready to close. I forced out the words. "I...don't know what to say."

"I can give you a day or so to think about it. Maybe take the time to go online and become familiar with the band? Just get back to me by tomorrow night. I can't wait much longer than that, since we leave in two weeks."

My eyes widened. "Two weeks? Wow."

"Yeah. Take that into consideration, too."

"How long is the tour? I never asked."

"It's four months. Again, this job only encompasses the North American leg. You wouldn't be working in Europe. So it's a temporary position."

Four months.

I can handle four months, right?

Am I actually considering this?

"Okay, well, I appreciate the opportunity. I promise to get back to you tomorrow with an answer."

"Call me back at this number."

"Will do."

I hung up in a daze. *What the hell did I get myself into?*

After taking a long, hot shower to clear my head, I was no closer to a decision.

I decided to call Leah. We'd grown up together in Shady Hills, Missouri, and she still lived there. Leah was the only person from home I still talked to regularly besides my mother.

Since no one knew the real reason I'd ventured out to the desert today, when I started my story I told Leah a white lie about hoping to meet the band after getting a tip about a hidden recording studio out there from our mutual friend Ryder.

"I can't believe you lied to that manager guy," she said. "But what's the harm if he believed you, right? I mean, you *have* been looking for a job. Maybe this is fate. Besides, it's only four months. Do you know how fast that will fly by?"

"Are you saying you think I should take it? Go on the road with them?"

"You have nothing better going on, right? Seriously, this is the best way to kill some time while you're trying to figure your life out."

"If *I* don't get killed first."

"You'll be fine. You'll be surrounded by people. Nothing is going to happen to you. Think of it as an adventure. Do you know how many people would die for this job?"

"I feel kind of guilty that I don't appreciate it more. It should go to someone who does."

"Like this girl, Stacia, I work with," Leah agreed. "She has a tattoo of Tristan's face on her side. But that's not even the crazy thing. When he was in Missouri once, she found out he'd gone to a local salon for a trim. A woman who worked there knew how much Stacia loved him, and she swept up his hair and gave it to her. Stacia keeps it in a jar! Let that sink in."

"Stacia sounds nuts."

Actually, I might've been the nuts one. I was considering taking a job I'd been offered because of a gigantic lie.

As Leah chatted away about the girl she worked with and her nutty jar of Tristan's hair, I decided to throw caution to the wind. It would either be the biggest mistake I'd ever made, or the opportunity of a lifetime. But deep down, I knew I had to take it—for the same reason I'd found myself in the desert earlier.

I interrupted her. "Leah?"

"Yeah?"

"I'm gonna do it. I'm gonna go on tour with Delirious Jones."

Chapter 3

EMILY

No one told me just how exhausting working on a music tour would be.

Don't get me wrong. It was the most exciting thing I'd ever done in my life. But there was no time to breathe. The action was so fast and constant that every day blended into the next. It had only been a week. Those seven days had gone by in a flash, yet it felt like I'd been here forever and had no concept of the world outside.

There were no set hours. I basically worked all day, with random breaks in between. And I was on call twenty-four hours a day for "emergencies"—like if someone needed something that catering or a delivery person couldn't fulfill. Having things delivered was a challenge when trying to protect the privacy of the band and keep their location secret. So that's where I came in, constantly running from place to place.

Delirious Jones had two buses. The main bus carried the band members and their management. The other band employees and I were on the second bus. Then there were additional buses for the crew employed by the tour company.

Sleeping in a bunk with no windows took some getting used to. At night, when we'd take off for the next city, I'd put my earbuds in and listen to a podcast or an audiobook until I eventually fell asleep. I'd drift in and out of slumber all night, often woken by the sound of the motor stopping. The mattress, though, was surprisingly comfortable.

Thus far, the band had done four back-to-back performances, starting in Boston and ending in New York. I hadn't had many interactions with Tristan or the other guys in the band. Tristan Daltrey sang and played guitar, and Delirious Jones also included drummer Atticus Marchetti and bass player Ronan Barber. Their keyboardist apparently quit a few months back due to some personal problems, so a musician named Melvin Finkle was filling in for the tour. They'd apparently gone through a couple of temporary keyboardists before him.

The real work began when we arrived at a new location. The tour manager rented a car in each city, and I had to be at the ready to go get whatever the band or crew needed. I'd even been asked to hem pants once. This position should've been advertised as "jack of all trades." I mean, maybe it had been. But I definitely hadn't gone to college for this kind of work. Still, I was a firm believer that opportunities landed in your lap for a reason. And while I hadn't shown up in the desert that day expecting to land a job, I knew this would be good life experience for me.

Tonight was the first night we'd be staying in a hotel because there were two shows in a row in Columbus, Ohio.

I'd be rooming with one of only two other women on the crew, Layla, the tour photographer. Our room was modest, with two double beds.

As we settled in, Layla bounced on her mattress. "How are you liking being on tour so far?"

"I've been too busy to really think, you know?" I chuckled. "I blink, and then we're in the next city."

"You said this is your first tour. How did you end up here?"

"I'm still trying to figure that out." *Not a lie.*

Layla smiled. "Anything surprise you so far?"

"I wasn't expecting this level of fandom, you know? I can't even exit the field where the buses are parked to get to the parking lot without running into crazy girls."

"Yeah. It *is* pretty crazy. They all want a piece of them. Especially Tristan."

Tristan.

He looked so different now from the way he'd looked in the bathroom that day. His long beard was gone, replaced by much lighter facial scruff along a strong jawline. The brown hair that had been piled under a hood was now usually let loose, wavy and thick, falling over his forehead to frame his face. Tristan was gorgeous—rugged and tattooed all over from his arms to his chest and even up to the base of his neck. It was no wonder women went crazy over him, and his broody, powerful voice was just as amazing as his looks.

"I haven't gotten to speak to Tristan much since the tour started," I told Layla. "Or any of the guys, for that matter. What's your take on them?"

She shrugged. "Everyone assumes Tristan is the wildest of the bunch. You know, that lead-singer energy. That's the persona he puts on for the public. But in reality, I find him to be the most private—not necessarily the wildest."

I kicked off my shoes and lay back on the bed. "Interesting."

"When you take photos of people, sometimes you look into their soul in a way others can't. And in Tristan I see someone who's preoccupied, lost a bit, even if I don't understand why."

"There's more than meets the eye, then?"

"Yeah." She nodded. "Atticus is probably the wildest of the crew. And his eyes tell me he's troubled about something."

"What about Ronan?" I asked.

"Ronan is the funniest. His eyes are mischievous."

Both Atticus and Ronan were just as good-looking as Tristan. The three of them were like a rock-god trifecta.

"How come you're never taking photos at night?" I asked.

"The guys have a rule: no photos after the show. Probably because they don't want the world to know what they're up to. My job is to mainly document the musical aspects of the tour, not necessarily the other shenanigans."

"The women, you mean?"

She nodded.

My phone rang, and I held a finger up to pause our conversation. "Hello?" I answered.

"We have a request for condoms," Stephen, the tour manager, said. "I need you to take the car and get some. Bring them to Atticus's room."

I ran my hand through my hair. "Uh...okay."

"You okay?" Layla asked as I hung up.

"Yeah." I slipped on my shoes and chuckled. "I have to get condoms."

"Oh shit." She laughed. "Well, at least they're being safe."

"No idea what happened to the box I bought the other night."

"I have some ideas." She rolled her eyes. "I think you need to get, like, ten boxes."

"No shit. I think I'll do that." I stopped at the door. "Do you need anything while I'm out?"

"I don't want to trouble you."

"I'll definitely need to buy something else to distract from the condoms, so what do you want?"

"Bring me back a Diet Coke?"

"You got it." I winked.

I took the rental car and drove down the main road to the nearest Walmart.

After grabbing some snacks for the hotel room, Layla's Diet Coke, and five boxes of condoms to keep stashed away so I didn't have to keep going out to buy them, I went to the self-checkout register.

When I returned to the hotel, I dropped most of the stuff in my room first, then went to the other side of our floor to deliver a box of condoms to Atticus. I knocked on his door, and when it opened, I handed him the box as fast as I could. He took it without uttering a word. It felt like a covert operation, almost the way I imagined a drug deal to be. I'd barely noticed the shadow of a woman behind him.

On the way back down the hall, I heard a struggle as I passed a little alcove off of the hallway that contained a vending machine. I realized it was a girl being practically mauled by a man whose advances she clearly didn't want. He'd cornered her, and her arms flailed as she tried to push him off.

"Get off her!" I shouted as I leaped in and used all of my might to shove him away.

"What the fuck?" he spewed.

"Can't you see she's telling you to stop?" I panted.

"Oh my God, thank you," the girl whispered to me.

"What the hell is going on?" A voice came from behind me.

I turned, surprised to find Tristan standing there. But maybe I shouldn't have been. This floor had been blocked off for the band and crew.

"This guy was pushing himself on her, when she was clearly resisting," I explained.

"Are you alright?" he asked her.

"Yeah," she muttered.

Tristan turned toward the guy. "What the fuck is wrong with you, man?"

The guy looked at the floor. "I had too much to drink," he slurred.

Tristan took his phone out. "Not an excuse..." He spoke to someone before grabbing the guy by the arm and dragging him down the hall.

Left alone, the girl and I chatted for a bit. She looked about my age, in her early twenties. She explained that she'd met the guy downstairs at the hotel bar, and he'd invited her to come back to his room. Turns out he worked for the tour company, which is how he'd had access to our private floor. After following him upstairs, she'd decided she'd had too much to drink and told him she'd changed her mind. But he'd followed her down the hall, then forced her into the vending area.

After thanking me one last time, she went back downstairs in the elevator.

I was going back to my room when I heard Tristan's voice behind me.

"Emily. Wait up," he said.

I turned, surprised he remembered my name. "What's up?"

"Are you okay?" he asked.

"Sure, why?"

"You didn't seem okay when I left, and I just want to make sure you're good."

"Yeah." I forced a deep breath in and out. "I am."

He cocked his head. "You sure?"

"That was a little triggering for me," I admitted. "He was basically attacking her."

He frowned. "Triggering...because something happened to you?"

"Nothing happened to *me*, but..." I trailed off as a rush of heat warmed my cheeks.

"Can I get you a water or something?" he asked.

My head pounded. Everything that had just happened hit me like a ton of bricks. "You wouldn't happen to have ibuprofen, would you?"

"Yeah, of course I do. Somewhere around here." He gestured down the hallway. "Come on. I'll get you some."

I followed Tristan into his room, which was a full-on suite. Depending on the offerings of the hotel, I was told sometimes Tristan stayed in a penthouse; other times, he ended up with the best room on whatever floor the band's management had booked. There was no doubt he got preferential treatment as the star of the band. I wondered if the other guys secretly hated him for it. Each of the band members at least got their own rooms, while the crew had to share. Thankfully, I really liked Layla.

I stayed close to the door as Tristan sifted through some stuff. There were a bunch of papers with handwritten words scattered on his bed. A leather jacket lay over a chair. He'd lit a candle on the bedside table—smelled like vanilla. This scene was a little different than I might've imagined in here. Much more Zen.

He zipped open a bag. "I guess you didn't realize wrangling drunk assholes was part of your job?"

"Thankfully, it's not, usually."

"I kind of feel guilty now," he said.

"Why?"

"Because you wouldn't be here if it weren't for me."

"What do you mean? The condoms weren't for you..."

He froze for a moment. "Condoms?"

"That's why I was over here. To drop off condoms for Atticus."

"What a jackass." He rolled his eyes. "Anyway, what I meant was, you were nervous about taking this job to begin with. I told you nothing bad happens on tour. And then you ran into that situation tonight. I was the one who told Doug to hire you."

I nodded as understanding dawned. "Thank you for putting in a good word, by the way. I wasn't sure you remembered me. We haven't spoken since the tour started."

"Don't take it personally. Tour's just been crazy. I've been meaning to say hello. Just under different circumstances."

I nodded. "Why *did* you tell them to hire me? You don't even know me."

"I liked that you didn't know who I was. That was the first time in a long time someone's looked me in the eyes and seen a normal person, not some musician they've made a million incorrect assumptions about."

"I saw more than your eyes in that bathroom, unfortunately."

"Yeah." He chuckled. "Sorry about that."

"Don't be. I'm just kidding. I was the idiot who walked into the men's room. Served me right." My eyes traced the ink at the base of his neck, just peeking out from his white T-shirt. "Anyway, I probably would've recognized you from the Internet if you hadn't had that long beard."

"That's exactly why I had the beard. I grow one every recording season when we don't have to perform. It helps me not be recognized in public. I hated having to cut it before the tour."

"Makes sense."

Tristan opened another drawer and finally pulled out the ibuprofen. "Ah! Got it." He handed me two pills and a bottle of water.

"Thanks." I cracked open the bottle and took a sip before downing the meds. "I'm surprised you're alone tonight."

"Why is that?"

"I've heard you guys have a different girl every night on hotel stops."

"Wow." He scratched his chin. "A different girl every night. I think my dick would fall off. Where are you getting your information?"

"I don't disclose my sources."

He shrugged. "Some nights I just want to be alone. I do have to write music at some point, rest my voice, get sleep."

I nodded. Now the papers scattered over his bed made sense. "You write a lot on the road?"

"I write whenever inspiration strikes, but being on the road is actually when I'm most creative. Late at night on the bus, when everything goes quiet? That's what I like best about touring. That's my favorite time to write."

"That's my favorite time of the day lately, too. There's something so relaxing about staring out at the moving darkness."

He cocked his head. "What do you do?"

"On the bus? Read or listen to podcasts..."

"Sorry, I meant in general. What do you do when you're not held captive by a tour for four months?"

"Not much of anything, actually. I'm trying to find my place in the world at the moment. I just graduated from Nevada State University."

"How old are you?" he asked.

"Twenty-two." I'd googled his age but asked anyway. "How old are you?"

"Almost thirty-eight. Old as fuck, right?"

"You don't look thirty-eight. I would've guessed, like, thirty."

"What did you study at Nevada State? Blowing smoke up people's asses?" He winked.

I laughed. "It's true. You look younger. But I majored in communications."

"Nice."

I shrugged. "Well, it's been challenging finding a job with such a broad degree."

"You're in a good position," he assured me. "I envy you."

"Envy *me*?" I drew my brows in. "Why?"

"You're a blank slate with your whole life ahead of you. Some days I wish I could go back and start over."

"Why would you want to do that? You're a huge star. If you did even one thing differently, you might not be where you are today."

"Where I am today isn't all it's chalked up to be." He sighed. "Don't get me wrong—I'm very grateful for it all. But there's always a price to pay for fame. Like giving up your privacy."

"Yeah. I'm seeing that. You guys can't go anywhere without being mobbed."

"You clearly don't give a shit who I am, though. I need that sometimes." He smiled. "Your innocence is refreshing, Emily."

Innocence? "I may be young. But I'm *not* innocent." I scoffed.

"I don't believe you. I can see it in your eyes. You're innocent as hell."

"You're not a good reader of people, then."

Tristan crossed his arms. "Tell me the worst thing you've done, and I'll believe you."

No one had ever asked me such a direct question before. And something about looking into this man's eyes made me want to answer honestly.

So I did. "I killed someone."

Chapter 4

TRISTAN

I blinked. "You...killed someone."

She muttered something and shook her head, looking down at her feet. "I can't believe I told you that."

"Well, I asked, and you certainly delivered. But I *do* think it warrants an explanation. That's not the kind of thing you blurt out without further details, you know?"

She finally looked up at me. "I killed my mother's boyfriend—accidentally. It was in self-defense. Or rather, in defense of my mother."

Shit. I swallowed. "What happened? I mean, leading up to it?"

"I'd come home early from school. Walked into the house and found him choking her. She was gasping for air. I pleaded with him to let her go, and he wouldn't. I was sure he was going to kill her." She took a deep breath. "I grabbed a bat from my brother's bedroom and knocked him over the head with it. I didn't mean to kill him. But apparently, I hit some spot on the back of his head..." Her words trailed off.

"When did this happen?" I asked softly.

"My senior year in high school. So a little over four years ago."

"Holy fucking shit. That's a lot to go through." I shook my head. "Are you okay? I mean, mentally?"

"Not really." She looked down at her feet again. "I still feel guilty about it. And I have a savior complex sometimes. Any chance I get to help someone, I take it. You witnessed a bit of it tonight. I think I feel like I have to do good deeds to make up for the horrible thing I did." She closed her eyes briefly. "Henry, my mother's boyfriend, was an asshole. But he had kids. They no longer have a father. Even if he was a terrible person, I took him away from them. They didn't deserve that."

"No, but you didn't deserve to be put in that position. Sounds like it was either him or your mom. You shouldn't feel guilty. You saved her life. You did what anyone would do."

Her eyes lifted to meet mine. "Is that true? *Anyone* would've grabbed a bat and bashed him over the head with it?" Her green eyes flashed.

"Probably not anyone. That took balls." I exhaled. "I'm sorry you have to live with the guilt. And I can understand why you were so shaken by what happened out there tonight."

"It doesn't take much to trigger me."

"I'm sorry," I said.

"You didn't do anything."

"Like I said, I brought you here." I wished I could wrap this girl in my arms right now, but that would seem creepy. "Do you need help?" I asked instead. "Like, do you see a therapist? You should talk to someone if you're still struggling with everything."

"Well..." She sighed. "I haven't wanted to rehash it. But perhaps I need to force myself at some point."

"The band has a shrink, believe it or not. She does remote therapy. Doug got the idea a while ago when Atticus went off the deep end, and he thought we were going to break up. He told us we should all get our heads checked and then hired her—Dr. Jensen. I'm sure she can fit you in."

"I'm not part of the band."

"Everyone on this tour is part of the band. I'll make sure you get in with her, if you want to. And I'll make sure it's paid for if the insurance they gave you doesn't cover it."

"That's nice of you, but you don't owe me anything."

I ignored her comment. "What's your last name?"

"Applewood."

"I'll mention you to her, if you want. I can have her office reach out."

"That's very gracious of you. I'll let you know, okay?"

"You shouldn't have to keep it all inside. That's the worst thing we can do to ourselves. Suffer in silence." *I should know*. Though my problems as of late were *nothing* compared to what this poor girl had been through.

"Do you do that?" she asked. "Suffer in silence?"

It was like she'd read my mind. "My issues aren't like yours, but yeah, I do keep things inside. I'm definitely struggling with my own shit lately." I shrugged. "Isn't everyone, though?"

Emily nodded. "I'm sorry."

I could tell she meant it. Emily Applewood seemed like an empathetic person. A strong person. Tough life experiences only make people stronger. She was young, but some things age you fast.

I got lost in her eyes for a moment. She was beautiful—not in the fake way most of the women I'd been around recently were. But in a natural way. Her long brown hair was wavy and had a reddish tint when it caught the light. She had a small gap between her two front teeth that I found oddly appealing, sexy even, especially framed by full lips that were cherry red without lipstick. Not an ounce of makeup on her fresh face, yet she was perfect. Perfect on the outside, and perfectly imperfect on the inside. She wasn't trying to impress me. She wasn't trying to be anyone other than who she was. Emily had gotten a bum deal for trying to do the right thing. And that made me angry. Life wasn't fair.

"Anyway, I'd appreciate you not telling anyone about this," she said, fiddling with her hands. "I don't need people here knowing what I just told you."

I shook my head. "I would never, Emily." I took a step toward her. "*Never*. I hope you know that."

"Anyway…" She looked back toward the hotel room door. "I'd better go."

Fuck. I didn't want her to leave. I wanted her to stay and talk to me, tell me what had led her mother to date a man so abusive he'd almost killed her. Where was Emily's father? Where was she from? I was really curious about her—maybe because being in her presence was the first time I'd felt a normal human connection in as long as I could remember. But there was absolutely no good reason to ask a twenty-two-year-old to stay and chat in your room. She'd have every right to assume my intentions were questionable, since my reputation unfortunately preceded me.

"Yeah, okay," I said. "Have a good night. Thanks for chatting with me."

"Thank you for the ibuprofen." She smiled before heading out.

After she left, I stared at the door, wishing she'd forgotten something, wishing she'd come back. Even if that was just a fantasy.

I eventually settled in my bed, my failed attempts at writing music surrounding me. But I couldn't shake Emily from my mind. What she'd done to protect her mom...

I told myself to mind my fucking business, but the urge became too great. I grabbed my laptop and searched *Emily Applewood*.

Sure enough, a story popped up from a news station in St. Louis, Missouri.

A Shady Hills man is dead after being struck with a baseball bat, allegedly by his girlfriend's eighteen-year-old daughter. According to police, Emily Applewood arrived home Wednesday night to find fifty-four-year-old Henry Acadia choking his girlfriend, Terry Applewood. According to Applewood's attorney, Frank Simmons, Applewood pleaded with Acadia to let her mother go. When the deceased continued to attack the elder Applewood, her daughter reportedly used her brother's baseball bat to hit Acadia from behind. According to the medical examiner, Acadia suffered an injury to the oc-cipital-atlas region, which caused him to lose consciousness almost immediately. The injury was fatal. Given Acadia's documented history of domestic violence, police have not brought charges against Applewood and are ruling the incident as accidental.

That was it.

Damn.

A life-changing trauma, reduced to a simple para-graph. In the days after it happened, the news media likely moved on to something else, but for Emily, the horror of that night would continue forever, haunting her. Life was so damn unfair.

I should've stopped there, but I scrolled through the other hits on Emily's name, including her social media pages.

There was nothing recent. Her newest post was from about a year ago. She was smiling in the photo, her eyes holding a certain light that seemed lost now. A guy had his arm around her. I couldn't make out his face because he was wearing a hood and kissing her cheek. My chest tightened as I looked at the caption: *I'll miss you forever.*

Chapter 5

EMILY

A week later, we had our biggest, sold-out show yet in Detroit.

I'd learned that one of my favorite parts of the tour were the moments I could stand backstage and enjoy the performance for a bit, ignoring the controlled chaos around me. The moment the lights dimmed in a packed venue, I always got chills. Then came the roar of the crowd as the band emerged, followed by more hysteria as Tristan belted out the first notes. And the audience would go from excited to captivated as the show got underway. Hands waving, bodies swaying, the crowd joined in singing whenever Tristan pointed the mic their way.

After hearing the band's music over and over, I could understand why so many people loved them. I often had the songs stuck in my head for the rest of the night. And it wasn't just Tristan who shined. The chemistry between him, Atticus, and Ronan was palpable. They'd look at each other and smile in the middle of a performance, as if sharing silent messages only they understood.

For some reason, tonight Tristan had sounded a bit different to me, like the notes weren't coming as smoothly as he sang. It wasn't obvious, and at first I'd thought it was my imagination. But the more I paid attention, the more I noticed it.

I was back from the arena now and on the bus, using the bathroom after a long day. We'd have a few more hours here before we hit the road for the next city. Our departure time had been delayed so the band could explore downtown Detroit. But none of that for me. As I washed my face, I continued to ruminate. I still couldn't believe I'd told Tristan about my past the other night. What was I thinking? His eyes had made me want to open up. They were mysterious yet somehow familiar, comforting, and nonjudgmental.

My plans to get into my pajamas were thwarted by a text from Stephen. *Tristan needs lozenges.* Apparently, the other members of the band had gone downtown, with security in tow, but Tristan had stayed behind. Besides that night a week ago when we'd talked in his hotel room, I'd only encountered Tristan in passing. I'd be lying if I said I wasn't hoping for another moment alone with him. Even if that was crazy.

Often, late at night, I'd watch from across the lot as various girls disappeared into the band's bus. God knew what was happening in there. I could only imagine how many women Tristan and the guys had been with since they'd become famous. Even if he denied having a different girl with him every night, it must've been a hell of a lot of ladies.

I put my jacket on and used the rental car to go to the drugstore for Tristan's lozenges. Stephen hadn't specified what kind to get, so I grabbed a couple of different brands.

After returning, I walked over to the band's bus and entered, expecting at least a few people in the main cabin. But it seemed virtually empty.

"Hello?" I called.

"Hey..." A low, gravelly voice came from the back of the bus.

Tristan emerged from the back bedroom, looking painfully sexy in ripped jeans and a T-shirt that seemed practically painted on his muscular chest.

Clearing my throat, I looked around. "Everybody's out, huh?"

"Up to no good somewhere probably, yeah..." He walked down the aisle toward me, and my heart beat a bit faster with each step.

I held out the small brown paper bag. "I got your lozenges."

"Thank you." He took them, the brush of his hand sending a chill down my spine.

I inhaled his spicy scent as I stared at his strong, tattooed arms. The combination was magnificent. But as much as I'd wished for alone time with him, I had no reason to stay. "Well...have a good night." I turned back toward the front of the bus.

"Emily, wait."

I looked back. "Yeah?"

"Do you have somewhere to be right now?"

"Not really. I was just going back to my bus."

"You're off the clock, right?"

"Technically."

"Have you eaten tonight?"

"I had a slice of pizza."

"That's not enough. Feel like taking a ride? I hate going out alone, but I could use a change of scenery."

"Won't people mob you if we go out? The other guys took most of security with them."

"I know a place open this late where no one will bother us. Really good food, too, and not far from here."

It was a no-brainer. I couldn't pass this up. "Yeah. Sure. Okay."

"Cool. Let me just grab a hoodie."

Tristan pulled the black hood over his head as we ran across the parking lot, past security to the rental car. I drove while Tristan sat in the passenger seat, texting someone. He then punched an address into the GPS on his phone and directed me as I drove us there.

After a few minutes we arrived at a Middle Eastern restaurant with a house attached. The sign out front read *Abdul's*.

"We're eating here?" I parked in the lot.

"Abdul, the owner, is a friend of mine," Tristan explained. "Whenever I'm in Detroit, I try to hit this place up. They stay open late. I wasn't going to come this time, but you reminded me I was hungry."

"I remind you of falafel?" I laughed.

"You're more like kibbeh." He winked.

"What?"

He chuckled. "Come on," he said as he exited the car.

I followed him to the door of the house. A dark-haired man with a moustache let us in. He and Tristan chatted for a few minutes about the band, and then the man clapped him on the back.

"Make yourself at home," he told us, gesturing toward the living room. "I'll have someone bring you a platter."

"Thanks, my guy." Tristan patted him on the shoulder.

I looked around. The house smelled like the spices coming from the restaurant, and there were religious statues all around the room—mostly variations of Mary. "I feel like I'm being judged right now with all these Holy Marys staring at me."

Tristan nodded. "Abdul's mother was very religious. She passed away a few years back, but he hasn't had the heart to move any of her statues."

"Well, that's kind of sweet."

"You'll also notice a stash of gay porn DVDs in the corner. Goes well with everything else, doesn't it?"

"Well, that's interesting."

"Life's about balance, Emily." Tristan laughed.

God, he was gorgeous. The way pieces of his silky hair fell over his forehead. His hair was amazing. "No wonder that nutty girl kept it in a jar," I muttered.

"Hmm?" he asked.

Guess I said that aloud. I shook my head. "Nothing."

"Are you not religious?" Tristan asked.

"Why do you ask?"

"You said the statues make you uncomfortable."

"Yeah. I don't really like talking about religion."

He wriggled his brows. "We could talk about porn, if you prefer."

Religion it is. I rolled my eyes. "Religion scares me sometimes. Anything that dictates how you're supposed to act, threatening punishment..." I shivered. "Maybe it's because I feel I *deserve* punishment."

"Whoa." His expression darkened. "Only truly bad people deserve punishment, Emily, not those who get caught up in shit. Besides, we're all imperfect in our own ways."

"Some of us more than others..." I murmured.

"I don't think we were put on this Earth to be perfect. I think we were designed to fuck up, learn lessons, and take those lessons back to wherever we came from."

"And where exactly did we come from, Tristan?"

"Not sure what it's called. But I think we all came from the same place. There has to be a purpose to this craziness."

"So you think there's a larger meaning to this thing we call life..."

Tristan grinned. "Something about you makes me want to admit things I'd never say to other people."

"Like what?"

"One of my interests is studying near-death experiences."

"Really? When the heck do you have the time for that?"

"There's always time for Internet rabbit holes, Emily." He winked. "And, there are a lot of commonalities among people's accounts of what happens when you almost die. Too many similarities, if you ask me, for it to be a coincidence." He paused. "And now you're wishing we'd watched porn instead of having this philosophical discussion at one in the morning, aren't you?"

"No." I laughed. "Tell me what you mean, though. What do people say happens when they have a near-death experience?"

"Well, those who claim to have crossed over talk about seeing loved ones who've passed who guide them to the other side. They also realize that their soul has lived many lifetimes, sometimes needing to go back to Earth to learn lessons they failed to grasp in a previous life. Sometimes they're given a choice of whether to stay there or come back." He shrugged. "These are all anecdotes, of course, and we can't prove anything. But it's pretty fascinating to listen to their stories."

I nodded. "It is strange how we go through life not questioning these kinds of things—as if our purpose is to eat bagels and scroll on our phones all day. It does make sense that there's more to it than that."

"Yup." Tristan plopped down on the couch and kicked his feet up. "God, this feels good. Hear that?"

"I don't hear anything," I admitted.

"Exactly. It's heaven—and not because of the saints surrounding us. It's just cool to be away from the tour for a while."

A woman entered with a massive platter of food: hummus, pita, falafel, skewers of chicken, piles of black and green olives. She placed it on the coffee table, along with two waters and two cans of Coke. I only now realized how damn parched I was.

"Thank you," I said as she walked away. My stomach growled. The food smelled so good.

Tristan and I ate in comfortable silence as we sat together on the floor of Abdul's living room. Half an hour later, we'd made a pretty good dent in the food when he rolled his napkin up and threw it aside.

"That was fucking tasty. Hits the spot every time."

"Best Middle Eastern food I've ever had," I told him. "And it does feel good to just rest and eat in quiet. Tours are grueling—and I'm not even the one performing."

"You and the rest of the crew work your asses off just as much as I do—probably more."

Now that we were on the subject of the tour, I had to ask. "Was everything okay with you tonight?"

His smile faded. "Why do you ask?"

I chewed my bottom lip. "I got to watch some of the performance from backstage, and you seemed...I don't know...a little hoarse at times, maybe?"

Tristan stared at me for the longest time.

"What?" I finally asked.

He shook his head. "Nothing. I'm just—you're right. No one else has called me on it. I want to say I'm surprised you noticed, but I'm not." He sighed. "Guess I didn't do a good job hiding it after all. Did I sound that bad?"

While I hoped not to insult him, I wanted to be honest. "I've listened to enough of you live to know what you sound like at your best," I admitted. "You sounded different to me tonight, like you might've been struggling a little. But, Tristan, you're an amazing singer no matter what."

He exhaled. "Thanks for not bullshitting me. I'm surrounded by people who only care that I show up so they keep making money. None of them would ever bring this to my attention."

"Is there something going on with your voice?"

"There is." He nodded. "But I haven't told anyone."

Feeling dread in the pit of my stomach, I swallowed. "What is it?"

"I was diagnosed with polyps on my vocal cords. It's been challenging to hit the notes I used to. I've known about them for a while, but they seem to have caught up with me all of a sudden."

My heart sank. "Is there a treatment?"

"There is, but it's surgery. That totally freaks me out. I've read there's a risk of permanent damage. Can you imagine? And then a lot of times, the polyps just come back anyway. They say the best first step is to rest the voice, which I'm hoping to do once this tour season is over. Surgery is a last resort. I've just been struggling through it. And apparently, not hiding it very well." He shut his eyes momentarily. "It's scary when you've worked your whole life for something, and it could all be taken away. Let that be a lesson, Emily. Don't base your entire self-worth on something that could be fleeting."

"What would you do if you weren't a musician?" I asked.

"I don't know." He looked away. "The thought of that terrifies me. I don't have a plan B. I never did."

"But you don't have to work another day in your life, and you'd be okay."

He shook his head. "It's not about that. Without music, I wouldn't have a purpose. I'd have money, but money means shit if you don't have a reason to live."

Now I felt stupid. Financial security wasn't everything. As poor as I was, I understood that.

"This situation has made me realize I threw all my eggs into one basket," he continued. "And that was probably a mistake."

"You might not be where you are if you hadn't, though. So, it's a catch-twenty-two."

"That's true." He nodded.

I wracked my brain for something that might make him feel better. "So, if your near-death-experience theory is true, and there's some purpose in everything we go through, is there a lesson you think you were put here to learn? Maybe this challenge with your voice is part of it."

"Interesting." Tristan scratched his chin. "Maybe I need to learn to accept failure to truly understand that success doesn't define a person. Or maybe I need to figure out how to be at peace without success—just be at peace with myself and nothing else. Learn to love myself, I guess. There's no way to be sure what the hell it all means." He looked at me pointedly. "What happened with your mom's boyfriend could have a purpose, too, even if it's hard to see."

"Or maybe I was a really bad person in another life, and that was my punishment," I countered.

"Maybe what happened was *his* punishment. But your lesson. And maybe the lesson is that you need to learn to forgive yourself."

"Very convenient story you've crafted there." I sighed. "If life is a set of challenges, can I unsubscribe from the game?"

He smiled. "Not an option, beautiful. That's why we have to enjoy ourselves along the way. We have to make life about more than the uncontrollable shit that gets thrown at us. Happiness isn't something that just happens. It's a choice, the way we react to life. Each person's happiness is their own responsibility."

I tilted my head. "That sounds a little too simple. I choose to be happy, therefore I am?"

"Happiness is more the result of choosing not to engage in the bullshit that brings us down, the negative self-talk, the worry and fear. When you move toward things more likely to bring you joy, that's where choice comes in. And happiness is the result. At least in my experience." He took a sip of water. "Look, I'm not perfect at it. But I'll give you an example of one thing I did right. Tonight, I was feeling like shit. So I told the guys I didn't want to go with them to downtown Detroit. I almost made the mistake of staying alone and wallowing over my shitty performance. But when you came onto the bus, I took the opportunity to ask you to hang out with me. Now I'm happy instead of miserable. That was the result of my choice."

I smiled.

He smiled back.

His gaze was electrifying, and I found myself wanting things from him in a way I had no right to. This man made me feel special. He made me feel *everything*. That was the last thing I'd expected.

"Thank you for sharing your secret with me," I finally said. "I'll pray that the situation gets better..."

"You could pray in this room and maybe one of these statues would listen." He chuckled. "Anyway, since you've been so honest and told me your biggest secret, I figured I owed you one."

I nodded, even as my heart lurched. *If only that was my biggest secret.*

Chapter 6

TRISTAN

Another night, another crappy performance.

No one besides Emily had mentioned anything about my voice being off. Did they not want to upset me, or did they truly not notice? Maybe they just didn't want me to stop. Tonight's concert in Minnesota had been one of my worst shows in a while. And all I wanted to do now was close my door and shut out the world. But that was hard to do on this bus with the scene playing out just beyond my bedroom.

Women laughing. The smell of weed and alcohol seeping through the crack under my door. It wasn't anything out of the ordinary. If anything, this was the norm. I'd been known to party with the best of them. But lately, I needed an escape from it.

Before I could think about that further, the door to my bedroom opened. I could've sworn I'd locked it, yet in walked two women, a blonde and a redhead. They could've been twins aside from the difference in hair color.

I squinted to get a better look at them. They *were* fucking twins. They had the same face.

Without so much as an introduction, they crawled onto my bed. I'd been lying against the headboard and straightened to sit up.

In the not-so-distant past, I might've reached over to the condom drawer and let them do whatever they pleased. But I'd had a shitty show, and I wasn't in the mood to play along tonight. It took a lot to get my dick hard when I was upset about something.

The blonde leaned over and started unzipping my pants. I placed my hand over her wrist. The old Tristan would never have turned down a blow job from a gorgeous woman, no matter my mood. But tonight? I couldn't.

"Thanks, but no thanks. I'd like to be alone right now."

"But he told me you asked for us specifically," the blonde said.

"Who's he?"

"Atticus."

I shook my head. That guy was so full of shit. He was pawning these two chicks off on me because he'd probably miscalculated the number of women he told our tour manager to let on the bus.

"Well, he lied. I'm sorry. Thanks, but no thanks."

As quickly as they'd entered my room, they left. Relief washed over me. I sat at the edge of my bed with my head in my hands. The sounds from beyond the door told me my bandmates certainly hadn't turned anyone down tonight.

Feeling stifled, I decided I needed some air. We were set to take off for the next city in a couple of hours, so I couldn't go very far. Grabbing my black hoodie, I left my room and waded through the illicit acts in the main cabin before exiting the bus.

The cold air against my face was a welcome sensation at first, but then I realized I was freezing my ass off. When had it gotten so cold? And damn, I wanted a cigarette right now. That would warm me up. But alas, I wouldn't be smoking tonight; I'd quit when my voice started going to shit. I didn't need the effects of smoking on top of everything else, even if I wasn't always known for my great judgment. At least I'd gotten that one right.

I looked over to the bus parked across from ours. I'd bet it was mighty warm in there. I'd also bet there were no groupies to run away from. That seemed like the perfect escape right now. Didn't it?

I walked across the lot, unsure where I was going with this. Or, did I know precisely why I was headed this way? I wanted to see Emily and ask her if I'd sounded worse to her tonight. That might've just been an excuse, though. I had her number; I could've texted.

It had been a week since the jaunt she and I took in Detroit. I hadn't spoken to her at all since then, which was quite deliberate. Nothing good could come from her spending time with me, even if I'd had fun the last time we hung out. I'd probably divulged too much that night, but she'd made me feel comfortable.

When I stepped onto the bus, every head turned in my direction.

"What are you doing in here?" Veronica, our PR manager, asked.

"I can't come say hello? I haven't thanked you all lately for how hard you've been working."

Veronica narrowed her eyes. "You've never once stepped onto our bus, Tristan..."

"Well, then it's about time I did."

I looked over to the back corner. Emily was reading a book, but she closed it when she spotted me.

"Excuse me," I said as I moved toward the rear to talk to her.

Guess I hadn't wasted much time getting to why I was really here. I could sense everyone's eyes on me as I took a seat next to Emily.

"What are you doing here?" she asked, seeming genuinely surprised.

Fuck it. "Feel like taking a ride with me? Getting a bite to eat before we have to leave Minnesota?"

"It's late, and we're taking off soon. So no."

I checked the time on my phone. "We have over an hour."

"I don't feel like going out. It's cold."

Rejection wasn't something I was used to, but the fact that she didn't jump made me like her even more. *Fuck.* I was screwed. "You're right. It's cold as balls out there. I don't blame you."

"You could've asked one of those groupies who got on your bus tonight to go out with you," she said, her tone almost bitter.

Ah. "You noticed them, huh?"

"Yeah. I notice them almost every night."

Maybe she was being standoffish because she was annoyed with the groupie situation, rather than general ambivalence about seeing me. That gave me a little hope, even if I shouldn't have cared.

"What do you think goes on in there with them?" I asked.

She shook her head. "I don't want to know."

"It's not always what you think."

"Oh, really?" She raised a brow. "What...are you playing Monopoly with them? You expect me to believe there's anything going on in that bus besides the obvious—"

"That's part of the reason I came over here. I wasn't into it and needed to escape."

She tilted her head. "You weren't into tonight's particular selection of girls, you mean?"

"No. Megan Fox could've walked in, but I wasn't in the mood tonight."

"Even *I* wouldn't turn down Megan Fox." She finally cracked a smile.

I chuckled, loving her comeback. And loving the visual of Megan Fox and Emily that flashed through my mind.

"Good to know you swing both ways." I winked.

"Well, I don't typically. But you know...there are always exceptions." She picked some lint off her shirt. "So you left the groupies on the bus to come see me? Why?"

"I'm not into you like that," I assured her. "I just wanted to say hello."

"I'm no Megan Fox. I get it." She rolled her eyes. "Thanks for the compliment."

I felt myself sweating. Why the fuck had I said that? I cleared my throat and attempted damage control. "I meant I don't have ulterior motives." I looked around the bus, noticing a few eyes still on me from up front. "It's actually way better over here. Calmer. You think they'd let me switch buses permanently?" I teased.

"I wouldn't want you here," she said.

My eyes widened. "Why not?"

"You attract too much attention."

"Everyone's but yours. You didn't even know who I was when you met me. Which I loved, by the way."

"That's because you looked like a grizzly bear with that beard."

I cackled. "See? This is why I miss you, Emily. You make me laugh."

"I'm surprised you feel that way. You haven't said a word to me in a week."

"That's also a reason I'm here. I wanted to apologize. I should've at least come to say hello. Especially after we hung out in Detroit. That was fun."

"Well, I know you've been busy. The tour has been nonstop. And then there's your *extracurricular* activities."

"Do I need to clarify again that I don't always partake in the groupies?"

She shrugged. "Honestly, I can't blame you if you do. Not sure I would be any different in your shoes."

"The truth is, this lifestyle gets pretty old sometimes. My bandmates may not share that opinion, but most nights I'd rather be eating a burger alone in a McDonald's that's about to close than fucking some groupie who's only interested in me because of my money and fame. That's like my dream—to just sit alone in McDonald's and not be bothered."

She chuckled. "I find that hard to believe, but okay..."

"Why? Anything that comes easy gets old. It's the chase that's exhilarating. You know what's *really* exhilarating? Wanting something you can't have. *That's* exhilarating."

"There's not much you can't have, Tristan Daltrey."

"Not true."

"Name one thing," Emily challenged.

You. Licking a line over that little gap between your teeth.

"A normal life," I opted to say.

"You could have that. You could quit tomorrow. Get a job at a local hardware store somewhere in Kansas. Eat your burger alone at the nearest McDonald's at closing time."

"When you've invested so much of your life in trying to achieve something, once you finally get it, it's very hard to throw it away, even if you occasionally wish you could. I also feel like I owe it to my bandmates not to flake on them. But some days, it's definitely tempting to walk away." I sighed. "Anyway, I don't feel like walking away so much when I'm talking to you. You're the most normal person I've come across in a while."

"Mundane, you mean?"

"Far from it."

"Well, I don't like hamburgers, so I wouldn't be able to join you in that depressing McDonald's that's about to close."

I laughed. "You make me smile, Emily, from the moment I met you. You're real." I lowered my voice. "And you're one of the few people who knows what's going on with me lately. You know...with my voice. So it feels good to be around someone I can be honest with. That's all."

"How *is* your voice?" she whispered.

"I wanted to ask what you thought after tonight's show. Did you notice it getting better or worse?"

"I'm not a doctor."

"I know. But you have ears." *Cute ones that stick out when you wear your hair back in a ponytail.*

"You want the truth, I assume."

Feeling a knot in my stomach, I nodded. "Yes, please."

"You were sounding better to me after Detroit. But tonight you sounded a little worse again."

That felt like a gut punch, even if I knew it was true. *Fuck.* If she noticed, how many other people did, too? I nodded. "That's what I was worried about."

"It hurts me to have to admit that to you."

"Don't be hurt. It's good for me to know these things. I appreciate your honesty, Emily. More than you know."

"Are you going to see a doctor soon or..."

"I have an appointment when the tour stops in L.A. No one knows, though."

"No one else has said anything to you?"

"No. Which is really fucking weird, if you ask me."

She nodded. "I'm sorry you're going through this."

"It's not the end of the world."

"Yeah. But it's scary, I'm sure."

I stared into her green eyes for a moment, reluctant to leave even if the stares from the people up front told me I'd overstayed my welcome. "Are you sure you don't want to grab a bite to eat?" I picked up one of her hair scrunchies and began winding it around my hands as I waited for her response. There was something oddly calming about the mindless motion.

"We have even less time now than we did before. Plus, it's still warm and toasty on this bus, and I'm not moving."

"You're no fun," I teased.

"I'm not that hungry anyway. Layla got chicken fingers earlier, and I had some. I think I'm good for the night."

"Okay then." I pouted.

She turned to look out the window, and I admired her beautiful profile. I would've given anything to know what she was really thinking.

I kept twisting the scrunchie. "Are you happy, Emily?"

"On the tour, you mean?"

"In general, but sure, yeah, on the tour, too..."

"In general? I'm working on it. On the tour? Actually, yes. It's been an amazing distraction from reality. I can't say I'll be any clearer on what I want to do with my life when it ends, but it's a good experience. And it will look good on the resume, too." She yawned. "The one thing I've been struggling with is sleep, though."

"You're having trouble sleeping on the bus?"

"Yeah. It's psychological, I think."

"How so?"

"I have this fear that we're going to get into an accident. So I can't relax. I feel like I need to be on alert."

"You'd rather be awake and alert if the bus crashes? Wouldn't it be better to be asleep and not know what hit you?"

"No. I'd die of a heart attack from the shock of waking up that way. If I could see it coming first, I'd be better able to handle it."

I chuckled. "But you eventually fall asleep, right?"

"Gradually, my tiredness wins out, yeah."

"If I were on this bus, I'd sing you a lullaby or tell you a bedtime story."

"That would be awesome, but you should probably rest your voice." She smiled. "Why don't you go get something to eat if you're hungry?"

Because I'm not really that hungry. I just wanted an excuse to see you. "Yeah, maybe. I'm sure catering has something for me to eat back on the bus."

She arched a brow. "Not a woman, I presume?"

Emily's innuendo gave me a visual of eating *her* that I had no business entertaining, even in my imagination. I cleared my throat. "Not a woman, no."

"Not tonight at least." She winked.

If she only knew how uninterested I was in anyone else right now.

I glanced up to find Veronica shooting daggers at me. "Why is she looking at me like that?"

"Because she's the den mother of the crew, and she probably doesn't trust you."

She shouldn't.

I guess I wasn't as nonchalant as I'd hoped. "Does this seem suspicious? Me talking to you?"

"A little," she answered.

"I don't care what they think, if you don't."

"I do like talking to you," she said.

That sent a jolt of excitement through me. "I like talking to you, too, Emily." I smiled. "A lot."

Which is exactly why I should go.

I reluctantly stood. "Well, I'll let you get on with your night. Don't want to overstay my welcome. You were reading a book."

She picked it up and flipped it over. "It's not that good."

"Kind of like my performances lately." I winked and took a step back. "Have a good night."

"You, too."

I saluted her. "See you in Chicago."

"Yeah. See you there."

I couldn't help myself. "Maybe I can convince you to get a bite to eat with me there?"

She rolled her eyes. "Maybe."

I inwardly fist-pumped. "Cool."

High off the way she made me feel, I tripped on something as I walked away backwards. *Real slick.* Veronica gave me the stink eye one last time on my way out. She could probably see through my intentions better than I could. I'd tried to convince myself I just wanted to talk to Emily, but there was a lot more I wanted to do with her. *But I can't.* She was too good for me. That's one thing I knew for sure.

I headed back to my bus as if it were some kind of punishment.

Thankfully, the girls Atticus and Ronan had invited over earlier were gone. Good riddance.

"Where the fuck were you?" Ronan asked as I walked past.

I stuck my middle finger up and continued to my bedroom in the back. I most certainly wasn't going to admit where I'd been. Atticus and Ronan would give me so much shit.

Back in my room, I tossed off my shoes and lay down on the bed. My stomach grumbled, reminding me that I should probably eat something. But I didn't feel like talking to anyone long enough to go back out there and dig through whatever catering had brought to the bus.

I turned to my side and placed my hands under my head. That's when I smelled it—a flowery scent that was all too familiar. *Fuck*. Why did I smell like her? *Emily*. Then I noticed it.

Her scrunchie wrapped around my wrist.

Chapter 7

TRISTAN

The morning sun stung my eyes as I opened the shade on my bedroom window.

We'd rolled into Illinois overnight. We'd be playing at an arena in Chicago tomorrow evening, and I planned to spend today and tomorrow resting my voice and trying to get my head in the zone after my terrible performance in Minneapolis. There was no choice—I simply had to get it together.

Ronan burst into my room without knocking.

Why do I keep forgetting to lock that damn door?

"Hey, dude." He plopped down on my bed. "What was up with you last night?"

My stomach sank. I wasn't sure whether he was referring to my performance or something else. "What in particular?" I asked.

"You were all bitchy to everyone. Then you kicked those girls out of your room and left the bus. Don't think I don't have my eyes on you."

"Pretty amazing that you were tracking my where-abouts while you had a girl face down on your lap. You're multitalented."

"Ambi-DICK-strous." He winked. "What is that?" He looked toward my hand.

Shit. I hadn't realized I was playing with Emily's scrunchie again. I'd slept with it around my wrist. "None of your business is what it is…"

"You're hiding something. I can see it in your face. Who does that belong to? None of the girls who come on the bus wear those in their hair." He squinted. "But more than that… I noticed it wrapped around your wrist when you came back to the bus last night."

"How the hell did you catch that?"

"I told you. I have eyes on the freaking back of my head. I see everything, brother." Ronan smirked. "You were with someone…"

"No, I wasn't."

"You hooked up with someone when you left the bus, and you don't want to tell me? That's shady as hell."

"I didn't hook up with anyone."

"Then whose hair thingy is that?"

One thing I knew about Ronan, he wasn't going to let up. He would stay here and keep prying ad nauseum until I told him the truth. And he'd start getting other people involved for entertainment. The more I denied it, the harder he'd push. It would be easier to just admit the truth.

"I went over to the other bus to hang out for a while. I needed a breather from this one last night. That's it."

"You didn't answer my question, though. Whose hair tie is that?"

"It's Emily's." I swallowed.

"The cute girl who fetches shit for us?"

His comment offended me. "She's more than just cute. She's bright...witty. Way smarter than the airheads we normally encounter on the road."

"So you went to *visit her* on the other bus..."

"I think she's cool, yeah. I was chatting with her and started twirling this thing around my fingers. I accidentally walked away with it, which is why you saw it on my wrist. Sorry to disappoint you, but you're not going to find anything salacious about that."

He scratched his chin. "Hmm..."

"Hmm, what?"

"Just trying to figure out if I believe you."

"I'm not into her like that," I lied. "I just went over there for a breather and to say hello. I talked to other people on the bus, too." *For a mere two seconds.*

He squinted. "Still don't know if I buy it."

I pulled on the scrunchie and snapped the elastic against my wrist. "Don't you miss just hanging out with normal people who aren't part of this world? People who don't have any ulterior motives? Who don't want something from you?"

"Isn't she technically part of the tour?" he countered.

"Yeah, but she's far from part of the music scene and couldn't care less about all that. She didn't even know who I was the day I met her, when she came to interview in the desert while we were recording. Initially, that's what I liked about her. We weren't going to find anyone else to work on the tour who genuinely didn't have a clue about us. And I've gotten to know her a little here and there since then." I shook my head. "But there's nothing going on. She's way too young for me anyway."

Well, that last part was true.

Ronan arched a brow. "Never stopped you before."

"Hooking up is different than getting involved with someone."

"Now you're getting *involved* with her?"

He was pissing me off. "No. But she's not the kind of girl you mess around with. You know? She's been through a lot..." I had to stop myself. I didn't want to talk about Emily's business. Even that bit I'd divulged was too much. He'd ask more questions if I went any further. Ronan was the nosiest person I'd ever met and had the biggest mouth, too. "Why am I explaining myself to you? You need to mind your freaking business about where I go and what I do."

He smacked me on the shoulder. "You *are* my business. Always will be. I tell you all of my shit—unsolicited—and you give me nothing in return. It's like you think I'm gonna judge you when I'm the least judgmental person."

Ronan had a point. He might've been nosy, but he didn't have a judgmental bone in his body. My trepidation about opening up to him, particularly regarding my vocal issues, had everything to do with my own shame.

"I'm sorry. Things have just been...tough lately." I hung my head.

"Your voice, you mean?"

Fuck. I lifted my gaze. "You noticed?"

"Yeah, I've noticed. I obviously haven't said anything to you. But I noticed. Atticus has too."

My shoulders hunched in defeat. The fact that they knew and didn't mention it made me feel even worse, like they'd been whispering behind my back. Now I'd be fuck-ing paranoid.

"Why the hell *didn't* you say anything to me?"

"Because what good would that do? We're on tour. We can't stop this train. Pointing it out would make you self-conscious. That would probably make whatever is go-ing on worse. That which you focus on only grows bigger."

"Aren't you curious as to what's causing it?"

He shrugged. "I didn't ask because I feel like that should come voluntarily from you. Like I said, focusing on it will only make it worse. More real. Didn't want to make an issue of it." He placed his hands on my shoulders and looked me in the eyes. "They still love you, man. Everyone loves you." He paused. "That said, what the hell *is* going on?"

"I have polyps on my vocal cords. That's why my voice is off. Doctor says the only way around it is surgery. But that could risk permanent damage."

"Fuck." The expression on his face freaked me out a little. "And you've had to keep this from us? Why didn't you feel like you could tell us?"

"I guess I didn't want anyone freaking out about it like you seem to be now. But to your point, the less I dwell on it, the more I hope it fades into the background." Thread-ing the scrunchie around my fingers, I said, "Do you think anyone else has noticed?"

"Like the fans, you mean?"

I held my breath. "Yeah..."

"I haven't heard any rumblings, and I'm normally pretty in tune to the gossip. I've been hitting all the music threads online. I'll let you know if I come across anything.

It's not so obvious. I notice it because I play with you all the time."

I'd bet it was more obvious than he seemed to think, especially if Emily, who was fairly new to our music, had noticed it.

"Well, if it gets any worse, it *will* be obvious," I said.

"Is there anything you can do in the meantime? Medication or therapy?"

"Rest and voice therapy are the only things I can do right now. But neither is feasible in the middle of a tour. So I really need to focus on fixing this shit once we have a break. I just hope I don't lose my voice entirely in the meantime."

True worry filled his eyes. "If you need anything, man. Let me know. I'm gonna start researching, too. What did you call it? Lollipops or some shit?"

"Polyps. And you're a fucking idiot." I laughed.

"You know me. I find stuff that others don't. If I have to make you a fucking witch's brew, I will. Throw some holy water on you. I'll do whatever I need to."

I rolled my eyes. "Thank you. I appreciate that, man."

"We're gonna get to the bottom of it." He gently punched my arm. "Nice way to get us off the subject of Emily, by the way—dropping that bomb about your voice."

"There's nothing more to say about Emily, because there's nothing going on."

"There's got to be some reason you felt compelled to leave the bus last night to go talk to her," he pushed.

"She and I are friendly. We hung out in Detroit," I admitted. "I took her to Abdul's. We ate and talked. That's it." I sighed. "She's cool. Reminds me of the calm and peace of the life I had before I left home."

"You mean eons ago when you were a teenager?"

"Yes, jackass. I'm not a damn teenager anymore—obviously. But I feel like myself around her. You've never met anyone who made you feel like that?"

He grimaced. "I'm not really looking to be reminded of my life before music. It was pretty crappy and nothing I want to remember."

I ate my words and nodded. I'd had a pretty stable life growing up, but Ronan had come from an abusive home. His parents were both alcoholics, and he looked at this as an escape from all that. He didn't have any nostalgia for his childhood.

"I get it, man," I said. "Maybe I'm just getting too old for this shit. More and more, I've been thinking about what life might've been like if I hadn't left."

"Yeah, you'd be piss-poor and out of shape. Probably far less tattoos."

I chuckled. "You don't know that."

"Look, there's no sense in thinking about what might've been. You could also be dead—could've gotten hit by a truck stumbling home from some no-name bar in the bumfuck town you grew up in." He put his hand on my shoulder and shook me. "What you should be focusing on is how you can make your current life—the only life you have...by getting your voice back in check."

I took a deep breath. "You're right."

"Don't think I have no ulterior motive here." He snickered. "If you go down, the rest of us go down. We all need you."

The pressure in my chest built. "I realize that. We've worked too hard to get where we are to have me take us down."

"It'd take a lot for you to lose them. People love you. Even at your worst, you're better than most." He sighed. "As much as I hate to admit it, you're the draw. It's fucking *you*. Bass players, drummers—we're more replaceable than someone with the voice you have. It's one of a kind." He pointed at me. "And remember this moment, because my damn ego won't let me repeat what I just said."

"Understood." I smiled, thankful for Ronan and relieved that I'd gotten some of this off of my chest. It did make me feel better.

"What's going on in here?" Atticus interrupted, whipping the door open. "Some kind of private talk? What did I say about you two assholes ganging up on me?"

"Not everything is about you, Atticus," Ronan said. "Anyway, we're just adjourning. I need to go have a smoke." He headed out.

"I'll join you," Atticus said, following him.

Relief washed over me that Atticus didn't pry. I panicked for a second, worrying that Ronan was going to tell him everything, but maybe that would be easier than having to rehash it. He'd said Atticus had noticed my voice anyway. The less talking I did about the situation—and the less talking in general—the better.

A few minutes after they left, Atticus's nephew, Kieran, walked in. "Do you have a second, Tristan?"

"Yeah. Sure. I've got a little time."

Apparently, my room was a revolving door this morning.

Kieran was Atticus's sister's son. Atticus was like a dad to him, since Kieran's father had passed away. Kieran had been traveling with us. He was just out of college and looking for an adventure before having to enter the workforce, so Atticus had suggested he join the crew for both the US and European legs of our tour. Even if Atticus didn't say it, I knew he loved having family around.

"What's up?" I sat on the edge of my bed.

"I wanted your advice on something."

"What can I help you with?"

"Well, basically you're a baller. Women are obsessed with you. And I want to know if you have any secrets or tips for me."

I chuckled. "Is something prompting this conversation?"

"There's a girl I like. But I don't know if she's into me, and I want to figure out what I could be doing to make myself more appealing. Like, I know women are into you because you're a star and all that, but I figure you have a lot of experience and might be able to guide me as to how I should act to give myself the best chance."

I cleared my throat. "Well, first of all, you shouldn't be *acting* at all. There's no better way to be than your authentic self. Anything else is going to get you nowhere fast, because it's hard to keep up a façade for long."

I'm one to talk lately.

"What if my authentic self is pretty damn boring?" he countered.

"I think most people find themselves boring. Because we live in our own shoes twenty-four-seven. We get sick of ourselves. You know? And we're our own toughest critics. But there are a few things you can do that might help capture someone's attention."

He sat down. "I'm all ears..."

"Okay, first, you never want to let her see you sweat. If a girl thinks you're too into her, that's going to be a turn-off. So, as much as you might like someone, you have to ease up on the attention, at least at first."

I chuckled to myself, thinking about my bus visit last night. *Do as I say, not as I do.*

"So how do you know how much attention to pay to someone you like?" he asked.

"Subtly show you're interested without getting in her face too much or constantly talking her ear off. No calling or texting her too much. That kind of thing. Basically, baby steps. Ease into things."

"Okay...good advice." He rubbed his hands together. "What else?"

"While you should always be yourself, little enhancements won't hurt. Make sure you smell good. A little of the right cologne goes a long way. A good smell can be an aphrodisiac."

"I don't wear cologne."

"Never too late to start."

He eyed my bottle of Armani cologne, then walked over to the bureau and sprayed some on himself.

"That's just a minor thing. Not a deal breaker," I continued. "But you're gonna want to exude confidence, and smelling good helps—especially when making a move. If she senses you're not sure of yourself, it's going to give her pause and make her wonder if there's a reason she should be thinking twice about you."

"What if you can't help seeming nervous to ask her out?"

I waved my hand. "Don't overthink it. Just pull the trigger and accept the consequences, good or bad. You're not gonna be any less nervous if you sit there and think about it."

"Okay." He nodded. "Anything else?"

"Yeah. Enjoy being young. You have so many opportunities ahead of you. And if this girl you like doesn't pan out, you have a lot of time to meet someone even better, because time is on your side."

"I guess that's true. Thanks."

I nodded. "Who's the lucky girl?"

"It's Emily. She works on the tour." He smiled. "You know her?"

Chapter 8

EMILY

Kieran placed his napkin in his lap. Our waiter had just brought two orders of the spaghetti carbonara at an Italian restaurant about a mile from our hotel.

"So, are you excited about the stop in St. Louis?" he asked.

Kieran knew our next stop after Chicago was only about an hour from my small hometown of Shady Hills, Missouri. I always had mixed feelings when I went home. But seeing my mother would for sure be a highlight, despite the painful memories there.

"I am," I said. "It'll be nice to see my mom and not have to stay at the hotel. I got special permission to leave the tour for a bit."

I'd opened up to Tristan pretty easily, yet I wouldn't dream of telling Kieran the truth about my past. Right off the bat, somehow I'd sensed that Tristan wouldn't judge me. Sharing that with him had been a risk, but I didn't regret it. Kieran, on the other hand, seemed like the type of person who might be shocked by my truth.

"There's nothing like an actual house with home cooking," I added. "You forget how much you miss it."

"I hear ya. I'm already dreaming about the next time I get to go home and eat." He smiled. "What do you think you'll do once the tour is over?"

"I'm not sure. That's why this experience is good for me. It's sort of like a palate cleanser. I'm hoping by the end of it I'll have some clarity about which direction I want to go careerwise."

"What are you narrowing it down to?" He twirled some pasta around his fork.

"Well, my major was communications, so I was thinking of applying for some PR positions or maybe marketing jobs. I might have to work some internships, though, to get more experience before applying for paid positions."

He nodded. "That sounds like a great idea. It's amazing how similar our situations are. That's exactly why I asked my uncle Atticus if I could come on this tour. I needed something to do while I figured things out…"

Kieran reached for the jug of water on our table and poured more into my glass. He was so considerate and respectful. Perhaps that's why I struggled to feel anything. As of late, I seemed to have a penchant for rough-around-the-edges, older men I had no business crushing on. Tristan had popped into my mind way too often tonight.

Ever since he'd come to see me on the bus, I'd been thinking about him, though we'd had no further interaction. So when Kieran had asked me to dinner this morning, I figured I had nothing to lose—anything to get my mind off my sudden obsession with Tristan Daltrey would be good.

The Chicago performance wasn't until tomorrow, so this was a night off for the band and crew. I couldn't help but wonder what Tristan was doing, how he was spending his free night, and whether he was nervous about the show, given his voice issues back in Minnesota. I found myself more and more nervous for him with each performance. Being the only person he talked with about his struggles felt like a weight on my chest.

I continued to force myself to make conversation with Kieran. "So, how does it feel to have a famous uncle?"

"Atticus is more like a father to me," he said. "My dad died when I was younger. He's not around as much as he'd like to be, but he makes up for it whenever he's home. He takes my brother and me on these weekend getaways, just the guys. He's really cool."

"It's nice for you to have that. I'm sorry about your dad."

"Thanks." He sighed. "What about your parents?"

"My dad left us—my brother and me—when I was three. My parents were never married. Growing up, my mother had a lot of boyfriends who'd come and go. It wasn't the most comfortable home life, but we did the best we could."

When our dinner was over, Kieran and I walked back to the hotel. As we bid each other goodnight at the elevators, he leaned in and placed a chaste kiss on my cheek. It was awkward and sweet at the same time. My body had no more reaction than if a baby blew a raspberry on my face. I knew in that moment there was no romantic future for us, as nice as he was.

I went back to my room to find Layla lying on her bed, watching TV. She sat up when I entered. "How was it?" she asked.

"He's so sweet."

Her brows lifted. "That's it?"

I kicked off my shoes, hesitant to say anything negative. "I don't know. It's not really a good idea to get involved with someone on this tour anyway, you know? If it doesn't work out, then what? You're stuck having to see them all the time. There's no escape."

"You couldn't have felt too much if your first thought is to look for reasons why it would be a bad idea." She saw right through me.

I sighed. "There was nothing wrong with him. He's super nice. But I have this problem where I tend to be attracted to guys who are all wrong for me."

"Join the club." She pointed to herself. "So Kieran has a lot of good qualities, and that makes him less attractive?"

I lay down on the bed. "It's not that I *want* someone to be an asshole. But when he comes across as near-perfect, it sort of lacks excitement, yeah. This is proof that I'm too young and immature to be in a relationship with someone who's worth it."

"I'm thirty-eight, and I still haven't stopped picking the wrong men. So trust me, it's not an age thing."

"I don't think I should be dating right now. And Kieran doesn't seem like the type of guy you string along. He deserves a nice girl. I don't ever want to break someone's heart again."

"Again?" She tilted her head. "Sounds like there's a story there. Are you a little heartbreaker, Miss Emily?"

A wave of sadness hit me. "Yeah. There is a story there. One I don't want to get into right now. But let's just say, I live with a lot of guilt over the way things ended with my first love."

"I'm sorry." She frowned. "That sucks. But at least you're learning from it, using it as a reason to be cautious with other guys."

"I guess," I murmured.

Just then my phone vibrated with a text from Stephen, the tour manager. It said Tristan was badly in need of allergy medication and asked me to go to the store to get some. I was off the clock starting at eight on nights we didn't have a show, but it was understood that if someone needed something in an emergency, I would deliver.

I looked up from my phone and hopped off the bed. "Tristan needs allergy medication," I told her. "I'm gonna run to the pharmacy."

"What a pain in the ass," she muttered.

I shrugged, putting on my shoes and grabbing my coat.

After I left the hotel, I searched for the nearest pharmacy on my phone as I walked through the parking lot to the rental car.

When I returned, I took the elevator all the way up to Tristan's penthouse suite. Unlike the other rooms in this hotel, this one didn't use a key. To enter, you had to have a passcode. Stephen had sent it to me in his text. As the elevator rose, my heart beat faster at the prospect of seeing Tristan.

The elevator opened to a spacious living area with a killer view of downtown Chicago. Tristan, though, was nowhere to be found. Or it seemed that way at first. The bedroom door was halfway open, so I walked toward it.

Before I could call his name, I froze. Tristan was in the room—but he wasn't alone. He was lying on the bed, and there was a woman with him—a woman *straddling* him. *What the fuck?* He was shirtless, but otherwise they were both clothed. Still, she was basically giving him a lap dance.

I didn't know what was wrong with me, but I couldn't move. Instead of running away, my eyes were glued to the situation. The room was silent, aside from her breaths. I couldn't look away—the way his head bent back, the way he bit his lip, the way she moved over him. She wasn't naked, but she might as well have been with the way she was grinding over him.

My eyes fell to his big, veiny hands holding her hips. What would they feel like gripping my body? Despite what he'd said before about groupies not doing it for him, he sure seemed turned on right now. My stomach twisted. More troublesome than the jealousy, though? *I* felt turned on, too.

Yet instead of leaving, I continued to stand there, imagining she was me, imagining what it would feel like to use his body to pleasure myself—to feel his hardness beneath me, that heat between my legs. My mouth watered. Distracted, the paper bag holding the allergy medication slipped from my hand to the floor.

Tristan turned, and his eyes widened as they met mine. After a few seconds of looking into his eyes, my legs regained the ability to move, and I hightailed it out of there.

Pulse racing, I pushed the button to the elevator more times than necessary and got in as fast as I could the second it opened. But before the doors closed, a large hand slipped between them.

Chapter 9

EMILY

My heart thundered against my chest as Tristan entered the elevator, shirtless and glistening, making my foolish knees weak. His musky scent filled the tight space as he panted. I could feel his breath against my face. It caused my senseless nipples to stiffen and every hair on my body to stand at attention.

What the hell is going on?

I pressed the button to go down, but we didn't get very far before he pushed the stop button and stood in front of the panel, blocking access.

"What the hell are you doing?" I asked, unsure which I felt more of, anger or arousal.

"What the hell are *you* doing?" he clapped back.

"What does it look like I'm doing? Leaving. I came to drop off your medication. And now I'm trying to get the heck out of here."

"Why did you run away like that?"

"Are you serious?" My eyes went wide. "You *know* why. You need me to freaking spell it out?"

"It freaked you out to see me with someone in there?"

"No." I looked down at my shoes. "I wasn't freaked out. It was just...unexpected and uncomfortable." I lifted my gaze to meet his incendiary stare.

His eyes bore into mine. "But you stood there watching for at least a minute..."

Shit. Shit. Shit. I said nothing, because there was no denying it.

"How was your date with Kieran?" he asked.

"How did you know about that?"

"I know everything." He tilted his head. "So how was it?"

"It was okay."

"Just *okay*?"

"He's...super nice."

"He is. Kieran is just about the best there is. He'd be great for you."

"He told you about the date?"

Tristan nodded. "He really likes you. I was the one who encouraged him to go for it."

"Did you now..."

Why did that disappoint me so much? I was even more disappointed in myself for feeling this way. I knew nothing could happen with Tristan, but I'd loved his attention and the idea that maybe he liked me.

He kept prodding. "So you didn't have a good time?"

"I did...but I think he and I are probably better off as friends."

"Friends?" Tristan winced. "Ouch. That's the kiss of death." He chuckled. "I don't have a single female friend. That should tell you something."

"Well, I'm not gonna date someone on this tour regardless, even if I were into him in that way. I figured there was no harm in a simple dinner, but I'm not interested in anything more than that with him. I'll feel bad if he expects something, because you're right. He's a good guy, and he doesn't deserve someone wasting his time."

"Well, I bet he'll ask you out again. If that's how you feel, though, let him down easy."

"I wish I didn't have to let anyone down." I crossed my arms. "Anyway, you say 'let him down easy'—is that what you do with all the women you hook up with? They never see you again. Something tells me you don't send them all letters of explanation as to why you don't contact them."

He stepped back. "Okay, first off, groupies pretty much know the deal going into it. You don't enter a man's room while he's on tour, throw yourself at him without so much as saying a word, and expect him to call the next day. That's one of the only things that makes this lifestyle easy. Everyone is normally on the same page. No one expects anything from each other."

"Yeah, well, that page is definitely frayed around the edges at this point..."

The corner of his mouth curved upward. "You don't seem to think very highly of me."

"I'm not down with the whole rockstar lifestyle," I huffed.

"I can tell. Although...you seemed pretty interested in what you were seeing when you stopped at the doorway and watched a moment ago."

I felt my skin crawl. "I wasn't watching you like *that*."

"How else do you watch someone? What does that even mean? I heard the paper bag crinkle. That's how I knew you were there. I didn't say anything because I wanted to see what you'd do. I expected you to leave, but you didn't." He cocked his head. "Why?"

Without a suitable answer, I improvised. "I didn't know whether to leave the bag of medicine or knock and interrupt whatever you were doing. My indecision kept me there." I breathed out. "Why did you order something to your room if you were with someone?"

"I didn't know she was going to come by. Plus, nothing really happened. I wouldn't have been ashamed if you'd walked in or even interrupted. We weren't having sex. And I wasn't planning to."

I shook my head. "You're so full of shit. Something *would've* happened if I hadn't interrupted you."

"Are you psychic now? How would you know what would've happened? I think I know better than you what my intentions were."

"You claimed you weren't interested in groupies as of late. Apparently, that changed." I blew a breath up into my hair. "Are you gonna move this elevator or what?"

"I needed a distraction tonight. That's why I let her in."

"A distraction from what?" I asked, placing my hands on my hips.

"I've been preoccupied with my shitty performances. I'm not feeling as motivated as I should for the show tomorrow night."

"So you figured you'd invite someone over to fuck the worry out of you?"

"Don't say things like that."

Is he serious? "Why? Because you think I'm too innocent?"

"No. Because it makes me want you to say it *again*, and I'm trying not to sexualize you, even if that's a losing game."

My heart beat faster. *He's attracted to me?* I felt my cheeks heat.

"You're all red. You're getting very worked up," he said.

"Yeah, well, I don't appreciate you insinuating that I was watching for fun like some kind of perv. You've made me a bit testy."

Even if I am a little perv.

"I'm just teasing you, Emily. And I kind of like you testy. It's a fun side to you. Incidentally, there'd be nothing wrong with that, you know—watching from the sidelines. We're all pervs in one way or another." His smile grew wider.

He seemed to be enjoying this situation a little too much. And that made me wonder... Not sure why it hadn't hit me before. My eyes narrowed. "Did you call me there so I'd walk in on that?"

"Why would I do that?" His face still showed a hint of amusement.

"So I'd *catch* you with her?"

"Yeah. I got what you were insinuating. But *why* would I do that?"

I shook my head. "I'm not entirely sure, but I find it suspect that the door was open when I got there, and you don't seem to have red eyes or a runny nose that would warrant allergy medication."

"I didn't leave the door open. She did."

"You could've closed it. You knew I was coming to your room to deliver something."

"Actually, I didn't. I texted Stephen. I had no reason to believe he was going to send you. I thought you were out with Kieran, remember? Figured you weren't even around." His eyes pierced mine. "But to entertain your theory, let's say I did leave the door open so you could watch. What would that make me?"

"A prick who gets off on using his sexuality to shock people."

"And if you intentionally watched me about to have sex with someone, what would that make *you*?"

"There was nothing intentional about it..."

"A little voyeur is what it would make you." He grinned mischievously. "If there's no truth to it, why is your neck turning redder by the second, Emily?"

God. I hated that I always turned so damn red when I was flustered. *Damn Irish skin.*

"Are you attracted to me?" he asked.

A rush of adrenaline sliced through me. I felt exposed. And worse, I didn't know how to deny my attraction without turning into a freaking lobster. "Why are you asking me that?"

"Because you seem flustered." His voice was low, seductive. "It seems like maybe I have an effect on you. Do I?"

"Only an egotistical person would assume that."

He held up his hand. "Guilty..."

"Why would it matter if I were attracted to you?"

"You're dodging the question." He inched closer, causing the hairs on my arms to prickle.

I felt ready to burst. "Of course I'm attracted to you. So is half the world. You're extremely handsome. But that doesn't mean I should do anything about it."

Then I looked down and noticed something for the first time. *What the hell?*

"Why do you have my scrunchie around your wrist?"

Chapter 10

TRISTAN

Fuck.

What the hell was I thinking?

I'd forgotten to take this off earlier. Stressed to the max about the Chicago show, I'd been messing with this damn scrunchie a lot, stretching and twirling it every which way. As much as I *had* orchestrated some of what went down tonight, the scrunchie was a total slip-up on my part.

"It's yours," I admitted, as if there were any doubt.

She stared down at it. "I know. But how did you get it?"

"I walked away with it accidentally the night I visited you on the bus."

"Why are you wearing it around your wrist? Your hair isn't long enough to warrant that."

I laughed, never imagining she'd consider I was using it for my hair. "I like to twist it around my fingers. Pull on it. It's a nervous habit."

"You've been corrupting my poor hair accessory all this time without my knowledge?"

Better than other things I've dreamed about corrupting lately. "Once again, guilty." I looked down at it. "Honestly I didn't realize I had it around my wrist."

"Well...you can keep it if you enjoy it that much." She shook her head. "Weird as it may be."

"Thanks. But let's get back to the subject of you being attracted to me."

"Let's not. Let's instead ask what's up with your alleged allergies. You don't seem stuffy."

I loved that she was calling me out. "My eyes were watering earlier," I lied. "I wanted to take something as a precaution. Sometimes when I stay in hotels, my allergies act up. Not sure if it's something in the cleaning shit they use or what..."

Except in this case, it was an excuse to see you.

I'd requested the meds knowing damn well they'd ask Emily to deliver them. Except after I texted Stephen, I felt really damn guilty about it. I knew she was out with Kieran and hadn't been sure whether she was back yet. But maybe I'd *wanted* to interrupt. That made me a piece of shit. Kieran was Atticus's nephew, for Christ's sake. What kind of man tries to disrupt the date of a kid who looks up to him? But I was fucking jealous. It was the first time in my life I'd felt this way. And it would've been nice if the object of said jealousy wasn't a girl practically young enough to be my daughter.

"Interesting how your allergies seem to have disappeared." She crossed her arms.

It would've served me right if they'd sent someone else to deliver the meds instead of Emily. In the midst of waiting for her to show up, a groupie named Angel came to my suite. Atticus had given her the code and sent her upstairs. He did shit like that all the time. In the past, it used to be a welcome surprise. But lately, I found it annoying.

Yet I'd decided to let things unfold with Angel, hoping Emily would walk in on us. Not because I wanted to freak Emily out, and believe it or not—not because I liked the idea of her watching, though that was an unexpected surprise. I'd let her walk in on me with Angel for her own good, my way of warning her away from me.

But I hadn't accounted for her standing in the doorway and watching. I'd only let Angel give me a lap dance, but when Emily didn't leave, the whole thing became about putting on a show for her. I was a sick fuck that Emily watching had turned me on so much. When she'd run away, though, I worried I'd upset her.

And now here we were. Stuck, thanks to me.

"Are you going to move this elevator?" she asked again.

"I'm having way too much fun teasing you." I moved aside. "But if you want to push the button, go ahead. No one's been stopping you this entire time."

Much to my pleasure, she didn't budge.

"I have a question," I said.

"What?"

"Why did you really stay at the doorway when you could've just left the medicine? Was it shock? Or something more?"

She glared. "How about you tell me why you called for medicine to treat a fake allergy instead?"

I laughed guiltily. "You answer first."

She looked away a moment. "I was just curious, I guess. That's why I stayed."

That was probably as honest an answer as I was going to get. I decided to reciprocate. "And I called you to bring me medicine because I wanted to see you, not because I needed it."

Her cheeks reddened. "Oh."

"So...you were curious..." I pressed.

She shook her head. "It wasn't a voyeurism thing. At first I *was* in shock. Not sure why. I just assumed you were alone if you weren't feeling well. But then the shock wore off and...I don't know. I just..."

She seemed a little worked up. And though I was sort of getting off on that, I needed to pipe down. "You don't have to explain," I said. "I'm sorry for messing with you tonight."

"You're making me flustered, and I don't like it." She looked beyond my shoulder. "Shouldn't you be getting back to your friend in there?"

"She'll be fine."

Emily rolled her eyes. "If she has any self-respect, she'll be *gone*."

"Let's hope she is." After a moment of silence, I added, "I wasn't going to have sex with her."

"I didn't need to know that."

"Well, you seemed to assume that was my intention, so I wanted to clarify. I'm sure it looked like that's where things were headed."

"Why would you start something if you weren't going to have sex with her?"

I didn't have an answer for that, since I couldn't admit the truth—that it had all been a show. That I'd done nothing but think about *Emily* lately. And sometimes, I fantasized about her sweet, innocent eyes looking up at me while I fucked her in ways she'd probably want me to go to hell for, even if I knew it could never happen.

"How are you feeling about tomorrow night?" she asked.

"Not very confident." I exhaled. "I told Ronan about my voice issues."

"You did?"

"Yeah, he brought it up. He was the first of the guys to do that, though apparently, he and Atticus had been talking about it behind my back. I told him the truth about the polyps on my vocal cords."

"I'm glad. I think the hardest part has probably been hiding what you're going through from them."

"He was cool about it. He wants to research things I can do while on tour. Knowing Ronan, he'll come back with some woo-woo shit he wants me to try or tell me I need to smoke pounds of weed."

"Well, sometimes you don't have anything to lose by trying out-of-the-box things. Though, not the pounds of weed necessarily." She laughed. "But maybe other unconventional stuff."

I wanted to ask if she would be into trying new things, too—namely, older men.

She gestured to the panel behind my shoulder. "Are we planning to move this elevator anytime soon? I already admitted why I stayed at the doorway. Not sure there's much more you're gonna get out of me tonight."

"If I hadn't stopped the elevator, you wouldn't have given me a chance to talk to you. I like your company."

"Well, you don't need to hold me captive to get it."

"The way you ran off tonight, I kind of did. Also, if I hadn't pulled the medicine excuse and just called you to hang out with me, would you have come to my room?"

"No," she answered emphatically.

"So I have to resort to creative ways to see you." I gestured to the panel. "Anyway, I've already pointed out that you can press the button anytime."

Emily looked over at it but didn't push. It pleased me to know that she was choosing to be here with me right now.

"Why do you like my company, anyway?" she asked. "You could get almost anyone to hang out with you..."

"When I'm with you I feel more like myself," I answered.

She blinked. "I don't know what to say..."

"You don't have to say anything about that at all. But I *would* like to know more about you, if you're willing to share."

She licked her beautiful, red lips. "What do you want to know?"

"Why haven't you posted on social media for over a year?"

She took a step back. "How the hell do you know that?"

"I googled you once."

"When?"

"The night you told me what happened with your mother's boyfriend."

Her bottom lip trembled. "You thought I was lying?"

"No, Emily. Not at all. It was just...more like a fascination with you. I wanted to know more but didn't want to upset you by asking for details. So I went in search of the information myself. That's it. I swear. I'm sorry if that seems intrusive."

Her voice shook. "I haven't posted because I don't have anything interesting to post."

I took a step closer to her. "Your last post was a photo of you and some guy. You alluded to missing him. What happened between you and him?"

Her breath hitched. Then she turned away.

Fuck. I'd struck a chord.

"I'd rather not talk about that," she murmured, her eyes filling with tears.

Nice going, asshole. First you trap her in an elevator. Now this. Why the hell did I have to pry? I wished I could take back my question. I placed my hand gently against her cheek. "I'm sorry I upset you."

Emily sniffled. "You didn't do anything. It's me."

"Yeah, but I brought up a subject that clearly triggered you. And I shouldn't have been so damn nosy." I wanted to hold her, but I knew that wouldn't be appropriate. Instead, I did what I should've done all along and pushed the damn button to move the elevator—not up to my room, but down to the ground floor.

"Thank you for setting me free." She smiled. "Even if this was oddly entertaining."

"Until I made you cry, yeah."

She wiped her eyes and laughed a little through her tears.

"Any chance I could convince you to come back upstairs with me?" I asked, holding both palms out. "I swear to God, I'm not insinuating anything. I just want to make you some tea and be sure you're okay."

Her forehead wrinkled. "You want me to hang out with you and your groupie up there?"

"I doubt she's still there. If she is, I'll kick her out."

"You're so respectful."

"I offer respect based on whether someone deserves it."

"Thanks, but I'm gonna head back to my room."

Good girl. I don't blame you.

Stay away.

"Okay."

She slipped the scrunchie off of my wrist. At first I thought she was taking it back, but instead she flung it at me playfully as the elevator doors opened.

Then she left without saying another word.

I held the doors open, smile plastered on my face and not even feeling guilty for how much I liked watching her ass as she walked away.

Chapter 11

EMILY

Backstage in Chicago, I leaned against a partition, drinking a soda and watching the show. Tristan was performing one of Delirious Jones's most popular songs, "Maybe You."

This was always the song where I noticed if his voice was faltering, because it required him to really belt out certain notes. My heart was in my throat as I listened closely, praying his voice wasn't getting worse. I almost hoped I'd lose my keen sense of hearing so I could tell him he sounded better and mean it, because he'd surely ask me. So far, though, he sounded good. Relief washed over me.

Then I hiccupped.

Goddamn it.

Hiccup.

I should've known not to drink it so fast. Every time, this happened.

I focused on my hiccups a moment, and evidently the song ended. Everything from there happened so fast.

I heard him calling my name.

Tristan calling my name.

Tristan calling me to the stage.

My eyes widened.

No. No. No.

I moved farther into the backstage area, but someone from the crew pushed me to the stage. Tristan waved me over, but I couldn't move. He waved me over again. One foot in front of the other, I made my way slowly over to him.

Then I was right next to him, under the blinding lights.

Tristan asked me a question, one I was too shocked to comprehend—I had no idea what it was. Then he put the mic in my face for an answer. A giant hiccup escaped into the microphone.

The crowd erupted in laughter.

And I was living my biggest nightmare.

I gave the peace sign and ran off stage.

"What the hell just happened?" someone called as I returned backstage.

Fuck if I know.

～

Later that night, I was safely back in my hotel room with no intention of leaving until morning. Then the tour manager sent me the most bizarre text.

> **Stephen: I can't believe I'm saying this, but Tristan needs you to get him bed pads.**

Emily: Bed pads?

Stephen: Yeah, like pee pads that go on the bed so people with incontinence don't leak onto the mattress.

What the?

Emily: Why the heck does he need those?

Stephen: He told me not to ask.

Emily: Are you kidding?

Stephen: Afraid not.

"What the hell?" I said aloud.

Layla stopped pouring her glass of wine. "What?"

"You don't want to know," I said as I found my jacket.

That son of a bitch. Was this some kind of a joke? And if I was really mad about it, why did I have a goofy smile plastered on my face right now?

I practically ran out of the hotel and hopped in the rental car, headed to the nearest pharmacy. I blew in and out of there as fast as humanly possible, because who wants to be seen buying bed pads?

When I returned, I used the passcode to enter the elevator that led to Tristan's penthouse suite.

When the doors opened, he was standing with a shit-eating grin on his face, his arms crossed like he'd been just waiting for me to appear.

"Urine pads, huh?" I threw the large plastic package at his head, prompting him to duck.

"How else was I gonna get you here?"

"You could've picked something a little less embarrassing."

"What would be the fun in that? Plus, I figured I hadn't quite embarrassed you enough tonight already."

I stared at him incredulously.

Then his expression softened. "I'm so fucking sorry about earlier, Emily. I never imagined you'd have the damn hiccups when I put that mic in your face."

"Why would you call me onstage anyway?"

"I've been calling members of the crew onstage every night. You know that. To thank them for their hard work. It's a little tour ritual. Then, I ask a funny question for each person to answer. Tonight was your turn. It wasn't meant to pick on you or anything."

I placed my hands on my hips. "You could've given me some warning."

"There's no fun in that. The best part is seeing the surprise on people's faces when I do it. I didn't know you were going to swallow a frog right before I called you out. You can't blame me for that."

I had to laugh. "I was so in shock I didn't process what you asked me. I still have no clue what the question was."

"You didn't hear the question, or you pretended not to?"

"I didn't hear it!"

"I asked you the most embarrassing thing that's ever happened to you."

"Ironically, it was that hiccup."

"Well, there you go. You answered correctly, into the mic." He laughed. "See? No one's going to be talking about my shitty voice after that. Thank you for stealing the show."

"I thought you sounded better tonight," I said, relieved to be able to say that and mean it.

His face lit up like a Christmas tree. "Really? Don't bullshit me, Emily. I can handle the truth."

"I wouldn't. I don't have any reason to lie."

"Well, thank fuck someone around here is honest with me. I didn't say a freaking word all morning and afternoon, hoping that resting my voice would help. Seems it did."

"If shutting up helps, you shouldn't be talking to me right now."

"Okay, fair point. But talking to you is my reward for a job well done. I can be quiet in my sleep tonight and all day tomorrow."

I shook my head. "You're too much."

God, he looked so freaking hot right now. His dark hair was damp from the shower, falling over his forehead. He wore a sleeveless shirt that really showcased his muscles and tats. I would never tire of looking at all of his ink. My body tingled from being in close proximity to him. Goose bumps peppered my skin.

"I know it's late. But hang out with me for a while."

"I can't."

"Why?" He flashed me a wicked grin. "The pee pads would be for nothing, then."

"Next time, please make it *anything* besides pee pads."

"You called me out on my fake allergies. Since you know I just order stuff as an excuse to see you, I figured I'd have a little fun with it." He batted his lashes, which were dangerously long for a man. "Come on. I've got good food for us."

"It's not appropriate for me to be hanging out with you, given my job here."

"Says who? I make the rules, if you hadn't noticed."

I looked out the window toward the skyline, feeling myself cave. "I don't know…"

"I just want your company. Nothing more, Emily." He made an X over his contoured chest. "Cross my heart and hope to die."

A whiff of his amazing scent floated in the air toward me. I *wanted* to spend time with him. That was the problem. What had started as general curiosity about this man had turned into nothing short of an obsession I could never admit to. It was far more than a crush at this point. I'd stolen a music magazine someone had on the bus so I could look, up close and personal, at the photo of Tristan's shirtless chest. I wanted to memorize all of his body art.

So, yeah, I *definitely* needed to leave. But instead, I asked, "What do you have to eat?"

"It's not as good as Abdul's, but Stephen went out and got me Middle Eastern tonight."

"Is there falafel?"

"Maybe." He winked.

I walked into the penthouse suite, marveling at the way the city lights illuminated the room. I stopped in front of the window and noticed his powerful stance behind me in the reflection on the glass. Now my body had gone from tingling to on fire. The hairs on my arms stiffened as he spoke softly behind me.

"Let's eat."

Tristan arranged the food on the counter. We each made a plateful and took it over to the living area, where we ate casually, sitting across from each other on two different couches. My nerves started to calm.

The peace was short-lived, though. In the middle of our meal, the elevator doors opened and in walked a beautiful woman with legs for miles and long, bright blue hair. Her slender arms were covered in tattoos, and her fake breasts spilled out of a black leather corset.

What the hell? I put my plate down and sat up a bit, feeling my throat about to close.

Tristan's brows drew in as he stood. "Can I help you?"

"Atticus said you sent for me."

"I'm sorry. He lied. I didn't send for anyone..."

"Oh." She looked down at her feet. "Sorry."

"No worries. Have a good night."

She turned around and got right back into the elevator.

An awkward silence hung in the air as Tristan sat back down.

"Figures that would happen when you were here." He scrubbed a hand over his face. "I've been trying to convince you I'm not with a woman every damn night, yet somehow they keep magically appearing."

"I guess you weren't lying when you told me he sends you girls."

"Yeah. I told him to stop, but he doesn't listen."

"Why stop?" I asked scornfully before taking a long sip of water to squelch my unfounded jealousy.

"Because I don't like those kinds of surprises anymore."

My cheeks burned. "If I wasn't here, would you have invited her to stay?" I braced for his answer.

"Not tonight. But I think the real question is..." He tilted his head. "How different would it be for me if you weren't on this tour? Your presence has been a good distraction. So I think it's safe to say my headspace might be entirely different if I didn't have *you* to look forward to. The person I am without you on tour might have been more likely to let her in, yeah—out of sheer boredom."

"Are you implying that your lack of interest in groupies is because of me?"

"I look forward to seeing you. My focus has therefore shifted. It's not even a sexual thing, but—"

"Oh, right. I'm no Megan Fox," I interrupted.

"I never said that."

"What you did say was that you don't have friends who are women, yet you insist you're not interested in me sexually. That's a direct contradiction. So needless to say, I'm a little confused as to what the deal is here."

His eyes seared into mine. "You're the realest human I've met since I got caught up in fame. And since that night you trusted me enough to confess what happened with your mother's boyfriend, I've wanted to know more about you. But I haven't wanted to overwhelm you with questions. I'm trying to get my fix in subtle installments. And, yeah, maybe you're my first female friend." He winked.

"Is it, like, morbid curiosity you have about me?"

"Not morbid. But curiosity? Yes. Absolutely."

I was supposed to be the curious one in this equation. How had this turned into a two-way street? I didn't know, except to say that no one made me feel the way Tristan did when he looked at me—like I always had every ounce of his attention. He'd made it clear with his actions that he *was* interested in me. Besides, he could have any woman he wanted sexually, so it couldn't have been only about attraction. I wasn't used to this kind of attention. And, I had to say, as much as I wanted to resist, it felt good.

"What else do you want to know, Tristan?"

He made himself more comfortable on the couch. "Start from the beginning. Tell me about your childhood."

"There's not much to tell except that my parents broke up when I was three. My brother Max is a few years older than me and lives with his girlfriend in Oklahoma now. So I don't see him much. Anyway, my parents were never married. But my dad left us when I was so young that I don't even remember him."

"Where is he today?"

"Probably still in Missouri somewhere. But I'm actually not sure. Sad, huh?"

"For *him*, yeah. He doesn't know what he's missing."

"I don't think he cares..." I chuckled angrily. "And sadly, neither do I anymore." I thought back to a dream I'd once had. "Once when I was around thirteen, I had a vivid dream that my father showed up at my door with an Easter basket and a live bunny. The basket was filled with pink flowers. Peonies. The bunny was just sitting in this huge pile of pink peonies. It was the cutest little light brown bunny with floppy ears. He handed me the basket and asked if he could make up for some of the time we'd lost. The dream ended before I could give him an answer. I remember waking up and feeling so sad—not because of my father, but because the little bunny wasn't real. Neither were the peonies. That's when I realized I really had given up on him."

"Wow." Tristan nodded. "That's so interesting. Once someone disappoints you that badly, they don't deserve anything more than to be overshadowed by a rabbit and peonies."

"Yeah," I muttered. "Exactly."

"So it was just you, your brother, and your mom?"

"Yup. Well, us and her many boyfriends. I got so used to the changeover every couple of years that I almost came to expect it. We all know how that last one ended, though…" I shivered. "Ironically, there hasn't been anyone serious since him."

"She never dated again?"

"As far as I know, she hasn't. At least no one serious. I think that situation scared her off men."

"That guy…did he beat your mother more than that one day?"

"Yeah. He was the worst of the bunch. I guess you could say she saved the best for last." I looked away. "During those years, I was so wrapped up in high school, I turned a blind eye to it for a while. I felt guilty leaving her alone with him, though. But she claimed to love him. Things just kept getting worse. He started getting real paranoid, accusing her of cheating on him." I tightened my fists. "Then the day I came home and found him choking her…" I cringed, thinking back to that nightmare. "I had to act fast." My breath shook.

"It's okay." He reached his arm out. "You don't have to go into the details."

"You know how the story ends anyway, right?" I let out a long exhale.

Tristan nodded and just looked at me for a moment. "What was life like after that?"

"I lived with a lot of guilt. Even if he deserved what happened, it's hard to live with something like what I did. I began to self-sabotage a lot of the good things in my life. I knew I needed a massive change in scenery, so it became my mission to get the hell out of Shady Hills."

"What kind of self-sabotage?"

"I had a boyfriend at the time that happened." I swallowed hard.

"What happened with him?"

Am I really going here, too? "Jacob was everything to me. We were friends long before we ever dated. The dating part was a small chapter of our overall story. We'd been friends almost our whole lives, actually—since we were really young. In high school, we tried our hand at dating. I never wanted to hurt him, but after the incident with my mother's boyfriend, I fell into a dark place. I felt like I didn't deserve Jacob. I wanted to spare him the grief of dealing with me while I worked through my issues. I also knew I needed to leave town, and he was a year younger than me. He had his entire senior year left while I was going to college in Nevada." I shook my head. "So I ended things with him—for his own good. I thought we were too young to be that serious, too. I didn't want to ruin our friendship by staying romantically involved."

"You regret it?"

"Only the part where I broke his heart."

Tristan blinked. "You're not still in love with him?"

His question hurt my chest. If there was one thing I knew for sure... "I will always love him."

"Where is he now?"

I shut my eyes, willing the pain away. "He's dead."

Chapter 12

TRISTAN

My heart sank. Had this kid killed himself because she'd ended things? All of a sudden the photo of her and that guy on her social media made sense—the one she said she'd miss forever. That must've been him.

"How did he die?"

"Car accident. He was riding in the back of a car with these guys who stupidly decided to race another car. They hit a tree, and Jacob didn't survive."

My stomach tensed. "I'm so fucking sorry."

"I was at college when I got the call. He and I were still in touch from time to time, but things had been different since the breakup. He didn't want to think about me dating guys while I was at school. And I wanted to give him the freedom to enjoy his senior year. I never imagined that something like that could happen. It stole any chance I had to make things right with him again."

This girl had been through more pain in a couple of years than anyone should have in their lifetime.

"I have to learn to forgive myself," she added.

"Forgive yourself?" I blinked. "You didn't cause his death."

"No, but I made a part of his life painful. I wish I could take it all back. And of course, I can't help but wonder how things might have turned out if I'd still been home in Shady Hills, if I'd never left. He might've been with me that night and not in that car."

"You can't think like that, though. For all you know, you might've been with him in that car."

"Sometimes I wish I was."

I frowned. "Don't say that, Emily."

"I thought you liked my honesty."

"I do. But I don't want you to think like that. And if you truly believe that, you need to change your perspective."

Her eyes grew watery. "Jacob was honest and kind-hearted and a representation of all that is good in the world. After what happened with my mother's boyfriend, he did everything he could to help me see things in a different light. And I thanked him by breaking up with him. It's really hard to spin it any other way."

"You had your reasons. Good, logical reasons. And you were so freaking young."

"He needed to be free of me. And I needed to go away to college without any responsibilities. I needed to grow up. He was the only boyfriend I'd ever had. But he still deserved better than for me to end things with almost no warning."

I shook my head. "Like we talked about before, there's a lot we don't understand about life—about why things happen the way they do, why good people die young. All we can do is the best we can. And, Emily, I haven't known you very long, but I know *you're* doing the damn best you can with what you've been dealt. And I'm proud of you." I reached for her hand. "It's an honor to know you."

"I wish I felt like I was doing my best," she admitted, taking my hand. "All I see when I look in the mirror is someone who's hurt people."

"That's what I mean by perception. When you get the right therapy, you won't see it that way anymore. You don't need to work through this alone."

She took a deep breath and let go of my hand. "Well, that's my life in a nutshell. Not much more I can say. Broken childhood. Killed a man. Lost a boy I loved with all my heart. I've felt outside of myself and floated through life ever since. I graduated from college and somehow ended up in Chicago buying pee pads for one of the most famous rockstars on Earth."

"Well, I, for one, am damn grateful for that." I smiled, and she returned it. Thank God she was smiling again.

She blew out a long breath. "I've had enough of talking about me, if that's okay?"

"Of course. But thank you for sharing as much as you did."

"I gave you way more than you bargained for."

"I can handle it all. I'm always here if you need to talk. I mean that, Emily. Day or night."

She nodded and looked at me a moment. "Tell me about *your* childhood."

"Not sure I can remember that far back." I winked.

"Well, you *are* old as fuck." She laughed.

Once again, I gave myself props for making her smile. Truthfully, I felt almost guilty thinking about how much easier I'd had it growing up.

"I had a nice childhood. It was pretty typical up until a certain point. You know, the classic situation. My dad coached all my sports teams while my mother made cookies for the school bake sale—that kind of thing." I paused, reflecting. "Then when I was about twelve, everything changed. My parents got divorced, and my dad remarried a couple of years later. It wasn't traumatic or anything, but it did turn my world upside down in a way."

She nodded. "I can't imagine having all that and then losing it. That might be tougher than not knowing what you're missing."

"It sucked at the time. But it's all good. I'm grateful for the normalcy I did have. I'll always cherish those early years."

"How old were you when you left home?"

"I moved to L.A. at sixteen. Whenever something difficult happens in my life, I throw myself into music. I was writing lyrics from a very young age. Taught myself how to play guitar at, like, thirteen. The time when my parents got divorced was ironically the time that everything started happening for me. I eventually found a talent manager. But he was California-based and wanted me out there, which is why I moved."

"How did you manage moving away from home at that age?"

"My mom moved with me."

"Ah, I didn't know that."

I chuckled. "I don't know if that would've happened if my parents had still been married. My father had firm roots in Iowa and wouldn't have been okay with just leaving."

"Where are your parents now?"

"They're both back in Spirit Lake, the town where I grew up. When my career took off, and I was old enough to be on my own, my mother moved back home. My dad ended up having two more kids with his new wife. So I have a half-brother and half-sister."

"Are you close with them?"

"I wish I could tell you yes. We're cordial, but not too close. That's partially because they were so young when I left home. I never really got a chance to know them. I visit them at holidays and stuff."

"Wow. You really left everything behind, then."

Everything.

And everything at that time had a name.

Cheyenne.

Thoughts of her invaded my mind. Back then, she was the one thing I'd left behind that mattered, the only thing I knew I'd miss.

Cheyenne would most definitely be a story for another day. But Emily wasn't the only one who had regrets about their first love.

Chapter 13

EMILY

My phone rang while I was out running an errand during our stop in St. Louis.

When I saw it was my friend Leah from home, I picked up.

"The hiccup heard around the world..." were the first words out of her mouth.

"Where did you see that?" I asked.

"Are you kidding? It's all over the Internet."

Great. I'd been so busy that I hadn't gone online much lately. But I should've known someone had captured that and posted it.

"I can't believe he called you to the stage. That's so cool."

"Actually, I wish he hadn't."

"I would die if that man so much as walked by me, let alone brought me up onstage with him. I mean, I'm not Stacia with her freaking jar of hair, but Jesus..."

"I'm not starstruck when it comes to him." *Only mildly obsessed.* I cleared my throat. "Tristan and I have actually gotten to know each other."

"Are you serious? I guess I assumed you didn't have that much contact with the band. You've been holding out on me."

Not wanting to get into it, I downplayed things. "There's not much to tell. The nature of my job means I interact with him from time to time. We've talked a bit. That's all."

Talked a bit. We'd had intimate conversations, I'd told him most of my secrets, and I felt like he could see through my soul. *Talked a bit, yeah.*

"What have you talked about?"

"All sorts of things. Life. He's not as egotistical as you'd think someone with his level of fame might be. He said he appreciates me because I never treat him any differently because he's famous."

"Well, that's cool. It would be disappointing to find out he's an asshole."

"He's definitely not."

"What about the other guys? Atticus and Ronan are so freaking hot. I swear, the three of them together..."

"I don't really know them as much. Atticus and Ronan are the wild ones. They like to party more than Tristan. They work hard but play harder."

"They're a little younger than Tristan, right?"

"Yeah. Tristan is almost thirty-eight. Atticus and Ronan are in their early thirties, I believe."

"What about the other guy?"

"The keyboardist? That's Melvin. He's nice but not really part of their close circle. Anders is the original one, but he's in rehab, and they don't know when he's coming back."

"They must get a ton of girls, huh?"

"They do," I agreed, ignoring the knot in my stomach.

"Can't say I blame them. I'd be dangerous in their shoes if I had a dick," she joked.

"Wouldn't we all." I chuckled.

"I'm sorry I won't get a chance to see you while you're in town," she said. "I can't believe I'm away visiting Chase while you'll be in Shady Hills."

Leah had recently met a guy from out of state. But it worked out just as well that she wouldn't be home while I was in town. I wouldn't have much time to hang out with her since I mainly wanted to spend time with my mother.

"No worries. Enjoy your time with Chase." I paused. "Anyway, I have to run. I've got to get down to the arena."

"Wait, before you hang up. Do you mind if I repost the hiccupping video on social media and say you're my friend?"

I rolled my eyes. "Go for it."

Leah giggled. "It'll be my fifteen seconds of fame."

"Glad to help."

~

Despite his better vocals at the last show in Chicago, the raspiness I'd noticed when Tristan wasn't having a good night came back for the St. Louis performance this evening. It made me sad for him, especially since he'd thought he'd been turning a corner by resting his voice during the day. There was a second show planned here tomorrow night, so he wouldn't even have a full day to rest it this time.

I didn't see Tristan after tonight's show because I left before it ended to go to my mom's. Since my hometown was an hour from St. Louis, I'd gotten special permission to leave the crew and spend the night at home. I'd gotten the day off tomorrow, too, but would have to rejoin everyone after the second St. Louis show tomorrow night in order to board the bus and leave for the next city. This was my one and only chance to see my mother, and I was so grateful for the time off.

When the car dropped me in front of my mom's house, I took a deep breath. Coming here was always a mix of emotions. So many good memories, but many bad ones.

The smell of chicken cooking in the crockpot greeted me when I entered the house and dropped my bag.

My mother came running. "You made it!"

After a long hug that was followed by my quick recap of tour life thus far, I joined her in the kitchen. Together we prepared the chicken enchiladas she'd started.

"I can't believe my beautiful baby girl is here."

"I'm so glad this worked out," I told her as I shredded some cheese.

"Your aunt Jean sent me the video of you hiccupping."

I stopped shredding for a moment. "The whole world has seen that, apparently."

"It doesn't seem to faze you." She chuckled.

"Nothing fazes me anymore, Mom."

She flashed me a sympathetic look, seeming to understand what I meant. "Please tell me you're happy."

Happy was a stretch. But things had been better lately. "For the first time in what feels like forever, I'm content. This position leaves me little time to think, which is apparently exactly what I needed."

She nodded. "I'm so glad you took it. Too much time to think isn't good."

"I'm sorry I got here so late. But at least I don't have to rush out in the morning. I got the day off and get to hang until you have to go to work tomorrow night."

We continued to chat as we sat together and shared the enchiladas, and after we'd cleaned up, I ventured to my old room. A charm bracelet Jacob had given me years ago sat atop the bureau. That was all it took to make me want to cry. Being back here was always an adjustment at first. So many memories at every corner.

My phone rang, interrupting my thoughts.

A rush of adrenaline hit as I answered. "What's going on, Tristan?"

"Well, that totally backfired." He groaned.

"What backfired?"

"I was so fucking braindead tonight after the show that I forgot you said you were taking off for your mother's house. I ordered freaking Bengay to my suite, and they had Mario deliver it. What a total buzzkill, and it completely defeated the purpose. He wasn't very happy with me."

I burst into laughter. "Thanks for the report. I needed that tonight. But you're an idiot, Tristan. Serves you right. That's what you get."

"I'm sorry to interrupt your family time. I just...felt like hearing your voice. I know it's late, but I'm a selfish prick so..."

"It's okay. I wasn't sleeping anyway."

"Did you have a nice night with your mom?"

"Yeah. We made my favorite enchiladas, and I told her all about the tour. She's actually a fan of you guys now. She started listening to your music when I found out I got the job."

"Do me a favor and thank her for creating you for me, okay?"

My cheeks hurt from smiling, but the lingering silence on the other end of the line was deafening. "Are you alright?" I asked.

He sighed. "Are you asking me that because I'm calling you so late, or because you noticed my voice was off tonight?"

"Both, I guess."

"I'm not okay, to be honest. I wish I could cancel tomorrow night's show. I've never canceled a show, Emily. Not once."

"Is that an option?"

"Not without serious repercussions, pissing off thousands of people."

"What would happen if you got sick?"

"I'd cancel, and everyone would have to deal with it."

"You've really never canceled a performance before? In your whole career?"

"Never."

"Well, then I'd say you're due. I think you need to tell Doug the truth about everything. Tell him you need a day to rest your voice."

"I don't know." After a long pause, he said, "Maybe you're right. Maybe I need to."

"Hang up with me, and go talk to him about it now," I insisted.

"I'm not ready to get off the phone with you yet."

"Go tell him you need a night off, then call me back. I'll be here."

"Alright. Gonna do it." He sighed. "Thank you, Emily."

"Of course."

Time crawled after we hung up. I worried for him. A single night off was one thing, but what if he needed more? What if people figured out why he'd canceled? The press could be brutal. There was no shame in it, of course, but I knew Tristan well enough to know that having this go public would devastate him. And the fact that *I* was feeling devastated right now indicated just how much Tristan meant to me. That was scary.

Almost an hour went by. It was nearly one in the morning when my phone finally rang.

I picked up. "Hey, what happened?"

"I did it. I told Doug everything," Tristan said. "He agrees we should cancel tomorrow so I can rest my voice." He sighed into the phone. "At least it's the second show here, and we were able to get one in. That's not going to satisfy the people who bought tickets for tomorrow night, though."

"You don't owe them anything, Tristan."

"I won't be able to sleep tonight. I'll be staring at the ceiling, second-guessing my decision."

"Have you heard from the guys since you told Doug?"

"They're still out partying. They'll find out soon enough. Honestly, I wish I didn't have to be here when they do."

I didn't know what came over me, but it felt like the right thing to say. "Why don't you come here?"

"To your mother's house?"

"Yeah. You can rest here tonight and tomorrow, away from everyone. We'll go back to the bus tomorrow night."

"I don't want to intrude on your time with your mom."

"Are you kidding? She'd die to meet you. She's asleep now, of course, but we can explain everything in the morning. Or *I'll* explain, since you'll be silent. I mean it. If you come here, you can't talk. You need to rest your voice."

"Yes, ma'am. Whatever you say."

"You're coming?"

"Already putting on my jacket."

"How are you getting here?"

"I'll call a car."

"Under your name?"

"Hell no. I use Stephen's account when I want to remain incognito. I'll put my shades on and my hood. I'll be good."

After I gave him my address, we hung up, and I wondered if I needed my head checked. Not only would my mother *definitely* get the wrong idea, I wasn't even sure what my intentions were. It wasn't just that I had a massive crush on Tristan. I cared about him a lot. All I wanted was to protect him—not only from the world, but from his own harsh self-judgment.

I waited by the window until I saw the bright lights of a car pulling up in front of the house. The car door slammed shut, and then a dark shadow of a man dressed in black approached the house. With every step he took, my heart beat faster.

Chapter 14

TRISTAN

Emily opened for me before I even reached the door. She looked so damn beautiful standing there. Her long brown hair blew in the breeze as she stepped out to greet me. I didn't give two fucks what was appropriate right now; I wrapped my arms around her and pulled her into a hug, letting every ounce of tension release with my exhale.

"Thank you," I said, taking in a long whiff of her flowery scent as if it were my oxygen. "You have no idea how nice this is, to be away from everything."

Her warm body was an intoxicating mix of comfort and electricity. She molded perfectly to me as her heart beat against my chest. I felt secure in a way I wasn't used to. Already this was a place I never wanted to leave.

She pulled back and led me inside. "Don't forget. You can't talk."

"Can I at least whisper?"

"Only if you have to."

Emily's mother's house was small but homey. The entryway had a coat closet off to the side. The living room had lots of windows and several plants. I immediately noticed a photo of Emily hanging on the wall. She couldn't have been more than thirteen. She still had the same small gap between her teeth, but the smile on her face in that image was different than her smile now—more genuine, less hesitant. The things that had darkened her smile were yet to come when that photo was taken.

Emily moved toward the kitchen, leaving me standing in the middle of the living room.

"Where are you going?" I asked.

"I'm going to make you some tea with lemon and honey. It'll be good for your voice."

Couldn't argue with that. "Thank you. That's very sweet."

Being here was heaven. My life was divided between hotel rooms, tour buses, and my vast, but empty, mansion in L.A. Spending time in an actual, lived-in, welcoming home was a treat.

I lay back on the couch, appreciating the way my body sank into the cushions. Appreciating the quiet. I felt incredibly safe here, away from all my troubles.

Several minutes later, Emily brought me a cup of steaming hot tea. She placed it in front of me on the coffee table, and I could smell the lemon.

"Thank you. I don't deserve this treatment." After blowing on it, I took a sip, the water just hot enough to soothe without burning my throat. When I looked over at her, I caught her staring, which she often did. She turned away quickly. I loved catching her in the act, but it always made me wonder what she was thinking, whether she stared because she found me attractive, or if she was thinking something else.

I looked around. "I love this house. It reminds me of my own growing up."

"It's small but has a lot of character, although my mother would be freaking out right now if she knew you were here and she hadn't vacuumed."

As if I could notice dust when all I wanted to do was stare into Emily's green eyes. "You have no idea how much it means to be able to decompress here without anyone breathing down my neck."

She nodded. "I sensed you needed a hideaway."

"You were right."

"This was my only opportunity to give it to you."

I set my tea on the coffee table. "You once said you had a savior complex. Are you trying to save me right now? Because it's working."

"You don't need to be saved. You just need to understand that you're not perfect. And that's okay. You've accomplished more in your life than most people ever will. You deserve some grace and some peace."

"*You're* my peace lately, Emily. I feel more at peace knowing you're on the tour. For the first time in a long time, I look forward to seeing someone every day, having someone to talk to who won't judge me, someone who doesn't give a shit about my celebrity status. Everything's going to hell in a handbasket around me, and yet I've never looked forward to each day more."

Her gaze shifted to the floor, and I hoped I hadn't taken my honesty too far. I looked around, desperate for a change in subject. "When I lose everything, maybe I can get myself a place like this. It's more homey and comfortable than my place in L.A."

"It'll go well with your McDonald's plans."

I snorted. "Is there one nearby? I'd take you there, but it's way past closing time, isn't it? That would defeat the purpose."

"You're not gonna lose anything, Tristan. Even your worst is better than most musicians at their best."

I smiled. "Ronan says the same thing."

"He's wise."

"Either that or he smokes a lot of weed." I laughed. "Anyway, no wonder I keep both of you around. It's good for my ego." I squinted. "I thought you didn't even like our music. What the hell is happening there? Is it growing on you or something?"

"It's not that I didn't like it. I just wasn't familiar with it. But now that I've listened to it, I'm a genuine fan. Although, not the type of fan who'll tattoo your face on my body or keep a jar of your hair."

"Say what?"

She shook her head. "You don't want to know."

"I think you're right." I shifted on the couch. "So, tell me specifically what you like about our music."

Emily didn't hesitate. "I love how it's not just one thing. It's a blend of hard rock with alternative elements and a little pop."

"What else?" *You're really shameless this evening, Tristan.*

"You deliver every word with intensity and emotion. In combination with Ronan's bass and Atticus's timekeeping on drums, it's such great synchronicity. It's a reflection of the relationship you three have."

"Anything else?" I asked, beaming with pride.

"Yes. Lyrically, your songs aren't simple. Each one is well thought out, and there's a real vulnerability there.

That's why so many people love you. Because they can relate."

"I don't care if you're stroking my ego right now. That was beautiful. Thank you."

I could kiss you for that.

I *wanted* to kiss her.

But I wouldn't.

Instead, I took a sip of my tea and shut my eyes for a moment. Both of us should be getting some sleep, but I was nowhere ready to say goodnight to Emily.

"Are you tired?" I asked.

"I should be, but I'm not."

"Neither am I. But say the word if you need to get to bed."

We talked for a while until she put her foot down.

"That's enough chatting. You need to rest your voice." Emily got up and disappeared down a small hallway before she came back with a blanket and a pillow.

"Do you think the couch is comfortable enough?" she asked.

"It's perfect." I'd have slept on a rock just to be here.

"We don't have any extra bedrooms. My mother turned my brother's room into her office and sewing room after he moved away."

"The couch is more than fine."

"Then I'll see you in the morning," she said.

I sat up suddenly. "Wait, what if your mother wakes up and finds me here?"

"I'll set my alarm so I wake up before she does. She usually sleeps in pretty late anyway."

Famous last words.

Because the following morning, I was woken by a scream.

Chapter 15

TRISTAN

My heart raced as I shot up off the couch. "I'm sorry! I can explain. I'm—"

She narrowed her eyes. "Wait, I know who you are. I just—"

Emily came rushing out of her bedroom, her hair a tousled mess. "Mom! I'm sorry. I meant to get up before you. This is Tristan Daltrey."

"My God, Emily. I *know* who he is." She held her hand to her chest. "But...how come you didn't tell me he was coming over?"

"I didn't know until after you fell asleep."

I cleared my throat before practically vomiting out a bunch of words. "Your daughter was kind enough to provide me with a safe haven last night. I've had some problems with my voice lately and had to cancel the show that was supposed to be tonight. I didn't want to face any-one and deal with all of their questions, so she suggested

I come here. Emily is one of the few people who knows what's really going on with me."

"I see. I'm sorry to hear you're having trouble. And well..." She laughed nervously. "I'm sorry for being so startled. Welcome."

I placed my hand over my chest. "*I'm* the one who's sorry for startling you." Damn, my heart was still pounding.

"No worries." She smiled and held out her hand. "I'm Terry."

"It's a pleasure to meet you, Terry." I took her hand, trying to seem innocent instead of like the predator she probably thought I was. I felt like a high school kid who'd gotten caught in his girlfriend's room with his pants down. Or at my age, maybe the high school teacher.

"Tristan needs to rest his voice today, Mom. So we shouldn't talk to him much."

"I can whisper..." I said.

Terry clapped her hands together. "Let me make everyone some breakfast. Pancakes sound good?"

"That sounds amazing," I said.

"Thanks, Mom. That'd be great."

I felt so undeserving of this treatment. Especially when my thoughts about Emily were anything but pure. If her mother knew, she'd kick me out the door instead of making me goddamn pancakes.

After Terry disappeared into the kitchen, I walked over to Emily. "I feel bad. What happened to your alarm?"

"She beat me by a matter of minutes. Trust me, though, she's fine with you being here."

I ran my hand through my hair. "I have no idea how she could be."

"I spent half my life waking up to strange men she'd brought over. This is the first time I had the honor of returning the favor."

That seemed a little fucked up. "Not sure how she could be fine with some dude who's closer to her age than yours camping out on your living room sofa. If I were her, I'd be suspicious."

She ignored my concern, placing her index finger at my mouth. "No talking."

She's lucky I didn't bite that finger. I wanted to. "You're so bossy." My eyes lingered on hers for a moment then fell to her lips.

Emily turned toward the kitchen, and I followed. Her ass looked good this morning in black yoga pants that clung to her like a second skin. I willed myself not to get a hard-on before having to face her mother again. But damn. She'd tied her hair up in a ponytail, revealing her slender neck and those ears that protruded. Apparently, being in proximity of her mother did nothing to quell the ache inside me for this girl.

The smell of brewed coffee was heaven. Emily's mom made a bunch of pancakes and set a large stack on the table. It was one of the best breakfasts I'd had in a while. It tasted like freedom. Like small-town heaven. This reminded me so much of home.

Every time I opened my mouth to speak, Emily glared at me like a drill sergeant. But it felt rude not making conversation with her mother after she'd been so hospitable.

I turned to Emily. "Can I whisper for a few minutes, please?"

She shrugged.

"I can't tell you how nice it's been having your daughter on tour with us, Terry. She's conscientious and hard-working and honestly, a breath of fresh air."

Terry smiled over at Emily proudly. "I'm grateful that she's having this experience. She hasn't had it easy in life." Her mother pursed her lips, stopping short of saying anything further.

"She's told me some things..." I said as I looked over at Emily, unsure how much to divulge.

"I told him about Henry," Emily clarified.

Henry Acadia. The guy she'd killed defending her mother. I'd never forget his name.

Her mother's eyes widened. "You did..." She exhaled. "I'm surprised. You don't tell anyone about...what happened."

Emily looked over at me. "There was something about Tristan when I first met him. I felt like I could trust him."

Hearing that twisted me up inside. It touched me that she trusted me, but then again, *should she?*

"I would never tell anyone," I told Terry. "I suggested to Emily that she see our band's therapist, actually. She's really great. And I think she could help her with some of the trauma."

Terry nodded. "I've been telling her she should do that for years. Maybe she'll listen to you before she listens to me." She looked down into her coffee cup for a moment. "There's a lot I wish I could take back about Emily's childhood. I owe her so much. I owe her my life. I just want her to be happy and find something she loves doing. Perhaps find a good partner. As long as she's happy. It kills me that I can't make that happen for her." She reached over to her daughter. "She deserves the world."

"I couldn't agree more," I said.

Terry smiled, lightening the mood. "I still can't believe Tristan Daltrey is sitting in my kitchen."

I felt my face burning. I really wanted her mother to like me. Because *I* liked Emily. But once again, I reminded myself that messing around with Emily wasn't an option. She deserved stability, and that wasn't something I'd ever be able to give her.

I stood and took my plate over to the dishwasher, then returned to retrieve Emily's. "I don't want to intrude on your mother-daughter time. I saw you have a nice yard. It looks like a beautiful day out, and I brought a notebook with me. I'm gonna head out back and write some lyrics." I looked over at Emily. "I trust you approve since that doesn't include talking?"

Grinning, she nodded. "You've already far exceeded your speaking limit today."

That afternoon, Emily and her mom went to get their nails done together.

While they were gone, I sat in the yard to clear my mind, unfortunately not feeling creative today. Not much songwriting got done, but it was still nice to sit in peace, ignoring the phone calls and texts that came in from the guys. I'd owe them a massive explanation when I got back to the bus tonight, but I needed this mental break, and that meant putting my phone on mute and silencing all notifications. I'd never realized how healthy unplugging was for the soul. The stress felt like it was melting away with each second I stayed away from my phone.

Later, I was back inside on the living room couch when Emily returned. I was surprised to find she was alone.

"Hey." I stood. "Where's your mom?"

"She had to go straight to her job."

"Where does she work?"

"She works the dinner shift at a local diner, three to eleven. She wasn't able to get tonight off."

"Ah, I see."

"We have a few hours, though. Are you hungry?"

"Yeah." I nodded. "I could eat."

Emily and I ended up ordering food to be delivered and had a relaxing meal outside on the back deck. After we ate, we went back inside and hung out in the living room. We had about an hour before we needed to call a car to return to the tour.

"I'm sure your mother gave you the third degree today," I said, hoping I sounded casual.

"What makes you think that?"

"She had to have asked what the hell you were doing hanging out with me..."

Emily shrugged. "She wasn't mad, but she did wonder if there was anything going on between us."

My pulse began to race. "Did you tell her there wasn't?"

"I did." She stared into my eyes. "That's the truth, right?"

"Right." But as the seconds passed, I gave in to the urge to confess. "I need to be honest with you about something."

She shifted in her seat. "Okay..."

"When you told your mother this morning that you trust me, that meant a lot. But I shouldn't be fully trusted. Because I've been lying to you."

Concern crossed her face. "About what?"

"I've lied in the past when I said I didn't like you *that* way." I let out a shaky breath. "I like you *every* way. Even the ways I shouldn't. But I have no business crossing any lines with you, and I don't intend to. As you already know, I'm a lot older, and my lifestyle is all wrong for you. So, basically...my intentions are pure, but my desires aren't. I just thought you should know. Maybe you won't trust me as much."

She swallowed hard, her eyes falling to my lips. "Doesn't sound like you trust yourself..."

"I definitely don't fully trust myself around you anymore. Especially when you look at me the way you do sometimes...like you're looking at me right now."

She drew in a shaky breath. "You've never been with anyone as young as me?"

"I didn't say that. But you're not a one-night kind of girl. I like you, more than I've liked anyone in a very long time. I don't want to mess with your heart. A girl like you needs someone nice to settle down with, not some self-absorbed asshole musician who's always on the road and can't even go anywhere without security. I don't want that for you. I want better."

Emily turned her nose up. "Well, lucky for you, I'm not interested in you romantically." Her face was red as a beet. I couldn't tell if she was lying or if I'd just made her really uncomfortable.

"Good." I nodded. "Smart girl," I added, barely audible. My eyes never left hers as we sat in silence, the soft hum of the furnace the only sound. The air felt charged with electricity, every moment and every breath amplified. Despite my applauding her supposed lack of interest in me, I wanted nothing more than to taste her lips right now. It was like nothing I'd just said mattered. Because if she'd been interested and willing, I would've kissed the hell out of her.

Emily shifted closer to me, our knees now touching. My dick stiffened as I became more aware of the heat of her body, her flowery scent. I still somehow managed to refrain from leaning in and taking her mouth with mine, but though Emily had said she wasn't interested in me, the look in her eyes sent a different message.

Yet despite my hopeful interpretation, I needed to respect what she was telling me, with words, that is. In fact, I hoped it was true, that she had no interest in me beyond friendship. That would make my dilemma a hell of a lot easier.

"Maybe we should head back," she finally said after clearing her throat. "You still have to have your talk with the guys. You can't avoid them forever, you know?"

"Okay." I let out a long breath. "Yeah."

The last thing I wanted was to leave, but this was her house, and if she was done here, it was time to go. Perhaps that was the best decision, given the tension in the air right now.

I expected her to get up, to start gathering her things. Instead, she stayed sitting next to me, not moving an inch. I prayed she couldn't tell I was getting hard.

When she finally did move, it wasn't to get off the couch. Emily leaned in and shocked the living hell out of me.

Chapter 16

EMILY

I couldn't tell you what came over me.

Was it the way he was looking at me—like he wanted to devour me—or just the way I'd been feeling about him for so long? What made me lose control like that?

But after I leaned in, I stopped short of actually placing my lips on his.

Instead, I chickened out and retreated, stumbling on my words. "I lied when I said I wasn't interested in you. I just don't *want* to be. It's dangerous and can't go anywhere and—"

He grabbed my wrist. "Were you just about to kiss me, Emily Applewood?"

"I considered it."

"Why the fuck did you stop?"

"Because I thought better of it."

"You mean you let your mind get in the way of what you really want?"

I shook my head and moved my gaze away from him. "I *can't* want you, Tristan."

"But you do. Is that what you're saying?"

When I didn't answer, he placed his hand on my chin until I looked him in the eyes. Even that little bit of contact made me weak in the knees.

"Emily, I told myself I wasn't allowed to kiss you. That I wasn't going to do something that made you think I wanted more from you than your friendship. But you wanting to kiss *me*? That's a fucking game changer." He licked his lips. "Lean in again. This time, I'm gonna catch it."

Unable to resist, I succumbed to the magnetic force between us, leaning in halfway. The next thing I knew, Tristan had wrapped his big hands around my face, his calloused fingers firmly against my cheeks. My body went weak against the couch as he leaned over me, pressing his lips to mine and pushing his tongue inside. *Oh.* I sighed into his mouth, relishing the reciprocal groan that vibrated over my tongue, the warm heat of his breath traveling down my throat.

The muscles between my legs contracted as he circled his tongue around mine. My body caught fire.

The kiss grew deeper, more frantic as my panties grew wetter by the second. I had never experienced this level of sexual excitement before, where I'd wanted someone so badly that nothing else in the world seemed to matter. Raking my fingers through his thick, messy mane of hair, I was desperate for more.

As if he could read my mind, Tristan flipped me around to straddle him.

He looked up at me, his beautiful blue eyes drunk with desire. "You are a fucking dream, Emily."

Between my legs, I felt the heat of his massive erection through his pants. That should've been my signal to rip myself away from him, but instead I bore down, pressing my clit into his bulge as he throbbed beneath me. Unable to control my need, I gyrated my hips to feel more of him. This had to be what taking a drug felt like. Because even though everything in me said to move my body off of his, I couldn't. It felt too good. I couldn't stop if my life depended on it.

"That's it. Grind against me. Do whatever you want. Use me for your pleasure." He groaned. "Fuck."

As my hips moved faster over his crotch, I kissed him with equal fervor. Tristan tasted divine as I savored every inch of his hot tongue. I tightened the muscles between my legs to keep from coming, all the while feeling selfish for using his body to satisfy my starvation. It had been so long since I'd been touched and *forever* since I'd been touched by a man. I'd only ever been with boys. This felt different. Much different.

A moment later, he flipped me back around to hover over me on the couch. He looked deeply into my eyes. "When was the last time you had sex?"

"Two years ago," I panted.

"That's a long fucking time. Who was it?"

"A guy from college. It was horrible. I didn't even come."

"And before that?"

"Jacob." I swallowed. "He was my first and the only other person."

He closed his eyes, seeming conflicted. My heart raced as I waited for him to say something.

Tristan finally opened his eyes again. "I'm not having sex with you. But I want to make you come. I want to watch your face and experience every second of you coming apart. I want to make you forget everything that's ever bothered you. Will you let me do that?"

Having completely lost my inhibitions, I nodded, desperate for whatever he was willing to give me.

"Are you sure your mother won't come home?"

"She won't. She can't leave work."

"Can we go to your room, just to be on the safe side?"

"Yes." I would've gone anywhere he wanted just to have his mouth back on mine again.

Taking his hand, I led him down the hall to my bedroom. I locked the door behind us and we tumbled onto the bed. Tristan put his gorgeous, tattooed arms on either side of me. Then he lowered himself to kiss me. Once again, I was lost in his breaths, his taste, the friction of our mouths. His erection pressed into my abdomen as our kiss deepened. Pulling his hair, I felt starved for more.

"You're so fucking hungry for it, Emily, aren't you?"

"Yeah," I muttered, bending my head back as he sucked on my neck.

"Me too. And I can't wait to devour you."

Allowing myself to get lost in him was wrong. I'd regret it tomorrow. As far as I was concerned, though, that was a problem for future me. Current me was too damn busy.

Until now, I hadn't realized how different it would feel to be with a man, how much more my body could react just from kissing him, from the feel of his scruff against my face, from his deep groans. I'd only gotten a taste today, and already I couldn't imagine ever being satisfied by anything less than this.

Jacob had been practically a kid when we were together. We were both over eighteen when we'd had sex, but very inexperienced. And the guy I'd slept with in college was completely forgettable. Tristan had me practically orgasming from kissing. I didn't know my body was capable of feeling so sensitized. It couldn't possibly get better than this.

With our lips still locked, Tristan slid one of his hands down to unbutton my jeans. Even the feel of his hand was enough to set me ablaze. He slid my pants down, and I worked to kick them off. Then I felt his warm palm cup me through my underwear. I jerked my hips, pressing my clit into his hand. He moved his palm in firm circles, never interrupting our kiss.

He slipped a finger into my panties, then another until three of his fingers were inside of me. "Oh God," he mumbled as he moved his fingers in and out, fucking me with one hand while the other squeezed my breast through my shirt.

"I can't believe how fucking wet you are." Rubbing his fingers along my clit, he spread my wetness around. "That feel good?"

I could hardly speak. "Ye...yes."

While I respected his decision not to rush into anything, I would've given anything to feel his cock moving in and out instead of his fingers. But Tristan had drawn a line. I was equally disappointed and grateful, since I was apparently not able to make responsible decisions today.

He fucked me with his fingers faster as he kissed me harder, never taking his lips off mine. My breathing quickened; I felt ready to lose it. But Tristan stopped kissing me suddenly. Cold air replaced the heat on my mouth as I yearned for the return of his lips.

He lowered his gaze to his hand, watching the way his fingers moved in and out of me.

"You have the most magnificent pussy. I wish you could see how beautiful it is." He pressed the thumb of his opposite hand against my clit as he sank his fingers in as deep as they would go. Then he began moving them. "Listen to that, how wet you are."

While I never wanted this to end, I felt myself coming undone.

As my breathing became more labored, he rasped, "Let go. Come all over my hand, baby. I want to watch you come."

Those words pushed me over the edge. The muscles between my legs tightened around his fingers, his thumb pressing into my clit as a powerful orgasm ricocheted through my body. It was euphoric, and he was so right, because in those seconds, not a single thing mattered in the world—not Henry nor Jacob dying, not any of the guilt I knew would come. It was just me and Tristan—his touch and his taste, our mutual desire causing me to lose all sense of reality, all sense of right or wrong.

He stayed with me until my muscles pulsed the last few times.

"That was so fucking beautiful," he whispered.

I could hear the wetness as he pulled his fingers out of me. My eyes followed as Tristan brought his fingers, covered in my arousal, to his mouth. He licked them clean as if it was the best thing he'd ever tasted. That made me tingle all over, nearly reviving my need to orgasm.

"I think I just found my new addiction." He slid his tongue across his bottom lip. "Fuck drugs. I could get high off *that*."

I reached up to thread my fingers through his hair. "You sure know how to make a woman lose her damn mind."

"Feel good now?"

"I don't remember the last time I felt this good, Tristan."

"Good." He lowered himself and enveloped my mouth with his, groaning over my lips. "Don't let me do anything more than that to you. Because once I fucking start, I won't be able to stop."

"Not sure I'm a very good influence, considering I'm the one who reached out to kiss you and started all this."

We lay across from each other in silence for a while.

"You surprised the hell out of me when you leaned in," he finally said.

"I surprised the hell out of *me*. But I agree, this can't be a thing. I just had...a moment. I've wondered what it would be like to kiss you for a while. I wasn't expecting the rest. But we can't do any of it again."

He groaned. "No way I can go through life without kissing you again. But I'll find a way to control myself beyond that."

I knew better. The more we were around each other, the more dangerous it would be. No way would I be able to resist doing more with him if he tried.

What have I done?

Reality came crashing down. My throat felt parched as I swallowed. "I don't like this feeling." Not sure I meant to say that aloud.

His brows drew in. "What feeling?"

"The *after*. It was amazing in the moment. But the after? The after will kill me. I'll be thinking of what we did all night tonight."

He pulled me toward him. "Then ride on my bus with me, so neither of us has to be alone thinking about it."

My eyes widened. "Are you crazy? How are we supposed to get away with that?"

"I'll make up an excuse as to why I need you there, if you want. But fuck what they think. I want you with me."

"You're gonna make up an excuse as to why you need me in your *bedroom*?" I laughed. "And what gullible people are going to buy said excuse?"

"I don't really give a fuck if they do or don't."

"Well, I do," I insisted.

He wrapped his hand around my hip. "The entire time here with you, I've barely thought about my voice. When I'm with you, I forget everything else and just enjoy being in the present. All I want to do is talk to you, look into your eyes, and now...kiss you and touch you. Bring you to orgasm. There's nothing else I care about at the moment."

I smiled sadly. "Becoming dependent on someone to forget about your problems isn't healthy."

"That's not *why* I want to be around you. Forgetting the bad shit is a result of being happy and present."

"I won't be around forever, Tristan. And I shouldn't get close to you like this."

"Says who?"

Of course, he didn't understand why I'd messed up so terribly in crossing the line with him. There was a lot he didn't understand about me. But rather than explain further, I looked over at the time. "We're gonna be late. We have to get back to the bus."

Tristan reluctantly got out of bed. He looked concerned as he watched me gathering my things.

"Hey." He placed his hands on my shoulders. "You alright?"

"Yeah. I'm fine." My stomach felt unsettled. Surely he could tell I was lying.

But even I couldn't pinpoint, nor articulate, what exactly was bothering me. It was so many things. The fact that I hadn't been honest with him. The fact that I wanted nothing more than to stay in this cocoon with him forever. The fact that seeing all those women throw themselves at him would be a lot harder now that my heart was involved. The fact that I might've had sex with him if he hadn't been so in control of the situation today. The list was endless. This was not at all where I was supposed to end up when this tour began.

As Tristan and I waited for our ride outside my mother's house, he rested his chin on the top of my head and wrapped his arms around me. I closed my eyes and allowed myself to be held by him, allowed myself to feel safe and cared for during this last moment of peace away from the tour.

Because I knew in my heart that everything had just gotten a whole lot more complicated.

Chapter 17

TRISTAN

After we returned to the tour, Emily went to her bus, and I went to mine to face the fire of my bandmates.

"So, like, what does this mean?" our interim keyboardist, Melvin, asked. "You're not getting the surgery, so it's just gonna keep getting worse?"

"Not necessarily. I'm trying to manage it—resting my voice when I don't have to use it. So all this talking right now isn't really helping me."

"Why not just get the damn surgery?" Atticus challenged.

I didn't want to admit I was scared. But that was the truth. "There are risks to that, and I need to do more research. I'm seeing my doctor when I get to L.A."

Atticus shook his head. "I don't understand why you haven't talked to me about this before."

"He talked to *me*," Ronan added.

Atticus glared at him. "That makes it ten times fucking worse," he spewed. "You open up to him about this and not me?"

"I just didn't want to alarm you. Ronan confronted me about it. That's the only reason I told him. I couldn't lie once he asked me a direct question."

"I notice everything while you guys have your heads stuck in your asses." Ronan raised his chin at me. "I also noticed Tristan getting out of a car today with Emily, though he's trying to convince me nothing is going on there. Might explain where he's been for the past day."

Atticus's eyes widened. "Emily the hot roadie?"

That comment irked me to no end. He'd better not have any freaking ideas about her. I'd kill him if he so much as *thought* about making a move on Emily.

"Yes. *That* Emily. But there's nothing going on," I lied.

Atticus flashed me a suspicious look. "You were with her the entire time you were gone?"

It made no sense to deny where I'd been, though I wouldn't be telling them anything *else*—more for Emily's privacy than my own.

"She grew up an hour away from here. I went to her house to get away from the tour for a while," I explained. "She knew I'd canceled and offered me a safe place to decompress."

"*She* knew you canceled the show before we did?" Ronan frowned.

"So what? She doesn't have a vested interest in anything. I felt comfortable talking to her about what was going on. She and I are cool like that."

Atticus shook his head. "You expect me to believe there's nothing going on between you and her?"

"I expect you to realize that it's none of your freaking business what I do."

"Well, no wonder you haven't been interested in anything lately besides retreating to your room after the show. Probably jerking it to thoughts of Emily," he chided.

I shook my head. "I need to be done talking now. I have to rest my voice."

No one argued with that as I headed past them to my bedroom in the back. Lying on the bed, I closed my eyes and vowed not to speak until we got to the next city.

I still couldn't believe what happened with Emily, the way she'd made the first move. Today shouldn't ever be repeated, but I couldn't possibly regret one of the best and hottest moments of my life. Who would've thought less was more? Holding back like I had, limiting myself to only pleasuring her, was one of the most erotic things I'd ever experienced.

And right now? I was so damn hard, I thought I might explode. It was a miracle I hadn't escaped to her bathroom and fucked my hand. But now I couldn't concentrate on anything else; all I wanted to do was taste her again. It had taken everything in me not to lower my mouth to her sweet pussy, but she'd given me more than I could've imagined to begin with.

Tonight I'd fantasize about what it would've been like to have more, to fuck her the way I wanted to. I'd already decided I shouldn't go there, though. Having sex with someone like Emily—someone I truly cared for—felt too intimate. It would mean something to me. And I couldn't afford to get feelings involved when I knew things would end as soon as the tour was over.

The bus lurched forward and began to move as we started toward the next city.

Having to endure the ride without getting to see or touch Emily would be torture. I wouldn't have minded exploring Shady Hills with her for days. Exploring *her* for days. Not sure her mother would appreciate my hanging around, though. How long could we keep her believing there was nothing going on? Pretty sure she knew better already.

I decided to call Emily's cell.

She picked up after a few rings. "Hey."

"Just checking in with you."

"I'm glad you did. How did it go talking to the guys?"

"It went okay. What choice do they have but to accept it? I'm glad the talk is over with."

"You shouldn't be talking to me. You need to rest your voice."

I sighed. She was right. "Will you text with me, then?"

"Yeah."

"Okay. Hanging up." I scrolled down to her name on my phone.

Tristan: Hi, Emily.

Emily: Hi, Tristan.

Tristan: Do anything interesting today?

Emily: You might say that.

Tristan: I'm still mad you wouldn't switch buses and stay with me tonight. Now I'm cuddling with Duffy and not you.

Emily: Duffy?

I looked over at the worn, gray stuffed toy I'd had since I was a kid.

Tristan: My ratty teddy bear from childhood. Where I go, he goes. The guys have given me a lot of shit for that over the years. But he's my good-luck charm.

Emily: That's actually adorable.

Tristan: Adorable for a nearly thirty-eight-year-old man to be sleeping with a teddy bear? Not sure. But I don't give a shit. It's the one thing I have from home, and he's sticking with me.

Emily: I can only imagine the things poor Duffy has witnessed.

Tristan: Thankfully, one of his eyes is coming loose. So he can't see very well.

Emily: Oh, that's good. LOL

Tristan: He wishes you were here on the bus with us, though.

Emily: I'd be safer on the BDSM bus.

I grinned.

Tristan: Ah yes, the BDSM bus and magic mushrooms.

Emily: Pretty sure the only magic mushroom is in your pants.

I bent my head back in laughter.

Tristan: I think you're right. And boy, you are fucking sassy tonight. I love it. Definitely seeing different sides of you today, literally and figuratively. ;-)

Emily: If today taught me anything, it's to stay on my own bus.

Tristan: Ouch. Am I that scary?

Emily: You're that good. And therein lies the problem.

Tristan: I barely showed you how good I am. I wanted to do more, but I need to be careful with you. I also don't trust myself not to take it too far.

Emily: I had no business messing around with you.

Tristan: Why do you keep saying that? We make the rules. And if I had my way, you'd be on this bus right now.

Emily: Didn't you have enough to explain to them today? You want to add why I'm suddenly traveling with you?

Tristan: I don't care what they think; although, I did deny anything between us when they asked earlier. But that was mainly to protect you. I didn't think you'd want them to know.

Emily: They suspected something?

Tristan: Ronan caught me with your scrunchie before. He also saw us getting out of the car together today.

Emily: I could get fired if they think we have something going on.

Tristan: I'll fire anyone who tries to fire you. There's no one who'd go against me. Plus, we don't have a company policy against dating people on the tour.

Emily: Have you ever dated anyone on one of your tours?

Shit.

Tristan: Never seriously.

Emily: You fucked someone who worked on a tour, then?

I sighed. I didn't want to lie to her.

Tristan: I had a thing with our former PR person. The one before Veronica. Last time we were in Europe.

Emily: I see. So this is what you do—hook up with people on tour.

Fuck.

Tristan: You asked me a question. I was honest. Don't use my answer as an excuse to minimize what's happening between us. I've been with a lot of women. That's not news. None of that has anything to do with you and me.

Emily: You and me? What am I to you exactly?

She'd given me an opportunity, and I didn't want to fuck it up. I took a moment to gather my thoughts before typing.

Tristan: You feel like home to me. You've felt that way from the moment I met you, even when you were a stranger. I'm still trying to figure it out.

When she didn't respond, I feared I'd said too much. But that didn't stop me from continuing.

Tristan: Every time I'm around you, I feel like myself, the person I was before all of this craziness happened. I love how honest you are. You make me smile. And you make me wish I had all the time in the world to figure out how to make you happy. Because when you smile at me, it brings me joy. I don't understand what's happening here. But I like you. More than I've liked anyone in a very long time.

The dots moved around longer than normal, but she finally texted back.

Emily: You make me smile too.

I breathed a sigh of relief.

Tristan: And sometimes I make you moan. Thank you for letting me do that, by the way.

Emily: Pretty sure I should be thanking you.

Tristan: I'd love the opportunity to do it again, even if you don't seem to think it's a good idea.

Emily: You were the one who said we needed to stop at kissing.

Tristan: I can be swayed.

Emily: It's not a good idea.

If she had doubts, I had to take a step back.

Tristan: No pressure from me. Just know my door is always open if you decide you need me.

Emily: Everyone else in the world has the passcode to your room, so why not me, right?

Tristan: I can't tell if you're mad or joking.

Emily: I'm smiling.

Tristan: Phew.

Emily: You should try to rest.

Tristan: Yeah, you're right. But just know that as I close my eyes, I'll be thinking of you—what we did and what we didn't do. And that will probably keep me up.

Emily: Goodnight, Tristan.

Tristan: 'Night, Emily. Sweet dreams.

Chapter 18

EMILY

I'd vowed to avoid Tristan tonight, if I could help it.

Staying away from him was one thing. Thinking about him constantly was another. I'd done nothing but that since our encounter at my mother's house a couple of days ago.

His voice sounded fantastic during tonight's performance in Louisiana—gritty yet velvety smooth, without the shakiness that had crept in previously. Tristan had a way of conveying emotion with every note, and tonight he seemed to be back at the top of his game.

Nonetheless, I found myself in an emotional tailspin. During the show, Tristan brought a woman from the audience onstage with him. That wasn't anything new. He was known for doing that, and the crowd always went wild, every woman hoping she would be the one he chose, to have the opportunity to touch him. He'd sing a certain song and dance slowly with the woman, often with their bodies pressed together. It hadn't bothered me before, but because of what had happened between us, or the fact that the fan he'd brought up tonight was especially attractive, this time things felt different. She was also aggressive, at one point grabbing his face and kissing him. It was clear Tristan hadn't been expecting it, but he didn't stop it either. A surge of jealousy tore through me, a reminder of how dangerous my feelings for him had become.

For the rest of the night, I felt sick. I helped load some things onto the buses after the show and prayed Tristan didn't contact me tonight. I didn't want him to sense that I was upset, nor did I think it was a good idea for me to be alone with him again.

We'd be playing two shows here in Louisiana, so tonight was a hotel night. After completing my post-show tasks, I went to my room and planned to take a shower and climb into bed.

But about 10:30, I received a text from Stephen.

Stephen: Tristan needs wart remover.

Emily: You've got to be kidding me.

Stephen: Not kidding you.

Could I make up an excuse and ask him to send someone else? I could say I was sick. My mind raced as I contemplated that. But alas, the urge to see Tristan overruled my better judgment.

Emily: On it.

"What do you have to get this time?" Layla asked as I rushed around to grab my things.

This one was so ridiculous that I didn't want to tell her. "Just some random stuff," I said. "Looks like Walmart closes at eleven, so I have to hurry."

Butterflies fluttered in my stomach the entire way to the store. I soon returned with two different kinds of wart remover—just for the hell of it—and went to Tristan's room.

This hotel didn't have a penthouse suite with a code, so he was in a regular room and would have to let me in.

After I knocked, I heard his gruff voice on the other side of the door. "Who is it?"

"It's the wart-remover express."

He opened and flashed a mischievous grin. "You're such a trooper."

"And you're a jackass." I threw the bag at his chest.

"Just remember, the more embarrassing the item, the more I miss you."

"Well, based on this, you must miss me a lot."

"I did." He snickered. "You're lucky I didn't order flavored lube. I debated it."

"Do you need anything in particular?" My tone was abrupt. "Let me guess, you want to know how I thought you sounded tonight?"

His smile faded. "You really think that's the *only* reason I called you here?"

Crossing my arms, I answered, "I think it's one of the reasons, yeah."

"You're my reward for a job well done, remember?"

"I'm your reward for a job well done and your distraction from your problems. That's a big responsibility and probably not healthy, Tristan." My demeanor hardened further as I again thought about that woman onstage.

His brows drew in. "What's wrong, Emily?"

"Why do you ask?"

"You're not looking me in the eyes, and you seem upset. I want to kiss you, but I'm afraid you'll bite my head off."

"Haven't you had enough kisses for one night?" I spat. He'd walked right into that one.

His expression darkened. "What do you mean?"

"Do you seriously not know?"

He shook his head.

"That woman you brought up onstage. You let her kiss you. Do you not fucking remember?"

"Ah. Shit." His eyes closed for a moment. "You're probably not going to believe me, but I *had* completely forgotten she kissed me. That's how little it meant to me." He closed the gap between us. "Emily, do you know how many women I've kissed? Not a single one has meant a damn thing in, God, I don't know how long—*years*—except our kiss."

How the hell was I supposed to stay mad after he said that?

I cracked a smile.

He looked relieved. "I got food for us."

For the first time, I noticed the spread behind him. "Middle Eastern? How did you manage that this late? Catering had Italian tonight."

"I know you like it, so I asked Mario to have it delivered."

"That was very thoughtful of you."

"Will you stay? I won't lay a hand—or mouth—on you, I promise. Just eating. Food." He winked. "Eating *food*. Nothing else. Promise."

A few minutes later, I'd forgotten all about the anxiety from earlier. Eating Middle Eastern food late at night while lounging with Tristan had become my happy place. It was our thing. This time we ate on the spare bed. He always requested a room with two beds, one for eating on and one for sleeping. Tristan sat up against the headboard while I kept a safe distance at the foot of the bed.

As we finished our meal, he smiled. "I haven't interrogated you in a while. Do you mind if I ask you some questions?"

I wiped my mouth. "Depends on what they are."

"There's a lot I still don't know about you. And my goal in life is to eventually know everything there is about Emily Applewood. But due to time constraints, acquiring that information has to come in phases." He grinned.

I swallowed, already feeling guilty for what I wouldn't be admitting. "Okay..."

"Do you believe in God?" He licked the corner of his mouth. "I mean, we've talked about your negative feelings toward religion. But we didn't dive too deeply into whether you feel like there's a higher power."

I tried not to overthink my answer. "I believe in... something. But I don't know that I trust in God the way I should. When you lose someone you care about, it makes you wonder if anyone is looking out for you or the people you love."

He nodded. "Stuff like that does make it hard to believe. I try to tell myself there are things we don't understand, that maybe some people have a certain purpose on this Earth, and their time is limited from the beginning—they aren't taken away, but maybe they agreed to that expiration date as part of their plan."

"So what would Jacob's mission have been if he died before ever really getting to live, never getting to see his dreams come true?" I challenged. "Make it make sense."

Tristan shook his head. "I don't have an answer, beautiful. But perhaps someone's purpose is not to achieve anything grand in life, but rather to touch the people around them. To leave an impression on this Earth. Some people change you just by having known them. I know that's kind of woo-woo and I sound like Ronan right now, but I have to think like that to accept tragedy."

"Have you ever lost someone?" I asked.

"You mean to death?"

"Yeah."

"No. So I probably have no right even talking about this shit. You're so much stronger than I am after what you've been through. You're so freaking young, but you've experienced much more."

"I'm not *that* young."

"Too young to be messing around with a nearly washed-up musician who's fifteen years older."

"You're far from washed up. *And* you sounded amazing tonight, by the way."

"See? I wasn't even gonna ask, because I didn't want you to think that's why I called you, because it isn't. But thank you for letting me know."

"You need to rest your voice more often. It does you good."

Tristan leaned back against the headboard and smirked. "Is that your excuse to leave?"

"I'm not in any rush," I admitted.

"Good, because I'm nowhere done with you."

"In what way?" I swallowed.

"Not done asking questions." He winked. "Get your mind out of the gutter, Applewood."

I tilted my head. "What else do you want to know?"

"What's the scariest thing you've ever done?" he asked.

Agreeing to come on this tour. I chose the second scariest thing.

"Probably facing Henry's kids after the...accident. Knowing they hated me for causing his death but looking them in the eyes anyway and apologizing for what happened."

"I can't imagine how tough that was," he said softly.

"There wasn't anything I could say that would make them feel better, so I didn't try. And sorry didn't seem to cut it. It was just one meeting, initiated by me so I could sleep better at night. But it was a horrible experience."

"You didn't owe them an apology, given the circumstances."

"I felt I did, even though what happened wasn't intentional." Starting to sweat, I needed to take the attention off of me. "My turn to ask a question."

"Go ahead. Ask me anything."

"Have you ever been in love?" My heart rose to my mouth as I awaited his answer.

"Once, yeah."

"When?"

"Back when I was sixteen. Right before I left Iowa for California."

"What was her name?"

His lips parted slightly. "Cheyenne."

"What happened?"

He looked at me like I should've known the answer. "I left for California..."

"I know that. But I mean...what happened before you left?"

"I told her I wanted to make things work long distance, but she didn't seem to want the stress of that, didn't believe it could work. Nor did she want to come with me—being in high school and all that. She was always supportive of my musical aspirations, but she didn't want to leave home. And I guess she didn't truly trust me, even though she could've at the time." Tristan looked away. "I loved her. Or I believed I did, as much as you can believe you love someone at that age. And despite her worries, I wouldn't have cheated on her, if she'd told me she wanted to make it work."

"You think you would've remained faithful all these years?"

"If we had stayed together, yes."

"Sixteen is so young to make decisions about your future."

"Yeah...but you know how it is when you're that age. You *feel* a lot older." He shook his head. "Sometimes being sixteen feels like yesterday." He turned to me and laughed. "For you, it practically is."

I rolled my eyes. "I feel like sixteen is a lifetime ago. It was before...everything. Before everything that changed my life," I murmured. "I wish I could go back to sixteen."

He moved closer. "Yeah. I'm sorry if I reminded you of that stuff again."

"Do you know what became of Cheyenne?"

He sighed. "I tried to keep in touch with her those first couple of years, but we drifted apart. She stopped calling me back, and I took the hint. By the time the boy-band thing happened, I'd pretty much scared her off for good."

"Hold up." My eyes went wide. "Boy band?"

"You didn't know about that?" Tristan chuckled.

"I didn't."

"It was when I was a teenager, before I met Atticus and Ronan. These other guys and I mostly played private events and never achieved the kind of fame we wanted. Not only was I singing, I was dancing back then, too. Had bangs so freaking long you couldn't even see my eyes, and baggy pants that looked like you could fly away in them. They hung halfway down my ass."

I giggled. "I can't picture you in a boy band."

"Try not to."

"I'm doing just the opposite right now."

"Promise not to laugh, and I'll show you a photo."

"I can do no such thing."

He found his phone anyway and pulled up an image from the Internet of the old band. They had matching outfits and were all kneeling with their fingers pointed toward the camera.

"Sexy, right?" He chuckled.

You couldn't even see his beautiful eyes with those crazy long bangs.

I snorted. "I prefer you now."

"Well, you, Emily, were probably all of what...three years old when this photo was taken?"

"That's kind of crazy."

He took the phone back. "I sometimes forget how damn young you are. I don't feel that much older than you. I don't know if that's a testament to your maturity or my immaturity."

Just then my phone chimed. It was a text from Layla asking if I was okay. *Shit.* She'd expected me to return by now, and it was irresponsible of me not to have thought about checking in. But I had a habit of forgetting my head whenever I was with this man.

"Layla is asking why I haven't come back. What am I supposed to tell her?"

"Tell her you're with me," Tristan said matter-of-factly.

"Not sure I want to admit that. She'll get the wrong idea."

He arched a brow. "She'd be somewhat right about the wrong idea, though, wouldn't she?"

"I don't want anyone knowing my business."

"But you have to respond to her. Otherwise, she'll worry about you."

"She'll worry more if I tell her I'm in Tristan Daltrey's room."

"Ouch." He clutched his chest. "That hurts, but it's probably true."

I shot her a quick text saying I was safe and hanging out with people downstairs and she shouldn't wait up. It sounded shady as hell. I felt guilty for lying. "I should go back to my room, but I don't want to."

"I'm not gonna suggest you leave. If I had my way, you'd be on my bus and in my bed. Every damn night."

"Well, it's a good thing you don't call the shots—I do."

"That *is* a good thing. We definitely need someone who's thinking above the belt to make such decisions."

"You're assuming I'm *not* thinking below the belt?" I quipped.

"Tell me more," he said gruffly.

"You know how hot you are. I don't have to spell out why it's hard for me to resist you."

Lying on his stomach, he inched closer. "I get hard just looking at the little gap between your teeth. Everything about you excites me."

"The gap in my teeth?" I poked his shoulder with my index finger. "I hate it."

"It's one of my favorite things. Every time you open your pretty mouth, I want to lick a line across it."

My nipples hardened. "That's all you wanna do?"

"Fuck no, that's not all I wanna do. I want to do everything to you. That's the problem."

Feeling drunk off the intense way he looked at me, I knew I was in trouble again tonight. I was addicted to him in every way—not only physically but to the attention he always paid me. That addiction blurred the lines between right and wrong.

"I'm scared, Tristan," I blurted.

"I wish you weren't." He rubbed his finger along my arm. "Tell me what I can do to change that."

There was *nothing* he could do. I wanted to scream that he didn't know everything there was to know about me, he didn't know why I'd gone out to the desert that day.

But I stopped myself. It wasn't the time for that conversation. It was *never* going to be the right time. And in the interim, I was losing the ability to control myself around him.

I *wanted* to have sex. My body was ready for everything with him. If he tried to go there, I wouldn't be able to resist. And that made me the most selfish person in the world.

I rubbed my thumb along the layer of scruff at his chin. He closed his eyes at my touch. Taking my hand in his, he kissed each of my fingers one by one. God, how I loved that. And when he looked up at me again with hooded, lust-filled eyes, I felt weaker by the second.

I reached out to massage his hair. "I wish I didn't love the way I feel every time you look at me. I'm headed for the biggest heartbreak of my life."

He frowned. "I know I told you not to trust me, but it was only a warning against things I might do to you that would actually feel good. Even if I cross the line, I'd only ever be making you feel good. I promise I wouldn't do anything to hurt you."

He didn't understand that I had a much greater chance of hurting *him* than him ever hurting me.

Chapter 19

TRISTAN

Emily started to fidget. She was very hot and cold tonight. One second she seemed like she wanted to jump my bones, and the next she looked like she wanted to flee.

"I think I should go," she said.

"Why? Is it something I did?"

"Nothing good can come of me staying the night."

"Something good *could* come. *You* could come. And that would be *very* good, wouldn't it?"

Her face reddened. "What about you, Tristan? You want to give me pleasure. But what about you?"

My starving dick twitched. "It gives me pleasure to give you pleasure." I tucked a piece of her hair behind her ear. "Taking it in baby steps like this is new to me. But I'm down for it. I don't need anything but to make you feel good."

"It's only a matter of time until you do." She tilted her head. "You asked me once when I'd last had sex. I never asked you. When was the last time you slept with someone?" She stiffened, seeming to brace for my answer.

155

"I haven't had sex with anyone on this tour."

Her eyes widened. "Because of me?"

Yes. "Not entirely."

"But partially?"

"Since we've been getting to know each other, you're the only woman I've been interested in. And while I can't say what I'd be doing if you weren't here, I *can* say I've had more fun imagining the things I'd do to you than actually starting something with anyone else."

Her blush deepened and spread. I wondered how far...

"Look at you. You're turning so red right now. Did I embarrass you?"

"The only thing that embarrasses me is my inability to control my feelings."

"We don't have to do anything tonight, Emily. We can just talk. We're really good at that."

"I know we are," she murmured.

"You're in the driver's seat, even if it might not seem like it. But I don't want you to leave. I want you to spend the night with me. If I can't have you on the bus, at the very least I want you in my hotel room where we can be alone, because it fucking makes me happy when you're around." I leaned in. "Wanna know how I made it through the show tonight?"

"How?"

"I was thinking about *you*. Every time I'd feel like I couldn't perform another song, I'd tell myself I was one step closer to getting to spend time with you. I can't tell you the last time I thought about a specific person so much while I was performing. You were right there with me to-night."

"Was I with you when you were kissing that woman?" she clapped back.

Thankfully, she was smiling.

I shook my head and covered my face. "Okay, I'll give you that one, smartass."

Emily chuckled. "You were really thinking about me when you were performing?"

"Yes. You're in my head." I pointed to my heart. "And you're here lately, too. So you might as well be here physically."

She looked away and let out a long breath.

I placed a hand on her chin, prompting her to look at me. "What's wrong, baby?"

Her eyes looked glassy. "You make me feel more special than I deserve."

I drew in my brows. "What are you talking about? You deserve the world, Emily. Don't let anyone make you believe otherwise."

She bit her lip, seeming troubled. Something felt off with her in general, maybe something she wasn't telling me. Though I had no idea what. I was missing a piece of her puzzle.

She stood up and moved away from the bed. "I do think I'm gonna head out."

I hopped up as disappointment settled in my stomach. I couldn't force her to stay if she wanted to leave.

"Okay." I managed a smile, so she didn't think I was mad.

We stood staring at each other in silence. She'd told me she was leaving, yet she hadn't moved.

I inched closer. "Bye, then." I took another step, moving in even more. "Have a good night." And then I moved in again so my lips were just over hers. "Sweet dreams." I took her mouth with mine and sucked on her plump lips. As I wrapped my arms around her, Emily relaxed into me, opening her mouth to welcome my tongue. She didn't really want to leave; this proved it. She whimpered, bringing my dick to attention.

"You're welcome to leave," I muttered over her lips before taking her mouth with greater force. She sighed and dragged her fingers through my hair. I inhaled her frantic breaths like oxygen. Every moan made me harder.

Emily opened her mouth wider as I led her back over to the bed. Her body bounced onto the mattress as she fell back. Feeling like a fucking animal in heat, I hovered over her as her chest heaved.

"I don't know what to do with you," I said, panting and conflicted. My body's intense need for her battled with my conscience, which still wanted to protect her, even if I knew I could never hurt this girl. I might not be right for her, might not always know what I was doing when it came to women, but somehow I knew I could never hurt *her*. Not intentionally, at least. Still, I needed to tread lightly.

When she pulled me down onto her and kissed me, my inner conflict was once again trampled by my body's wants and needs.

"I want to see you naked," I rasped.

She nodded as I reluctantly stopped the kiss to remove her clothes, starting with her shirt. I unbuttoned her pants before she helped kick them to the floor. I had her down to only a bra and panties. Lowering my head, I licked a line down her cleavage. Her tits were the perfect size, not too big and not small, just a little bigger than what could fit in the palm of my hand.

My dick was rock hard now as I unsnapped her bra and tossed it aside, my mouth watering for her nipples. I took one into my mouth, savoring the sweet nectar of her flesh. She hadn't been with anyone in over two years, and while for me the drought was a lot shorter, it was the longest I'd ever gone without sex. My body needed so much more than I planned to take tonight, and it was practically screaming at me to lose control.

Emily writhed beneath me, drawing my attention to her lower half. I slid her panties down as she spread her legs without me prompting her. I took a moment to kneel over her and just look. She was beautiful. Her long brown hair splayed across the sheets. My reflection in her eyes. Her nipples hard as steel and pointing at me. The beauty mark between her tits. Her gorgeous pussy. It took everything in me not to immediately begin devouring it, or worse, take my starving dick out and plunge inside. God, how I wanted to do that. I could only imagine how good that would feel, how fucking tight she'd be. I nearly came from the thought.

I took a moment to close my eyes and calm myself before lifting my shirt off. Her eyes fell to my bare chest before returning to meet my gaze. I couldn't take any more of the look-but-don't-touch game. Lowering myself once again, I took her mouth, groaning like a starved animal. Her naked breasts against my chest felt so damn good.

"Just tell me if you want me to stop, okay?"

She nodded through our kiss. My dick strained against my jeans, painfully hard. She pressed her bare pussy against the bulge in my pants, her wet heat taunting me in sweet torture. I'd never wanted anything more than to remove that barrier between us, to bury myself deep inside her. I wouldn't tonight...so I needed the next best thing.

"I want to eat your pussy." I kissed softly down her neck. "Can I?"

She let out a shaky breath, bit her lip, and nodded. "Yes."

Salivating, I slid down and took a moment to just look at her again. I couldn't remember the last time I'd wanted to examine someone's pussy like it was a goddamn piece of art encased in glass. But I loved looking at her, admiring her glistening folds and small landing strip.

I flicked my tongue along her slick and tender clit, savoring the taste of her arousal. I'd licked it off my fingers before, but there was nothing like feeling her wetness against my mouth while I tasted her. I circled my tongue around her swollen bud before inserting it inside her. In and out, I fucked her with it as she kicked her legs in pleasure.

Emily bucked her hips to press herself harder against my face, grabbing my hair to guide my movements. She wasn't afraid to move me around to suit her needs, and I buried my face deeper, my chin scruff covered in her juices.

Fucking hell, I wanted to devour every inch of this girl, wanted to consume her in every way. Never in my life had I been this feral over someone. I couldn't remember the last time I'd gone down on a woman or wanted it this badly. Certainly never wanted to bury my face in some random groupie's crotch. Normally I was on the receiving end of oral sex. But my desire to pleasure Emily far exceeded my need to be pleasured. All I'd wanted from the moment I met her was to make her lose her mind, to take her worries away. And this—fucking her with my mouth— was my favorite way to do that thus far.

As she dug her nails into the mattress, I ate her out faster, alternating between licking, sucking, and inserting my tongue. My dick felt ready to explode. Either she came soon, or I might come first—right there in my pants.

I stopped for a moment, replacing my mouth with three fingers inside of her. I wanted to see the expression on her face, and I couldn't with my mouth on her. I was slightly disappointed to find she wasn't looking down at what I was doing to her. I did appreciate that her eyes were closed and her head was bent back, very much in the zone and enjoying every moment.

When she opened her eyes and looked at me, I took that as my cue to return my mouth to her pussy. She gripped my hair again, and this time I closed my eyes to savor every last drop.

It took only a few more seconds before her body shook, legs trembling, muscles clenching. As her screams of pleasure echoed throughout my hotel room, all I wondered was when I could do it all over again.

Chapter 20

EMILY

I lay limp on the mattress, sated from that mind-blowing orgasm. Most of the tension in my body had been released, and I felt almost high.

Tristan had escaped to the bathroom shortly after I'd finished. He was taking longer than normal, and it didn't take a rocket scientist to figure out what he was doing in there.

Once he returned to the bed, he rested his chin on his hand and observed me a moment. "Am I dreaming, or are you really spending the night here with me?"

"I haven't decided yet." I smiled.

"Considering it's nearly morning, I think you've officially spent the night."

Shifting my body, I felt something underneath the pillow. I pulled out the rattiest gray teddy bear. My mouth fell open. "Oh my God." I held it up. "Is this Duffy?"

"The one and only." Tristan grinned sheepishly.

"You bring him into the hotel with you?"

"I can't risk someone breaking into the bus and taking him."

"Who in their right mind would steal this?"

"You never know. He's the only thing I own that I care about. They could take my Rolex, and I'd be fine with it. But this little guy is irreplaceable."

Oh my God.

There was a little tag sewn onto the side of the bear that read, *Property of Tristan Daltrey. Please return if lost.*

My cheeks hurt from smiling. "You realize how freaking precious that is, right? But it could damage your badboy reputation if people get wind of this."

He rolled his eyes. "The guys have threatened to out us plenty of times."

"*Us*...meaning you and Duffy." I laughed.

"Yes." He nodded. "He's in bad shape, but he's with me for life. Incidentally, even though he looks like death, I do keep him clean, which is why his fur has been compromised—from washing. His eye is starting to fall off, though, so I have to do something about that before it's gone for good."

My shoulders shook with laughter. Then I looked closer at the plastic eyeball starting to separate from the fabric. I hopped off the bed. "You just gave me the best orgasm of my life. The least I can do is sew your teddy bear's eye back on."

He sat against the headboard. "You can do that?" His eyes filled with hope.

"I keep a sewing kit in my purse."

"Wow."

"It's come in handy a lot lately."

I took out my kit and located the gray thread before I returned to the bed. Tristan watched my every move as I threaded the needle and positioned the eyeball to make sure it was even with the other eye. As I started sewing, I found myself a little nervous. I felt like I was performing surgery on his precious friend. Once I'd placed the final stitch, I handed Duffy back to him.

Tristan smiled at the bear. "This might be one of the sweetest things anyone's ever done for me."

To see this burly, tattooed god of a man looking down lovingly at an inanimate ball of matted fur warmed my heart and made my ovaries explode. "Well, I wouldn't want anything to happen to something that means so much to you."

"*You* mean a lot to me, Emily. I'm sorry if my saying that freaks you out, but it's the truth." He set the bear aside and moved closer. "I'm too old for you, and bad for you in every way, but I can't help how I feel."

My heart felt ready to burst. "Tristan—"

"I know I've been with a lot of women," he continued. "Girlfriends. Flings. One-night stands. But you're the first person in a very long time who makes me forget everything and everyone else. You've made me think it's possible to want to be with one woman."

His words stole the breath from my body. He'd echoed the way I felt about him. Tristan had become everything to me in such a short amount of time. And yet he knew nothing.

Nothing.

I'd gotten caught up in a way I'd never anticipated. I was having too much fun pretending. Forgetting. But while he didn't know everything there was to know about me, he still knew me at my core. There was nothing deceitful about my feelings for this man.

When I remained silent, he said, "Now that I've totally freaked you out with my proclamation, let's switch gears." He jumped up and pinned me under him. "I want to do it again."

"Do what?"

"Go down on you."

"Now?"

"More specifically, I want you to sit on my face this time."

Goose bumps covered my body. "Who needs sleep, I guess..."

I once again relished the feel of his heavy body over me, opening my legs to make room for him. Tristan's eyes were hazy as he lowered his mouth to mine. As he kissed me, he slid his hand under my shirt, cupping my breast.

No one had ever paid attention to my body the way Tristan had worshipped it tonight. And to have this gorgeous man, whom millions of women fawned over, giving me a thousand percent of his attention? I felt completely unworthy. We were in our own world, where I wished we could stay forever.

He squeezed my breast almost to the point of pain. I loved the way it fit so perfectly in his palm. My clit was already humming in anticipation, and despite my lack of sleep tonight, my body was alive. Though I knew I'd pay for it tomorrow.

After a few minutes, I felt his hand move to slide my panties down.

I lifted my shirt over my head, exposing my bare breasts, since my bra was still lying on the floor.

Tristan's stubble scratched my skin as he lowered his mouth to my breasts. My fingers raked through his hair as he pulled at one of my nipples with his teeth.

"I could eat you alive."

His words sent shivers down my spine, which landed straight between my legs. That was exactly what I wanted, for him to eat me alive, consume me in a way that would make me forget myself. There was no end to the things I wished he'd do to me.

Tristan kissed his way down my stomach. Then lower. He licked a line over my clit before he spread my legs apart. I screamed in pleasure as his mouth bore down on me.

"I'm so addicted to you," he mumbled over my flesh.

I raked my fingers through his lustrous hair as I closed my eyes.

Tristan broke my trance-like state when he moved back. "Get on top of me."

He slid down and worked to position me so I was straddling his head.

"Ride my face," he ordered, grabbing my waist and pulling me down onto his mouth.

I gripped the pillow in front of me as I bucked my hips, so sensitized from the power this position granted me. Gliding my clit along his mouth, I felt his groans vibrating through my core as he licked and sucked. I'd never done this before, and I wasn't sure I'd ever get over how damn good it felt.

Tristan used his hands to guide my ass over him, his facial hair scratching against my thighs as he began to fuck me with his tongue. I thrust my pelvis in rhythm with his mouth.

"Fuck, Emily. You taste even better the second time," he rasped. "I could feast on you forever. You're gonna make me come without even touching myself."

"Tristan…" I moaned, ready to come any second.

"I can't wait to feel you come all over my face."

I cursed at myself for wishing this would be the moment he gave in, flipped me around, and entered me. The thought of Tristan inside me made me throb even harder over his mouth. I lost it, my muscles contracting and a jolt of ecstasy tearing through me as I climaxed. He sucked harder on my clit, taking every last drop of my release.

"I can't get enough of you." He groaned under me, his face covered in my arousal. He licked his lips like he truly meant it.

After I came down from that second most amazing orgasm, I turned to face him. "Why is it always about me? What about you?"

"If you knew the things I fantasized about doing, you'd understand why I keep my dick in my pants."

"Like what?"

"Too much to list."

"Like what?"

"I don't want to lose you by telling you."

"What if I want to hear it? If you won't show me, you at least have to tell me."

"Okay, I'll give you the PG version." He paused, dragging his teeth along his bottom lip. "I think about sneaking onto your bus at night and letting you suck my cock until I come right over that pretty little gap in your teeth."

A chill ran down my spine. "What else?"

"I think about fucking your tight pussy so hard it ruins you for all other men. You'll only ever want me after I'm done with you."

"What else?"

"I think about smacking your ass till it's red, then fucking you from behind while I pull your hair. Then surprising you by sliding my dick into your ass, and you telling me how much you love it."

Damn. I gulped. "Just to clarify...that's the PG version?"

"You'd better believe it."

After Tristan talked dirtier to me than anyone ever had, he followed it up with the worst thing he could've done—he lay down behind me and held me. My body tensed as I tried not to feel the emotions that elicited. Never had I felt so safe and protected. And all I could think was, *This has to stop.*

Chapter 21

EMILY

The following day, Layla confronted me after lunch in the hotel.

"You never came back last night," she said.

Yeah. I'm quite aware of that. "I had a little...too much fun," I told her, determined not to admit where I'd been. I could feel my face getting hot.

She winked. "I figured it was something like that. You said you were hanging out with people downstairs. I assume you met someone interesting?"

"No one you know." My cheeks burned. "But yeah."

I felt guilty about lying to Layla. She had become a good friend, but I couldn't risk anyone finding out about Tristan and me. He pretended it didn't matter to him, but he didn't need the complication of his bandmates giving him shit or people whispering behind our backs.

"Well, next time I'll know not to worry if you don't return to the room." She winked. "Didn't think you had it in ya, kid."

I smiled, but there *couldn't* be a next time. After last night, I knew I had to do something. Tristan and I had crossed a line of intimacy that would be hard to come back from. I couldn't risk getting any closer to him. My lack of self-control had been eye opening. I'd lost trust in my ability to make the right decisions moving forward.

My phone chimed.

Tristan: Any chance I could convince you to come to my room and have an early dinner with me before sound check?

I was tempted, but I knew what I had to do.

Emily: I'm working.

Tristan: I can pretend to need something from you. Actually, I don't even have to pretend... I do need something from you. A kiss at the very least to get me through tonight. I can't stop thinking about you.

I should've been swooning, but all I felt was sadness. Despair. He deserved more than someone who hadn't been honest with him. My stomach felt unsettled as I typed again.

Emily: I really can't.

The dots moved around for a long time before he responded.

Tristan: Okay.

An hour later, everyone was getting ready for sound check when I arrived to drop off coffee for the crew backstage at the venue.

"Hey, you..." came a deep voice from behind me.

I turned to find Tristan standing there, looking gorgeous in his ripped jeans and a black shirt cut off at the arms. My body came alive at the sight of him.

"What are you doing here, Tristan? Don't you have to get ready for sound check?"

"I needed to see you, or I wasn't gonna be able to focus tonight."

I looked over my shoulder. "We should go somewhere else, then."

"Let's go to my dressing room," he said. "It's empty right now."

I followed him there, and we stood facing each other. He smelled like his cologne, but with a hint of something else.

I sniffed the air and narrowed my eyes. "Have you been smoking?"

He looked down for a moment. "I just had one."

"Why?"

"I was tense after our text exchange earlier. I needed to calm down."

"You were tense because of me?"

"You've got me feeling like a fucking lovesick teenager, Emily. I'm too old for this shit. When you blew me off earlier, I got a sinking feeling in my stomach." Concern filled his eyes. "I mean... Last night was amazing. Am I delusional? I need you to tell me if I'm coming on too strong. Or if I did something wrong. I feel this resistance from you. It's weird because I also feel like you really *want* to be around me, but something's holding you back. I'm not sure if it's more than your job here. I get that I'm not right for you but..." He exhaled.

He was hurt. *I'd* hurt him. As I looked into his beautiful, sincere eyes, I knew I couldn't do this anymore.

"You're absolutely right that I want to be around you. There's nowhere else I want to be when we're together. And you're also right that I'm resistant to us getting closer, but it has nothing to do with you or my feelings toward you."

He took a step back. "Oh God, this isn't the it's-not-you-it's-me spiel, is it? I thought you had more respect for me than that." He shook his head. "I'm sorry." He took a deep breath. "Just be honest. That's all I ask. I can handle the truth. If you're not interested in spending time with me anymore, I'll leave you alone. Simple as that."

This was my opportunity to cut the cord. "I can't do what we've been doing anymore, Tristan. I can't get closer to you...as much as I want to."

His phone chimed, and he looked down at it.

His eyes looked sunken when his gaze met mine again. "I'm late for sound check." He stared at me another second, then walked away.

I stood frozen in his dressing room. *You've done it now, Emily.*

Feeling empty inside, I made my way through the arena to the exit. In the distance, I could hear the echo of his voice. I only hoped I hadn't ruined his chance of having a good performance tonight. Although, staying here under these circumstances would now ruin his chance of having a successful tour.

During the show that night, Tristan's voice was undeniably off again. And while I knew I had no control over the physiological nature of his problem, I still blamed myself. In my heart, I knew I'd contributed to it. Just like I'd driven him to smoke earlier with my wishy-washy behavior. The smoking hadn't been good for his voice, either.

It helped that we were on buses again tonight instead of a hotel. That removed the possibility of Tristan calling me to deliver something to his room and kept the highway as a barrier between us. But it didn't seem like he wanted to speak to me anyway. He hadn't texted, which proved he was upset. Still, the fact that he was keeping his distance brought me immense relief.

It would make what I had to do tomorrow so much easier.

Chapter 22

TRISTAN

We rolled into Texas the next day. I'd finally dozed off close to morning after tossing and turning for most of our ride here. Last night in Louisiana had been one of the worst of the tour. Not only did my performance suck—that was the least of my problems—I couldn't stop thinking about how I'd fucked everything up with Emily.

Atticus sauntered into my bedroom. "It's almost noon. Rise and shine. It's time we had a talk, man." He sat at the edge of my bed.

The last thing I needed was his shit on top of everything else. "What is it?" I snapped.

"You've been different these past couple of weeks. I'm not talking about your voice, either. I'm talking about whatever the fuck you have going on with that girl. It's like your body is here, but your head isn't."

"*That girl* has a name."

"I shouldn't have to tell you that getting involved with her is a bad idea. Those reasons are obvious, but when it starts to affect your music..."

"The only thing affecting my music right now is my voice issue, which I only have so much control over. And whatever was going on with Emily I'm pretty sure is over now. Alright? So you don't need to worry about it. You also don't need to tell me why it was a bad idea to get involved with someone on this tour, or why it was a bad idea to develop feelings for someone who's practically half my age. I get it. But sometimes we can't help how we feel. Although, not sure why I expect *you* to understand that."

He narrowed his eyes. "What's that supposed to mean? I'm not heartless, you know. I'm just a realist."

"A realist who cheats on his girlfriend."

"Whoa. First off, she's not my girlfriend. And I'm not a cheater. Riley and I have an understanding. She knows I'm not interested in monogamy. It's an open relationship. That's very different than cheating."

"Don't you ever get sick of this lifestyle?"

"Sometimes. But the only woman I've ever loved is gone. I never needed anyone or anything else when I was with Nicole."

It was rare that Atticus brought up his ex-wife. There was an unspoken rule among us that Nicole's name was not to be mentioned, especially while on tour. It was the one thing that affected his performances. He bounced his legs. "Anyway, I guess I just don't give a fuck anymore. I might as well try to have fun and take advantage before I'm old as fuck like you."

"Go to hell." I laughed.

Atticus and Ronan would take any opportunity to remind me I was five years older.

"Seriously, though..." he said. "What happened with Emily?"

"Oh, now you know her name?"

"Yeah, I know the name of the person who's gotten into my lead singer's head and who's threatening to fuck up the rest of this tour for us."

"For the last time, she has nothing to do with my voice problems. Stop insinuating that."

"She *does* have everything to do with you alienating yourself from us lately. The night you took off? Canceled the show? That was a first."

"I just needed a break. God forbid I take one—"

"You haven't answered my question. What *happened* with her?"

"Fuck if I know," I said, looking over at the wall and wishing I could punch it. "She says she doesn't think it's a good idea to continue whatever it is we started. I really like her. I've had no desire to be with anyone else since the tour began. That's a first for me. But none of that matters if she's scared."

He lowered his voice. "You fucked her?"

"No. We messed around, though, and I took things too far." I looked out the window at her bus.

Atticus snapped his fingers in front of my face. "When was the last time you felt this way about someone?"

"Not since I was sixteen."

He nodded. "Cheyenne..."

"How the hell did you remember her name?"

"Because I never forgot that conversation we had when we first met. You got drunk and told me all about her. You were pretty broken up over it."

"Wow. I don't remember that."

"Well, yeah. You were drunk." He chuckled. "Whatever became of her?"

"I have no idea."

"You never tried to look her up?"

"No." I shook my head. "For a while, I didn't want to know, but now it doesn't matter. So much time has passed. But the closest I've ever come to feeling something for someone like that has been with Emily. Being on this rollercoaster of a career has numbed my feelings for a long time. It's hard to meet the right people when you're surrounded by mostly the wrong people. It's rare to meet someone you connect with. And when you do? You remember what it feels like to be human again."

"Why are you so sure it's over between you and her?"

"She made it clear she doesn't want to pursue anything further. The reason isn't as clear. But it doesn't matter. I need to back off. And today is day one of that. So you don't need to worry about me getting in over my head anymore." I sighed, hardly trusting my own assurances. "Now, what you *do* need to worry about is my fucking voice. I won't get to see the doctor until we're in L.A. I'm gonna need to go quiet again today."

"All I can do is pray, man. I don't have the right answers, nor do I understand all of the medical articles Ronan has been sending me."

"He has?"

He nodded. "Dude's been researching all these ways to help you. But it's kind of hard to make herbal tinctures on tour." He laughed. "I told him he needs to stick his tincture up his sphincter."

I let out a guttural laugh. "You gotta love that guy for trying. More than you do for me, asshole."

"Ronan's a better man. That's for sure. All I've been doing is complaining." He came over to pat me on the back. "Anyway, I'm glad we had this talk, even if it started with me chastising you."

"That's how all our talks start, don't they?"

His face showed a rare sincerity. "I know I can be rigid sometimes. But I don't want you to think I don't care about your happiness. If some girl makes you happy, makes you remember who you are and all that shit, more power to you—as long as you don't lose all the other parts of you in the process. You've worked too hard to lose your damn mind, you know?"

"Too late for that, man." I chuckled.

"You wanna head out for a smoke?"

I shook my head. "Nah. I slipped yesterday and had one, but I'm trying to be good."

"Well, good on you, then." Atticus gave me the finger before he left.

Once again alone with my thoughts, I specifically stopped myself from texting Emily. I didn't want to be that guy who couldn't take a hint when someone needed space. It didn't matter how much I wanted to see her, how much she calmed me. I needed to do what was best for *her*—and that was listening to what she'd told me she wanted.

I needed to get everything off my chest, though. If I wasn't going to call her, writing a letter would be my way of communicating. Texting seemed too informal for this, and I didn't want her to feel like she needed to respond. Writing a letter would make it impossible to cross the line or do anything stupid. Stephen could deliver it for me. I would say what I needed to say, then focus on getting my head back into the tour. Maybe I could put this damn angst to good use and write some fucking music again. Now, there was an idea...

Grabbing a notepad and paper, I tried not to over-think it.

Dear Emily,

You're probably wondering why the hell I'm writing you this letter when I could just walk across the lot and talk to you. But you clearly want space. Even if I don't understand your apprehension about me, I need to respect it. I'm not the kind of guy who pushes himself on someone who wants to be left alone. I can take a damn hint. In the spirit of respecting your privacy, I'm writing this letter instead of coming to see you. I want to reiterate that I only want what's best for you. And I might even agree that what's best for you is distancing yourself from me.

At the same time, we will inevitably run into each other. I don't want you to feel uncomfortable in those moments. But I won't instigate extra time with you beyond a professional, friendly relationship. No more ridiculous delivery requests; although, I'm gonna miss those.

You know how much I respect you. I could say a lot more about my feelings, but I don't want to make this harder than it already is. Just know that spending time with you has been the best. Even if it was temporary, I appreciated every second of it.

No hard feelings, okay? I'll always be here if you need me.

xo Tristan

I expelled some air and looked down at the words I'd written. This sucked, but I needed closure if I had any chance in hell of concentrating on my performances again. After folding the letter, I realized I didn't have a damn envelope. I couldn't just hand Stephen an unsealed letter. The irony wasn't lost on me that the person who would be tasked with running out to buy me damn envelopes would be Emily. So, I decided the best course of action would be to grow some balls, walk my ass down to her bus, and deliver the letter myself. I wouldn't stay. I'd just hand it to her and leave. Any extra time with her would defeat the purpose of writing down what I wanted to say.

I grabbed a hat, and just as I stepped off the bus, Stephen approached. He was holding...an envelope? What the heck? Had he read my freaking mind?

I looked down at it. "What's that?"

"It's a letter for you...from Emily."

What the fuck? "She gave it to you?"

"Before she left, she asked that I get it to you."

"Left?" My heart began to race. "What are you talking about?"

"Emily left the tour this morning."

⁓

I'd never paced so much in my life.

Twenty minutes had passed, and I still hadn't read her letter.

I'd done this. I'd caused her to leave. I'd taken it too far and hadn't gotten my letter to her fast enough. If I'd just called her sooner, she wouldn't have felt like she had to leave. She lost her freaking job because of me. *Jesus Christ. What have I done?*

I couldn't get myself to open it. I didn't want confirmation that it was my fault, that I'd scared her away by not controlling my carnal desires.

After several minutes of pacing, I finally grew some balls and opened it.

Dear Tristan,

Please forgive me for doing this. I should've had the courage to come say a proper goodbye. But I knew if I looked in your eyes, I wouldn't have the guts to leave.

By now, you know that I've decided to quit the tour. I can't stress enough that my reasons have nothing to do with anything you did or said. Or anything we did together. Trust me when I say that any conclusions you are drawing right now are not the right ones. I've led you to believe you know everything about me, but that's unfortunately not true. I have a very personal reason for needing to leave right now. And I never should've come here to begin with.

I owe you an explanation. A huge one. I promise you will see me again someday, and I will properly explain things when the time is right. But that time is not now. And so, it's not fair that

I allow you to get closer to me when I haven't been completely honest.

I realize that I am being cryptic. But I need to take a step back—for myself and also for you. You need to focus on the tour right now, focus on regaining the strength of your voice. My being here was distracting. It was also not the right way to solve my own problem. I'd thought working on the tour would be an escape, a good experience, but I hadn't anticipated our connection, that I could fall for you in the process. Tristan, you make me feel like the most special person on Earth. I only wish I deserved it.

Promise me you won't overanalyze this. Promise me you'll forget about me for now and focus on healing yourself and getting back to music. I don't want to be responsible for derailing anything. But when the tour is over and you're feeling better, come find me. I'll explain more then.

My address is 83 Cherry Lane, Henderson, Nevada.

Until we see each other again,

Emily

What. The. Fuck?

That wasn't what I expected. I was more confused than ever.

I sat with my head in my hands. I was clearly wrong about what the hell had been going on with her. This was more than her just being scared of me. And while that brought me some relief, it also made me realize Emily was more complicated than I'd ever imagined. Despite her absence, she'd continue to haunt me, but she was right. I was currently on a train I couldn't get off of, and as curious as I was to understand everything about Emily, I had no choice but to get through this tour. I owed it to the guys. And to myself, I supposed. It was time to get my shit together.

I knew for certain that I wouldn't be able to wait until the European leg was over to see her. So after the US tour ended, I'd go to Nevada. I'd have a few weeks off before going overseas. Until then, I needed to not let this consume me.

Later that afternoon, the strangest thing happened. Lyrics came pouring out of me, after weeks of struggling with my writing. As much as Emily had distracted me from my work while she was here, she was inspiring me now. It was her. It had to be. As I wrote about beautiful eyes masking despair, falling for a woman you didn't know but your soul did, I only hoped she was okay. She'd left a huge mark on me, and this creativity was proof of it. The heaviness in my chest was proof, too.

The music I wrote now might never see the light of day, but Emily was somehow healing me, even if she wasn't here.

Chapter 23

TRISTAN

Three months later, when the North American tour finally ended, the guys went to Europe almost immediately. They wanted to enjoy the sights for a few weeks before we started performing. As planned, I stayed behind.

Getting through the US tour hadn't been easy. But I'd managed to get my voice under control by going quiet like a monk most days. I made staying silent my job. In that respect, it helped that Emily was gone, since I hadn't been tempted to talk to anyone else like I had been with her. It was the first time in a long while that I made myself and my health a priority. I'd even learned to meditate and would put my headphones on and drown out the world for hours each morning as I listened to calming music.

Through it all, though, I'd been counting the weeks until the tour ended so I could see her. And now that the day had finally come, I was a ball of freaking nerves.

Stepping out of my rental car on her street in Henderson, Nevada, I knew Emily wasn't expecting to see me so soon. She'd probably assumed I'd wait until Europe was over. But I couldn't. Anyway, this was the compromise with myself that had kept me from abandoning the tour and jumping on a plane to Nevada, something I'd wanted to do almost every damn night.

Henderson was nice. While I'd been to Vegas before, I'd never been to this suburb just southeast of the city. Her neighborhood was pretty residential, with a park located at the end of her street. She lived in a small, one-level home that looked like a single-family residence.

Licking my lips anxiously, I walked up to her door and knocked. My heart pounded as I waited for her to answer. *Jesus.* I'd performed onstage for thousands of people, and my blood had never been pumping quite like this.

When the door opened, it wasn't Emily, though. It was another girl.

I cleared my throat. "Hi. I was wondering if Emily was home."

The petite blonde stumbled over her words. "Uh…"

It took me a moment to realize she was acting strangely because she'd recognized me.

She pointed. "You…you're…"

I held out my hand. "Tristan Daltrey. Nice to meet you."

"I know. Um…wow." She shook her head. "Emily… yeah. She's at work."

"Where is she working?"

"She got a temporary position with a local company. Marketing coordinator for a project."

"I see." I nodded. "Does she like it?"

The girl ran a hand through her hair. "She seems to."

"What time does she get home?"

"Around six. You're welcome to stay here and wait."

That was hours from now. Kind of dumb of me to expect that Emily would be home in the middle of the day. "I don't want to bother you," I said. "I can catch her later."

"Are you sure?"

"Yeah. But would you do me a favor, please, and not tell her I'm in town? I don't want to distract her. I'll just come back later when she's home."

"Okay..." She blew a breath up into her hair. "Won't be easy to keep this a secret. But I won't say anything."

"Thank you." I took a step back. "I appreciate that very much."

What the hell was I going to do in Henderson without being recognized for the next three hours? I was in no mood to interact with people today. I probably should've traveled with someone, had security or something, but I hadn't felt like dealing with that, either. This was a trip I wanted to make alone, and anyone I would've trusted to come along was in Europe at the moment anyway.

I decided to go back to the hotel in Vegas and hide out in my room. After stopping for a few autographs in the lobby, I was finally alone again. Why I hadn't rented a house was beyond me.

I sat on the bed, contemplating my return to Emily's later. I didn't have much of an appetite, but I ordered room service and ate as I flipped through the channels, never able to settle on anything. I just kept watching the clock, counting the minutes until I could go back to Henderson. I prayed that my being here wouldn't be an unpleasant surprise. I hadn't warned her I was coming, because I was curious about seeing her in her element, not via some contrived scene she might prepare for me.

At 5:45, I left the hotel and drove back to Emily's neighborhood.

I'd been prepared for her to seem shocked when she saw me, but the fact that she was standing outside her house, looking like she was waiting for me when I arrived told me that her roommate hadn't kept her word.

Emily looked even more beautiful than I remembered. She wore a black skirt and white blouse—very professional. I'd never seen her so dressed up. It made me feel like I'd missed years with her, not a few months.

As I stepped out of the car, she walked toward me.

"Hi, Tristan," she said calmly.

She'd definitely been expecting me.

"Hi, gorgeous. I take it your roommate told you I stopped by earlier?"

"She did. She managed to wait until I got home, though. But then she couldn't hold it in anymore."

"At least she waited until then. I didn't want to upset you or distract you from your work."

"It doesn't upset me to see you." She smiled. "I'm glad you're here."

I still had no idea what that really meant. "Fuck, I'm so tense right now." I let out a long breath. "I didn't think I'd be this nervous. But I'm so damn glad you're okay with me being here."

"Tristan..." she whispered, placing her hand on my cheek.

I took her hand in mine and kissed it. "I missed you," I said, my voice hoarse. "So much."

"I missed you, too." She turned toward her door. "Come in."

"Thank you." I followed and wiped my feet at the entrance before stepping inside.

I looked around. Everything was freshly painted and new. "Cute place."

"Thank you. It's obviously a rental. But the rent is very reasonable for a house."

"Where is your roommate now—what's her name?"

"Cami. She works at a casino most nights. So she just left."

"Ah. Do you always have a roommate?"

She nodded. "I couldn't afford it otherwise."

Right. Not everyone has money coming out of their ears, asshole.

I'd buy her a house if she'd let me. But something told me she wouldn't accept it and might think the gesture was a little crazy.

There was a cream-colored sofa with flower-patterned throw pillows and a small coffee table with some candles and a coffee table book. In the corner was a large white bookshelf with the spines of books arranged by color.

"Are those your books?"

She shook her head. "Cami's. She's a huge bibliophile."

"You get along with her?"

"Yeah. She's really nice."

"Well, I'm glad it's working out."

Silence filled the air as we stared at each other for a moment. Despite my nerves, I wanted to kiss her. But that wasn't the plan for today. Nowhere near it.

"I wasn't expecting to see you until after Europe," she said.

"I figured, but I couldn't wait that long. But I did my best to respect your wishes for as long as I could."

"When do you have to be in Europe?"

"I have a three-week break. Everyone else is already there. But I opted not to sightsee with them and all that crap. It was more important that I get to see you, rest my voice, and get my head in gear."

She nodded. "I see..."

Her breathing quickened, and she suddenly didn't seem to know what to do with her hands. She'd gone from cool as a cucumber to the total opposite in a matter of seconds.

The need to comfort her overtook my vow to respect her personal space. I took her hand. "It's just me, Emily. You don't have to be nervous. There's nothing you can't tell me."

Her voice trembled. "You don't understand, Tristan." Her eyes filled with tears.

What the fuck is happening?

I brought her close and held her. Her heart was going a mile a minute against my chest. Tightening my hold, I spoke softly in her ear. "You're not obligated to tell me anything, if you don't want to. You owe me nothing. I just needed to see you. To make sure you were okay. I've thought about you every day. I've written songs about you. I've held you in my heart. I don't understand everything, but I've never felt like this about anyone before." I moved back to look at her. "There's nothing you can tell me that will change the way I feel about you. But I'm not expecting anything. I'll settle for your friendship...to have you in my life."

She looked deeply into my eyes. "I'm not who you think I am."

I stiffened. "You're not Emily Applewood?"

She sniffled. "I am, but..." Emily looked down at her feet and shook her head.

As much as I was dying to know what the hell was going on, I hated seeing her like this. She needed to calm down. I placed my hand on her chin. "Can you do me a favor?"

She lifted her gaze to mine. "What?"

"I don't feel like you're ready to talk about whatever it is you need to say. I don't like seeing you so worked up. You've likely had a long day as it is. Will you let me take you out to dinner before we talk? I doubt you've eaten if you came home from work and had to deal with me being here."

Her eyes were red. "Not sure I'll have an appetite..."

"Try." I forced a smile. "Any good Middle Eastern places around here?"

Emily wiped her eyes. "There *is* one, actually."

I gestured toward the door. "Let's go."

When I offered my hand, she took it. But hers was trembling.

She gave me the name of the restaurant, and I popped the address into my GPS. Emily was quiet during the ride, and I didn't push her to talk.

The restaurant was about a fifteen-minute drive from her house. Once there, she seemed to calm down a little.

By some miracle, we were able to slip into the restaurant and to a corner table without me being recognized.

Emily insisted she wasn't hungry and was indecisive about what she wanted. So I picked a platter that had a variety of things for us to share. During dinner, Emily answered my questions about the temporary marketing job she'd taken and told me she planned to move back home to Shady Hills to save money once her contract was up. I nearly offered to pay her expenses so she could stay in Henderson, if that's what she wanted, but I reminded myself not to overstep my bounds or throw around my power obnoxiously. I didn't own her. According to her, I didn't even *know* her.

She picked at her food, still obviously nervous. My appetite wasn't the greatest either, but this time out had been good if it helped her to calm down even a little.

After dinner, we drove back to her place. Since her roommate remained at work, we were still alone.

She paced in her living room.

"You don't have to tell me anything, Emily," I reiterated. "I'm not here to put pressure on you. I'm here to offer my support, to return some of the positive light you've brought to my life. I'm not kidding when I say seeing you at the end was what got me through that tour."

"You don't understand. I don't have the option to *not* tell you. That's not my choice to make."

"Alright. I'm sorry. I'm confused."

"I know." She looked up at the ceiling and exhaled, closing her eyes for a moment, almost like she was praying. "I don't know how to start."

"Start from the beginning..."

She blew out a shaky breath. "I have to think about what that is..."

I placed my hand on her shoulder. "There's no rush. It doesn't have to be tonight."

"It's not going to be any easier tomorrow." She swallowed. "How long are you in town anyway?"

"A few days? But it can be longer if you need me."

"Give me a second," she said, moving over to the other side of the room. Staring up at the ceiling, she said, "It doesn't matter how many times I've rehearsed this. I just don't know how to tell you."

I watched as she paced some more and muttered something under her breath, as if she were practicing what she was going to say. I hated that she was so tormented. She'd seemed so honest about other aspects of her past; it was hard to understand why it was so difficult to open up about this one thing.

"Just start from the beginning," I suggested again. "One step at a time. It's okay..."

Emily finally shook her head and joined me on the couch. "Okay..." She took in some air. "From the beginning..." She nodded.

My heart raced. It seemed her nervousness was contagious. I was nervous *for* her.

"The beginning is Jacob," she said.

I nodded. "Your boyfriend who died."

"Yes."

A bunch of theories floated through my mind. She'd said she wasn't who I thought she was. Did she lie about how he died? Was she driving the car that killed him? Before I could continue hypothesizing, she spoke again.

"Jacob was my best friend from a young age. Even though we tried dating when we were older, first and foremost, he was my closest friend. I loved him with all of my heart and soul, and when he died, he took a piece of me with him."

"You told me he died in a car accident..."

"Yes. He did."

"You said you were away when it happened?"

"That's correct. I was at college."

"Okay..." I gulped.

"After he died, his mother gave me a box of his personal belongings. She said she was too distraught to go through them, but wanted me to have them."

I nodded to encourage her.

"One of the things it contained were a series of journals. He'd never told me he journaled. I didn't read them right away. But more recently, I finally had the courage to go through them. There were things about Jacob I never knew. I'm not sure his mother would've given them to me so freely if she'd known how personal they were."

"She obviously felt you could be trusted with them." *What does any of this have to do with Emily or her character?* "What did you find out?"

She hesitated. "When Jacob was sixteen, his mother told him he was adopted. That was devastating for him. Apparently, his parents had agreed to tell him on his sixteenth birthday. He'd talked to me about that back then. But he hadn't told me he'd taken steps to find his birth mother. Apparently, he found her about a year before he died. He'd gone to see her, and he'd written about it in those journals."

"Wow." I blinked. "That's so sad. I mean, that he'd found her and then died not so long after."

She teared up. "It is...so sad."

The pain she felt for her friend—ex-boyfriend—was palpable. She seemed to have a lot of trauma she hadn't dealt with when it came to him. I moved in to hold her, but she quickly stepped away. Taking the hint, I returned to my spot across from her at the other end of the couch.

She looked into my eyes for what seemed like a full minute. Was she having second thoughts about sharing all this? My mind raced as I tried to figure out where this was all going. Then she uttered the words I didn't know would change my life.

"His mother's name is Cheyenne."

Chapter 24

EMILY

Tristan jolted as if I'd punched him in the stomach.

"Cheyenne..." he repeated.

I nodded. "Cheyenne Benson."

I could see the transformation in his face as realization dawned. His eyes slowly widened to a blank stare.

This was the moment I'd been fearing for so long.

I wanted to explain why I'd let things develop between us, but that was last on the list of items that needed to be addressed.

Tristan placed his hand over his heart as if he might collapse. "I don't understand," he whispered, shaking his head. He turned to me, his voice shaking. "Are you implying what I think you are?"

Holding back tears, I nodded. "When Jacob went to meet Cheyenne, she told him she'd gotten pregnant with him when she was a teenager. She admitted that she'd never told the father. She said at the time she was scared and worried you would quit everything and ruin your career to stay back home. She also knew she wasn't ready to raise a child, so she made the difficult decision to put the baby up for adoption."

Tristan hung his head, his voice barely audible as his ears turned red. "I can't believe this."

I gave him a few moments to process before I went on.

"When Jacob asked her who his father was, she told him your name and who you were. He thought she had to be lying. He knew of you. Jacob was way more into music than I ever was. Then she showed him photos of you and her from when you were teenagers. She gave him some of them to keep. He didn't know how to handle it. He asked her if she thought you'd be open to finding out about him. Cheyenne told him she didn't know, that she hadn't spoken to you in years. She felt like she didn't know who you were anymore, but that the boy you'd been back then would've wanted to know."

"You're damn fucking right I would've," he growled.

It was the first bit of anger he'd shown. I was sure it was only the beginning. He deserved to be angry.

"Cheyenne told him she wouldn't blame him for reaching out to you. She seemed deeply regretful for having hidden him from you and apologized for not being able to go back and make things right."

Tristan placed his head in his hands and bounced his knees nervously. He finally looked up at me, his eyes cloudy with confusion. "I don't understand. How did you end up at the recording studio? You were...stalking me or something?"

My stomach lurched. I felt like I could throw up. "No. Not exactly." I shook my head. "I have a friend from high school who works in the music industry out in L.A. now. I contacted him, pretending to be a Delirious Jones fan, and asked if he knew how I might be able to get an autograph. He told me where you guys were recording your album. The information came so easily that I took it as a sign. My initial intent was to see if I could get access to you. I wasn't sure if I was going to tell you anything or just gauge whether you were a good person, one who would want to know the truth." I gulped. "I knew nothing about you aside from what I'd read on the Internet. When I stood in front of the building that day, I had no idea what I was going to say or do if I met you. Then the door opened, Doug saw me standing there, and he mistook me for someone coming to interview for the assistant job. So I went with it, never imagining where it would lead."

Feeling ashamed, I paused a moment. This sounded ridiculous, even if it was the absolute truth. Tristan stayed silent.

"I convinced myself that the best way to get to know you was to take the job. If you were a bad person or someone who might reject the idea of having had a son, I could rethink how to approach things. But quickly, I learned you were a good person, someone who absolutely deserved to know about Jacob. Someone who would want to know. But I also soon realized that telling you during the tour wasn't fair, because it would devastate you. Then I learned about your voice struggles, and I worried about your mental health if I were to throw this at you in the midst of it all. It became about *when* to tell you, not whether to reveal it at all. I didn't want to put you through this until you could properly process it."

He stared at me incredulously.

It felt like my throat was closing, but I forced myself to continue. "The chemistry we have, the strong feelings I still have for you—that was independent of everything else. I allowed myself to fall for you, to get lost in the experience, wishing so much that I was really the girl you thought I was. And it became harder and harder to acknowledge the truth, even to myself."

The vacant look remained in his eyes. "You should've told me..."

"Telling someone they have a child they never knew about, let alone that the child is dead, wasn't something I could just spring on you. And then my heart got twisted up in it. I started to wish I had met you under different circumstances, where I could've allowed myself to see where things would go. But that's not reality. That's why I left. Because I'd let things go too far. My feelings for you were blinding me, making me forget why I'd gone to find you in the first place. I wasn't trying to deceive you, Tristan." A tear rolled down my cheek. "Please know that. I just didn't want to devastate you in the middle of a tour. I didn't know how to tell you." My voice cracked. "I'm so sorry. I handled everything wrong."

His eyes held a torment I'd never witnessed before. "You're sure? You're sure he's my son?"

There was only one way to give him the assurance he needed. I went to get the box where I kept all of Jacob's belongings—the journals and his photos. After I returned with it, I took two of the latest photos of Jacob and walked them over to Tristan.

He looked down at the first image and was transfixed. I was certain he didn't need any more proof, because he could see for himself what I always had. Jacob had his eyes. Jacob's face was a younger version of his own. In the photos Cheyenne had given Jacob, Tristan was the spitting image of Jacob at the same age. Had Jacob had a chance to grow into a man, I suspected he would have looked even more like Tristan as time went on.

Still staring down at the photos, he simply said, "I can't believe this."

He continued staring at the images of his son, the one he'd never know. This wasn't about me—or us. It wasn't about the dumb mistakes I'd made. Tristan was in shock, and I needed to let him process.

After several minutes, he finally looked up at me again. "Why didn't Cheyenne contact me after he went to see her? I mean, she told him who I was. He could've come to find me, so why didn't *she* contact me at that point?"

"According to his journals, she left things up to him. And Jacob wasn't sure if he was going to find you. She apparently told him to let her know if he decided to reach out, and she would contact you first so you would be prepared."

"Why didn't he come find me the second he knew?"

"I think he was afraid…"

Tristan shook his head. "I can't believe this." Then anguish crossed his face. "Does Cheyenne know he's dead?"

I sighed. That was the other difficult part of this. "No one knew he went to find her until I read his diary a month before I found you. Jacob never told anyone about meeting with Cheyenne, and he died a year ago. I did try to find her first. But she was gone. So she doesn't know."

He narrowed his eyes. "What do you mean gone?"

"She'd moved from the address I had for her, the one Jacob had written down. And the person who lives there now didn't know where she'd relocated. I never had a chance to tell her. I decided to try to find you instead."

He held his stomach. "I feel sick." When I came over to comfort him, he warned me away. While that hurt, I understood. I wouldn't have wanted anyone to touch me, either.

"Tell me what you need, Tristan. I'll do anything to help you get through this."

He looked at me like I was crazy. "What I need you can't give me. I fucking need to turn back time. I need my son not to be dead. I need Cheyenne to have told me the goddamn truth more than two decades ago. I'll never get what I need."

My voice was barely audible. "I'm so sorry."

He stared back down at the photo. "She needs to know he died."

"I know."

Tristan rushed toward the door. "I have to fly to Iowa."

"Will you be able to find her?"

He paced. "I'm sure her family still lives in Spirit Lake. Someone will be able to tell me where she is."

"Are you going to try to find her before you go to Europe?"

"I feel like I have to."

My heart raced. "Do you need me to go with you?"

"No. I need to do this alone."

"Are you sure?"

"I'm sure. You need to work. And you've done enough."

I've done enough. I wanted to throw up. "Do you mean that in a bad way?"

His expression softened. "No, Emily. You were the only one who had the decency to tell me I had a son."

"You should hate me right now for the way I let my feelings get in the way of everything. I only made things more complicated, and I'm sorry."

He scrubbed his hands over his face. "You didn't do anything wrong. But I understand now why you felt it couldn't work between us. Everything makes sense, and yet *nothing* makes sense. The last twenty-plus years of my life were a complete lie." He placed his hand on the door-knob. "I should go."

"What if you can't find her before you have to go to Europe?"

"Then I'll go on tour with my fucking heart in my mouth and figure out a way to finish it. But I won't rest until I tell her. And I won't rest until I look Cheyenne in the eyes and ask her to explain why she never told me about the most important thing to ever happen in my life."

"Before you go..." I walked over to the box and took out Jacob's journals and the photos. I held everything in a pile, returning to where Tristan stood. "I want you to take these. You should look through everything. These are his most recent private thoughts. It will help you learn about him."

"Are you sure?"

"Yeah. You can give them back to me, if you want, when you're done looking through everything. Or you can keep them. You have more of a right to them than anyone."

He took them from me. "Thank you."

I wanted to ask when I'd hear from him, but I didn't. I wouldn't blame him if he never called me again. Even the pain of that felt better than having to hide everything from him. My feelings for Tristan were just as strong as they always were, so I could only hope both of us would find our way to some peace with all of this. I loved him. It was as simple—and as impossibly complicated—as that.

Chapter 25

TRISTAN

It felt surreal. Suddenly I was fifteen again, standing in front of Cheyenne's mother's door. I had no idea how much Mrs. Benson knew about any of this, or what I was going to say. I just had to wing it.

Back in Nevada yesterday, I'd booked a ticket to Iowa, flown here, and spent the night at a hotel near my hometown of Spirit Lake. Carrying Jacob's diaries with me in my backpack almost felt like they were some kind of good-luck charm, though I hadn't had the damn courage to read them yet. I needed to focus on the task at hand, not allow myself to get so emotionally involved that it paralyzed me. I'd barely allowed myself to think about my son, for fear that I'd break down.

I wasn't sure I could read the diaries anytime soon. How would I function on tour with the regret I knew I'd feel? The more I distanced myself for now, the easier it would be. The less real this situation would seem. But I felt guilty for not opening them right away. Then I'd remind myself that he was gone, and nothing could bring him back, certainly not reading his personal thoughts and feelings.

I still hadn't knocked on Mrs. Benson's door. Instead, I looked around for a moment, taking a long whiff of the fresh air in Spirit Lake. Nothing smelled like this. It smelled like my childhood. Not much had changed here. The same trees lined the street outside Cheyenne's childhood home. The same view of the lake in the distance. The paint on the exterior was the same, although flaking. The fence was the same, too, albeit a bit rusty.

The door suddenly opened. Startled, she jumped back.

I cleared my throat. "Mrs. Benson..."

"Oh my God. Tristan." She covered her mouth. "It's you."

I sucked in some air. "I know it's been a long time."

When tears formed in her eyes, I suspected maybe she felt guilty for keeping my son a secret. In any case, I wasn't here to have it out with Cheyenne's mother. I just needed to know one thing.

"I need you to tell me where Cheyenne is."

"She's living in Milford now, with her husband."

That was a couple of towns over.

"Do you have an address?"

Her breathing seemed shallow. "Is there a reason you need to see her?"

"I need her address," I repeated.

Mrs. Benson went back inside the house and returned with an address written in pen on a piece of paper. She handed it to me.

I'd planned to see my parents while I was here, but I was too anxious. I'd go see Cheyenne first and come back to Spirit Lake after.

~

I'd imagined this moment several times over the years but never thought I'd actually see Cheyenne again. Even as I stood at the doorway to her house, I couldn't believe it. My heart thundered in my chest as I forced myself to press the doorbell. It was the middle of the day, so I had no idea whether anyone was home.

But then the door opened, and Cheyenne stood there, looking almost the same as I remembered, her brown hair still long, the same beautiful blue eyes. Now they had slight creases at the corners. I looked into the eyes of my first love, yet love wasn't what I felt anymore. Cheyenne looked frozen but not exactly shocked. Her mother, I assumed, had given her warning that I was on my way.

"Hi, Cheyenne."

"Tristan..." she whispered.

"I think you know why I'm here." Sadly, she really didn't. She just thought she did. What I had to tell her was far worse than she could ever imagine.

She stepped aside. "Please come in."

I needed to get the hard part over with. No matter how much anger I harbored for the decision she'd made, she deserved to know. So I came right out with it. "He died, Cheyenne. Our son passed away in a car accident."

She nearly fell over, bringing her hand to her mouth. "What?"

"I'm so sorry to be the one to tell you."

As she began to cry, I somehow held back my tears. "It happened a little over a year ago. He never told his parents he came to see you. He wrote about it in a journal that was found after he passed. Jacob never had the chance to find me. A friend who read his journals came looking for you, but you weren't at the address he had for you anymore. So she came to find me instead."

"Oh my God," she murmured, holding onto a side table.

As much anger as I felt toward Cheyenne, all I could see was a mother who'd lost her child. There was no place for anger right now. In this moment, she and I were just two broken people who never had a chance to know our son. In my case, never had a chance to meet him.

I felt numb as I went to her kitchen and found a glass in the cupboard, pouring her some water.

With a shaky hand, she took the glass from me and gulped the water down.

I took an article from my backpack. I'd had it printed at the hotel back in Nevada.

"This is a news article about what happened. He was riding in a car with some kids who were racing. He was the only one who died. It was about a year after he'd come to see you." I swallowed, my throat parched.

"How could I not have known?"

"Bad luck and timing. No one read his diaries until recently."

She closed her eyes. "I can't believe I'll never see him again."

At least you got to see him once.

It took several minutes for her tears to stop enough that she could talk again. "I know you must be so furious with me. I can't even begin to—"

"Don't, Cheyenne. Sure, I'm furious. But that doesn't matter right now. You need to process this. I'm not gonna force you to explain yourself today. I'm pretty sure I know everything you're gonna say anyway." I shook my head and looked down. "Nothing you can say will bring him back."

The anger in my heart had shifted—at least for the moment—to a mix of sadness and regret. It didn't feel like I knew Cheyenne anymore, didn't really want to, and yet here we were, sharing a monumental pain no one else in the world could understand.

I couldn't breathe. I needed to go, but I didn't want to just leave her.

"You live with your husband?"

"Yes." She wiped a teardrop from the corner of her mouth.

"You shouldn't be alone right now. Have him come home. I'll wait until he arrives. I can come back before I leave town, if you want to have the other conversation, but I don't think we should be talking about any of that stuff right now. I just gave you devastating news, and you need to process it." I found a pen and paper on the desk in her living room. "Here's my number, if you need to reach me. I'll be at my mother's for a couple of days."

After I handed her the paper, I looked down. I hadn't noticed until now. "You're pregnant..."

She nodded.

"Do you have any other children?"

"No. This is the first since..." She stopped short of finishing the sentence. She didn't need to.

The minutes while we waited for her husband were quiet and painful. When I saw his car pull up, I left without saying another word. I didn't even look at him when we passed on my way out.

A raw feeling developed inside my chest. Cheyenne was pregnant, starting a life with her new husband. Meanwhile, the son I never knew had grown up without his actual parents. She'd get a second chance to start over, to do things right, and Jacob would never have a second chance at anything.

~

A half hour later, I pulled up at my mother's house, a brand new, sparse structure on the same plot of land I grew up on. I'd tried to convince my mother to let me buy her a house for years. She'd finally agreed to let me build her one on the property a couple of years ago.

When Mom opened the door, she had a huge smile on her face. All I'd told her was that I was coming to town. "Tristan!" She wrapped her arms around me.

"Mom." I rubbed her back, feeling awful for what I was about to do.

Her expression darkened when she pulled back and looked at me.

She wrapped her hands around my cheeks. "What's wrong? Did something happen?"

In that moment, I finally broke down, crying like a fucking baby in my mother's arms.

She held me tighter. "Tristan, my God, what happened?"

How was I going to tell her she'd had a grandchild she never knew about who was now dead? I was her only child. My mother had always wished I was the type of man to get married and settle down, but she'd resigned herself to likely never having any grandkids. This was going to devastate her.

"I'm sorry I'm not a better son, that I almost never come home. I'm sorry for so many things," I said, my voice shaky.

"You owe me no apologies. I'm so proud of you. Please tell me what's wrong."

We sat down, and I told my mother everything. She cried, and I held her like she'd held me after I told her the grandson she'd never met was no longer.

"Do you have any photos of him?" she asked.

I reached into my bag for the pictures Emily had given me. I'd only looked at them once, so it was like looking at him for the first time all over again. My mother's eyes filled with tears again as she stared.

"There were so many times when I thought about what might have happened if I hadn't moved away from here," I told her. "It always felt like I might've been missing out on a better life. But I had no freaking idea *how much* I was missing."

She finally looked up at me. "He was beautiful."

"There's no doubt he's mine, right?" I smiled sadly as I wiped my eyes.

"Not in the least. My beautiful grandson." She sniffled. "Wow."

Just then the doorbell rang. When I opened, the last thing I expected to find was Cheyenne.

Her eyes were red as her dark brown hair blew in the breeze. "Can I come in?"

"Sure," I said, stepping aside.

"Hi, Mrs. Daltrey."

My mother nodded once. "Hello, Cheyenne."

She held her stomach. "Do you mind if I sit?"

I gestured toward the couch. "Of course."

My mother left the room to give us privacy.

Cheyenne took a seat. "I'm not going to be able to sleep tonight if I don't explain myself to you." Her voice trembled. "I know it's hard to believe, Tristan, but I thought I was making the right decision at the time."

"It was a decision I should've been in on," I couldn't help but say.

"Of course, I realize that now. But sixteen-year-old me was scared and a little out of her mind."

"Did you know you were pregnant before I left for California?"

"No." She shook her head. "It was four months after. You'd already left, and that made it even harder for me to garner the courage to tell you. I realize now that I made a mistake. At the time, though, I blamed myself for being irresponsible. I was the one who'd forgotten to take my pill a couple of times. You'd done nothing to deserve that predicament. I knew if you found out, you'd give everything up and come back home. That's the type of person you are, Tristan. But I couldn't let you do that, especially when I knew I couldn't raise a child. I made the only decision that made sense at the time. But it was the wrong one. I know that now. I didn't have the right to make the choice for you."

"No, you didn't," I muttered.

"I don't know how I can ever make it up to you. I'll live with this guilt forever."

I sighed deeply. "I wish you'd at least contacted me when he came to find you."

"I felt it was *his* decision. I told him I'd support whatever he wanted. He was hesitant. I think he was afraid of rejection. Because of who you are."

That was a knife to the heart. The idea that my son would think anything was more important than him killed me. I hung my head. "If that was the case, he was very wrong."

"I didn't push it because I was scared of your reaction, too. But I believed he'd find you eventually. I'd asked him to let me know when he decided so I could tell you first."

I raised my voice. "You should've told me anyway."

"I know!" she cried. "I know. I made all the wrong decisions. I believed we had more time. I never imagined..." She placed her head in her hands and bawled.

Fuck.

I took a seat next to her but stopped short of touching her. "Try to breathe, Cheyenne. You can't afford to get upset in your condition."

She looked up at me, her eyes swollen and red. "How could you care about me at this point?"

"Because I'm not a cruel person. I understand why you made the decision you did. It just makes me sad. And you're right. I would've given up everything. I wouldn't have regretted it, either. That would've felt nothing like the regret I have now."

If I didn't figure out how to forgive her, it would eventually kill me. I wasn't there yet, though. "Cheyenne, go home and rest. You said what you had to say." Then I told her a lie. "I forgive you. Just take the time to mourn and stop feeling like you need to explain yourself. What's done is done."

She needed to leave. If she stuck around any longer, she'd sense my lingering anger and question whether I was being truthful. I worried about her health and didn't want to be responsible for something happening to the baby. She couldn't afford to lose another child.

Cheyenne seemed to calm a bit. I walked her out and realized her husband had been waiting for her in the car. He and I made brief eye contact as I shut the door.

Chapter 26

EMILY

Four long months had passed since I'd confessed everything to Tristan in Henderson. And so much had changed since then. For one, I was now living back home in Missouri.

I was currently in the middle of one of my shifts at Art's Grill. The air smelled like coffee with a hint of bacon grease at all hours here. I'd been working at this restaurant, where my mother also worked, in order to make money while continuing to look for a permanent job.

Even though I had supposedly been trying to move on—even had a new boyfriend—when I was doing mundane tasks like wiping down the tables, my mind always wandered to Tristan, wondering how he was doing, what he was up to, who he was with. Actually, I knew the answer to the latter. A couple of weeks ago, I'd gone online and a certain headline had smacked me in the face:

Delirious Jones Lead Singer Tristan Daltrey Seen Out on Dinner Date in Paris with Band's PR Manager

That had stung. Band management had switched PR people when they got to Europe. Instead of Veronica, it was this chick named Nazarene Mercier. She was gorgeous, with long, black hair and gigantic brown eyes. French, I think. Tristan told me he'd had a thing with the band's PR person in the past, and I wondered if it was the same woman. Maybe they'd brought her back. Maybe *he'd* brought her back and started things again. In any case, it had been hard to see those photos on social media. But it was what it was. Did I still think about Tristan all the time? Of course. But I had to accept that there was no chance for us.

Shortly before he left for Europe, Tristan had called to catch me up on everything that had gone down with Cheyenne back in Iowa. He'd thanked me profusely for bringing everything to light. But he'd also made it clear that we needed to move on. He hadn't said why in so many words, but the message was clear to me: he wasn't going to pursue anything with his dead son's ex-girlfriend. I couldn't say I blamed him. His reaction had been what I expected from the start.

Strangely, it had been a relief to get that closure. I didn't need to hope for a future with him, which would've been delusional. But the knowledge of where we stood didn't take away the ache in my heart. I felt it whenever I thought about the brief time when I'd forgotten who I was and all the pain that came along with that, the brief period when a man had looked at me like I was the most important thing in the world. And when he'd made me feel that way.

The life I lived now, however, was a stark contrast to the tour experience. When my temporary marketing position in Henderson ended, I could no longer afford my apartment in Nevada, even with a roommate. My mother had been urging me to come back for a while so I could save money, and I'd finally caved when things got bad enough.

I'd recently started dating Ethan, a guy I'd gone to high school with. He'd come into the restaurant one night and then started coming in more often. He eventually asked me out, and we'd been dating exclusively for about a month. Ethan was sweet and respectful and everything you could want in a guy. He'd come into my life at what seemed like just the right time, even if he didn't realize he was helping me try to get over a man who had infiltrated my soul. I'd told him only select things about my time on the tour, none of which included the fact that I'd been involved with Tristan.

Tonight at work was hectic as usual, with a steady stream of customers coming in for a late-night meal or piece of pie. In fact, I'd been so busy tonight that it took me a moment to notice the hysteria in one corner of the restaurant.

Patrons were surrounding someone. Then one of the servers said, "Holy crap. Is that who I think it is?"

Oh my God.

Tristan's dark hair fell over his face as he signed autographs, each person bouncing away in delight with their prize. He took a few photos with people before he turned and met my eyes.

My heart nearly leaped out of my chest as I approached him. "What are you doing here, Tristan?"

"Hi to you, too."

"Sorry. I guess I should've said hello first."

"I'm just kidding, Emily. I can understand why this is a total surprise."

"It sure is." I looked down at myself, wishing I had on anything other than my ugly server uniform.

"Now that the tour is over, I finally have a chance to breathe. I was hoping you and I could talk."

I looked over my shoulder to find the other servers watching us like hawks. "I'm on the clock for another hour, until ten."

"I'll wait for you."

"Here?"

"Yeah, why not?"

"Because you're a little distracting." I glanced around again.

"I'll leave, if you prefer."

I shook my head. What was I thinking? Yes, he was distracting, but no I didn't want him to leave. I'd missed him so much. His smell. Those gorgeous blue eyes looking back at me. I wanted to run away and jump into his arms all at once.

I finally seated him at a table in the corner, where I hoped no one else would bother him. Remaining tense for the rest of my shift, I glanced repeatedly at Tristan as I balanced trays of hot dishes and wobbly beverages. The weight of his eyes never left me, even as I tried to keep him distracted with food and drinks—on the house, per my manager. Mike was a huge fan, apparently.

When my shift was finally over, I grabbed my purse and went to his table, my stomach fluttering with antici-pation. How I'd missed his chiseled face, his radiant smile, the intoxicating way he smelled. But mostly I'd missed the way he looked at me, which hadn't changed. His eyes were still penetrating. Somehow our connection still felt as magnetic as ever. *What does that mean?*

"It's so good to see you, Emily," he said as he rose. "I'm sorry I didn't have the opportunity to come before now."

Heat traveled to my cheeks. "It's good to see you, too." I willed myself to act casual despite freaking out inside.

Tristan walked me out before we faced each other in the parking lot. "How did you end up working here?" he asked, looking back at the diner.

"This is the place my mother works. She was able to switch to the day shift, and I work some nights. Just passing the time until I can find a permanent job." I looked around, unable to ignore my coworkers' attention on us as they peeked through the window.

"Wanna take a ride?" he suggested.

"I have my car here." I pointed to my old navy Corolla. "I can't just leave it."

"I can drive you back to get it after."

There wasn't much to think about. It wasn't like I could say no when he'd come all the way here. It wasn't like I *wanted* to say no, either. Any time with him felt like a gift.

"Okay..." I shrugged.

The inside of Tristan's black Range Rover smelled just like him, heady and spicy, a painful reminder of having his scent all over my body. He started the engine and took off down the windy country road. "So, you're wondering why I'm here..." he began, glancing over.

"Yeah. Of course."

"I pretty much had to block out everything that happened before Europe in order to get through the tour."

"You seem to have found a good distraction, from what I read online."

"What do you mean?"

Blood rushed to my face. "You're dating the new PR manager. The whole world knows about it."

Tristan grimaced. "I guess I forget how that works sometimes. I don't pay attention to the press. But figures they reported on that."

That certainly wasn't a denial. I cleared my throat. "How's that going?"

"It's not too serious."

"Well, I'm glad you seem happy." I tried my best to not let my bitterness show.

"What about you?" he asked. "Are you happy?"

I raised my chin. "I'm dating someone, too."

He nodded several times. "Who's the lucky person?"

"His name is Ethan. I've known him since high school."

"Is he a good guy?"

"I wouldn't be with him if he wasn't."

His Adam's apple bobbed. "Well, if you're happy, I'm happy."

True happiness is what I felt with you before you knew who I was. Before I turned both of our lives upside down.

"You still haven't yet told me why you're here, Tristan."

"I need your help."

"Help with what?"

"Let me find somewhere to park so we can chat."

On pins and needles, I looked out the window as he drove down a side street and parked. He turned off the engine. Nothing but the sound of crickets rang out in the night.

"I know you and I have history," he began. "And I still haven't worked through all my feelings where that's concerned. I just pushed them aside. But I'm hoping you can look past the complicated nature of our relationship and help me. You're the only person who can."

"What is it?"

"I want to get to know my son. Who he was. Posthumously."

I blinked. "Okay..."

"You knew him best. I feel like I can't go on until I take some time to learn about him. To feel his spirit. I know he's not physically here anymore, but this town is where he lived. I want to go to the places he went. I want to eat at his favorite restaurants. Meet his friends. I want to know what made him smile. To see his childhood home and meet his parents. It's not the same as getting to know him personally, but it's all I have." He leaned his head back against the seat. "I've now read every page of his journals, but he only started those the last few years of his life. It's not enough for me, Emily."

"How long are you in Shady Hills?" I asked.

"Well, I've rented a house, and the lease is month to month. The guys and I still have some finishing touches to do for the new album—the one we were recording in the desert when you and I met. We rented a studio about an hour away in St. Louis, since there was nothing here in town. The guys are staying with me here at the house."

My eyes widened. "Everyone is living in Shady Hills?"

"Just Atticus and Ronan."

Nodding, I stared out at the street for a moment before turning to face him. "I think it's beautiful that you want to learn more about Jacob, but I'm not sure if I can handle being your personal tour guide."

Disappointment shone on his face. I regretted expressing my hesitancy. This wasn't about me...

"I can't force you," he said. "But I'm here in town regardless, if you decide to help. At the very least, I feel closer to his spirit just being here. It's rare that I have a break like this in between commitments. It didn't feel right going back to L.A."

I had to stop and think. If this would bring him some peace, how could I say no? I owed it to Jacob, didn't I? It would be hard to be around Tristan, but I needed to set aside my hang-ups and do it.

"His favorite place for breakfast was Sparky's. I have tomorrow free, if you want to meet me there at eleven AM."

Tristan's mouth curved into a smile. "I would absolutely love that." He let out a breath. "Thank you, Emily."

Tristan drove me back to the restaurant, and when we pulled up, my heart nearly stopped. Ethan's truck was parked next to my car. He leaned against it with his arms crossed.

"Where have you been?" he asked as I exited the Range Rover. His eyes moved to Tristan, who remained in the driver's seat with the car running.

"This is—"

"I know who it is," Ethan said. "They told me you took off with him, but I didn't understand."

I'd told Ethan about my time on tour with Delirious Jones, including the reason I'd set out to find Tristan. He knew everything—aside from the fact that Tristan and I had hooked up before Tristan knew who I was. I figured there was no benefit to Ethan knowing that. I'd never imagined Tristan would come to town and Ethan would potentially see the guilt written all over my face.

Tristan sized Ethan up before speaking through the open car window. "I'll let you get back to your night." He drove off without another word.

"What was that all about?" Ethan asked.

"Tristan is in between music stuff and staying in town for a little while to learn more about Jacob. He's renting a house here with two of his bandmates."

"What does that have to do with you being in his car?"

I shrugged, hoping to diffuse the situation. "He wanted to talk to me. He asked me to be his tour guide, help him learn about Jacob, since I was the person who knew him best."

"I don't know how I feel about that." He placed his hands at his hips. "You sure he doesn't have an ulterior motive?"

My face felt hot. "Like what?"

"Don't be naïve, Emily."

"You think he'd be making a play for his son's ex-girlfriend?" *Not knowingly, at least.* I laughed nervously. "It's not like that. Plus, he has a girlfriend."

Ethan's expression relaxed. "Okay. Sorry for overreacting." He sighed. "I just wasn't expecting this and didn't know what to think when they told me you left with him."

"I don't blame you one bit. If I'd known you were coming to the restaurant, I would've texted so you weren't concerned."

"Anyway…" He leaned in to kiss me on the cheek. "I missed you today. When I went by your mom's, she said you hadn't come home from work yet, which is why I stopped by to catch you here."

"I missed you, too," I said, praying he wouldn't continue to be suspicious, even if based on my reaction to Tristan today, he had every reason to be.

Chapter 27

EMILY

"I'll have the banana waffles." I put my menu down and slid it over to the edge of the table. "And he'll have a special order of waffles with pickles and bacon. And could you drizzle some mustard on top? I know that's a strange request, but if Chef Carl is still here, he'll know. He calls it the Jacob Special."

"Okee-dokee." The server smiled. "Carl is on today. Coming right up." The older woman didn't seem to recognize Tristan, which was a nice break from the norm.

Tristan's mouth hung open. "Are you serious? My tongue feels tangy even thinking about that. And not in a good way."

His *tongue*. The thoughts that elicited... "You said you wanted what Jacob would've had. That's what he ordered when he came here."

"Wow. Okay. Then that's what I have to get." Tristan looked around. "I guess I can see why he liked this place. It's old school."

Sparky's was a Shady Hills staple. It was warm and inviting with décor that combined vintage memorabilia and local artwork. There were mismatched, vibrantly colored upholstered chairs at each of the distressed wooden tables. Regular patrons occupied the counter.

Tristan and I sat across from each other at one of the tables. I'd been nervous to see him, but now that he was in front of me, it almost felt like old times. He had a way of making me comfortable even when I should've been nervous.

As he looked me over, I felt the room fading away.

"You look beautiful, Emily."

"Thank you." I cast my eyes down, feeling oddly shy. "You look good, too."

His gaze fell to my lips, causing my nipples to stiffen.

I cleared my throat. "You said you read all of Jacob's journals?"

"I did." He nodded. "Not right away. I hung on to them for months after you gave them to me. Toward the end of the tour, when I saw a light at the end of the tunnel and was confident I'd be able to finish my obligations without risking a nervous breakdown, I couldn't hold off anymore. I was blown away by a lot—namely that he wrote music. That twisted me up the most."

"Yeah. You have no idea how many times I've thought of that."

"It was clear how much he cared about you, too."

Jacob had written about how difficult our breakup was but that he knew we'd be in each other's lives forever. That had touched me. Jacob had just started dating a girl from his college in the months before he passed. He'd told me about her during one of our last phone calls. I remember feeling relieved because it had lessened my guilt about the end of our romantic relationship. But that's all I knew about her, because the date on his last journal entry was before he'd met her. Not sure why he'd stopped writing.

"What did you think of what he wrote about you?" I asked.

Tristan let out a long breath. "It hurt that he doubted my character, but I can't blame him. He didn't know me. But I hate that he was afraid to come find me."

"I'm sure you can understand why. In his eyes, someone like you could think he was out for money."

"Yeah, I totally get it. It just sucks. I never would've turned him away. Just the opposite. He wouldn't have been able to get rid of me."

His words tugged at my heart. "I know."

When the server set the plate of waffles with bacon and pickles in front of Tristan, the aroma brought on a wave of nostalgia. I couldn't help but laugh at Tristan's hesitation.

"Have I mentioned I hate pickles?" He grimaced. "And mustard? But I'm gonna eat the hell out of this for him." As I nibbled my own breakfast, I watched Tristan cut his waffle into pieces, being sure to layer each bite with all of the accoutrements. When he finally took a bite, he grinned with his mouth full sarcastically. "Mmmm..." Then he downed a bunch of water.

"Are you gonna be okay?" I chuckled.

He nodded, and I watched in amusement as he worked his way through the giant waffle, bite by bite.

"It actually gets easier with time." He rubbed his belly. "I guess I can kind of see why he liked it. It's got a certain bite to it."

I laughed. "There are other things he liked that are easier to stomach. I just started with this because it was his favorite. And, you know, it's kind of funny watching you suffer."

He grinned. "By all means, don't hold back. I want to learn everything about him. And if I haven't thanked you enough for doing this, let me thank you again. I appreciate you agreeing to be my tour guide."

"It's not a problem." I licked syrup off the corner of my mouth. "I'm glad to be able to do it."

"So...what did your boyfriend say when he saw you with me?" he asked a minute later. "He didn't look too happy. I hope I didn't get you in trouble."

I wiped my mouth. "He was a little freaked out at first, but I haven't told him what happened on the tour between us, so he doesn't have a reason to be suspicious."

"Ah...the old, what he doesn't know won't hurt him."

"There was no reason to tell him. I never thought you'd come to town. I wasn't sure I'd ever see you again."

Tristan pushed his plate away. "We should talk about us, though, Emily."

Us. My heart fluttered. "What about us, specifically?"

"I didn't handle things well when I found out about Jacob. After I left my mother's, I ran off to Europe when I should've gone to see you one more time. I owed you that. I don't want you to think our time together meant nothing to me. I just didn't know how to handle it, you know? Still don't, really."

"I'm the one who should be explaining myself, Tristan. I let things cross a physical line, knowing you were Jacob's father. What kind of person does that make me?"

His mouth curved into an impish grin. "A horny, gap-toothed little minx."

My eyes widened. "Excuse me?"

"I'm kidding...sort of." He chuckled as I sat there mortified. "Look, Emily...the truth is, I came on pretty strong. I was practically obsessed with you. Obviously, I had no freaking clue you were harboring my biggest secret. But I chased you pretty hard. You can't take all the blame for what happened between us."

"How can you forgive what I did so easily?"

"You didn't do anything intentionally. You gave in to your feelings, but it wasn't premeditated. You had your reasons for not telling me who you were during the tour. You didn't expect me to pursue you. You didn't expect us to have real chemistry. I can't fault you for that. You got caught up. So did I."

I shook my head, though I did appreciate his perspective. "I still think you're going too easy on me."

"For being human? I don't regret anything that happened. If I remove the obvious conflict of interest, there isn't a moment with you that I would want to take back. It was still one of the happiest times I can remember. And if that's fucked up to admit now, so be it. It's complicated. But so is life, Emily." He sighed. "So is this fucking life."

Tristan always had a way of making me see things in a different light. "Why do I always feel better after talking to you?"

"Likewise." He smiled.

"Where do we go from here?" I asked.

"Well, I'm hoping you'll be my friend."

"I thought you didn't have female friends," I teased.

"You're my only one." He winked.

Friends with Tristan? I would take that over erasing him from my life. "Okay, then, friend." I smiled, feeling my face tingle.

My body was the only one not in denial right now. Sitting across from him, there wasn't a moment when I wasn't acutely aware of my unwavering attraction. How I'd missed being in his presence, feasting my eyes on him. His tousled hair, unkempt but perfect. The way his piercing eyes directed all of their attention on me. His big, rough hands adorned with silver jewelry. The allure of his tattoos, too many for me to have memorized, despite *so much* staring at the magazine image of his naked torso. More than anything, his nearness was a constant reminder of how it had felt when he touched me, explored me with his mouth. It was the only time in my life my body had reached that level of arousal. I would never forget how that felt.

"Just like you used to say I reminded you of home, of your true self...you made me forget who I was, Tristan. You made me forget all the painful memories. I was a new version of myself around you, the bare-bones version of me without all the bad stuff. And in that sense, it was the true me you got to know. Unfortunately, I also lost sight of why I was there and that I had a job to do. That's why I left when I did, because I was incapable of handling things the way I should've." I started to get choked up. "I didn't want to leave you. It was the last thing I wanted."

He reached across the table for my hand. "You've had a lot on your shoulders, even before you came to find me. You need to give yourself a break, let it all go. Start fresh. You deserve that."

I nodded, but there was one problem with heeding his advice. Despite everything that had happened, I didn't *want* to let go of the connection Tristan and I had. If I let go of *everything*—the guilt and the bad stuff—the good memories would have to go, too. And that's why I'd probably continue holding it all.

He let go of my hand. "When will I see you again after this?"

"I have to work tonight, but I was thinking maybe tomorrow we could visit Jacob's parents, the Mahoneys."

Tristan straightened in his seat, seeming on edge. "You think they would want to see me?"

"After you found out the truth, I told them how I'd gone on the tour and found you. And I let them know why you're in town. They very much want to meet you."

"Wow. That sounds great, then. Thank you."

Tristan paid the bill, but we lingered at the table. His phone chimed at one point, prompting him to look down.

"Who's that?" I asked.

He looked up. "Nazarene."

Immediately, I regretted asking. It likely came across as jealousy to begin with.

The text was a huge reality check. Both Tristan and I had significant others now. Being with him again felt natural and brought back the best of memories, but any expectations my heart held on to were nothing short of delusional.

I stood from the table. "We'd better get going."

Chapter 28

TRISTAN

The following morning, I was at my rental house doing a third read-through of Jacob's journals. The first time you read, you always miss something. In order to burn it into my memory, I'd probably never stop reading them.

The toughest part for me was always the section where he wrote about discovering I was his father.

> *It still doesn't feel real. Tristan Daltrey is my father? Just last month, I was having a conversation with Jaden about the fact that I didn't respect the guy as a musician. I said he prioritized fame and fortune over artistic integrity, writing music without substance to appeal to the masses. When I watched him being interviewed, he always struck me as arrogant. I said the only reason Delirious Jones became popular was one song that went viral on social media.*

So many musicians deserve that esteem more. I feel guilty now for the shitty stuff I said, even if it still might be true.

I just don't know what to make of this. Cheyenne said it was up to me whether I wanted to contact him. But he doesn't seem like the kind of guy who would welcome this kind of news. What if he thinks I'm lying or trying to get money out of him? I'd rather not know him than be rejected.

I feel sick. Why couldn't my father just be some normal Joe?

Tristan Daltrey? Fuck, man.

I closed the notebook and took a few deep breaths. A knock at the door interrupted my wallowing. I lifted my gaze to find Atticus entering the room.

He took one look at me and narrowed his eyes. "What's got you down?" he asked.

"My son thought I was an overrated tool..."

"What makes you say that?"

"I was reading his journal again."

"Well, if he'd met you..." He paused. "He would've confirmed that."

"Thanks a lot, asshole." I chuckled.

"I'm kidding." Atticus pulled a chair out and sat backwards. "But try to stop torturing yourself with things you can't change."

"Easier said than done."

"I know this whole trip is about connecting with him, and that's not easy when he isn't here. But I hate seeing you so damn down like this. You need to cheer up, man. You should come with us to crash this karaoke bar tonight. The locals will shit their pants if you show up."

"I'm not sure how I'll feel after today. I'm supposed to meet Jacob's parents this afternoon."

"I didn't know you were doing that today."

"Yeah. I'm meeting Emily at their house later."

Atticus rested his chin on his hands. "How's it been—hanging out with her?"

"It's a little tense, but that's to be expected."

"You still like her?"

"Doesn't matter."

"I get that. But feelings don't just get erased because of circumstances."

"I *can't* like her. How about that?" I shrugged. "She's got a boyfriend now anyway."

"And you have a girlfriend."

"Yes. Thanks for the reminder."

He scratched his chin. "You know, I find it kind of weird how you *haven't* had a girlfriend all these years. And when that whole thing went down with Emily, you jumped right into a relationship."

"What are you insinuating?"

"Not saying it's a bad thing, but just that you might've jumped into something with Nazarene to forget about Emily."

"You're a friggin' genius," I said.

"Nothing wrong with that. Nazarene is a smokeshow. Can't go wrong there. But I feel like you connected with Emily on a deeper level."

I inhaled a deep breath. "I can definitely see why my son loved her so much."

Atticus raised a brow. "Just him who loved her, huh?"

Fuck. I couldn't even begin to ponder whether what I'd felt for Emily was love. I shook my head. "Like I said, doesn't matter."

"You seem to think Jacob would be mad at you for unknowingly messing around with his girl. How do you know he wouldn't understand?"

"He hated me enough as it was. Pretty sure that would only make things worse."

"He didn't hate you. He didn't even know you."

"What gets me is, he wasn't wrong with some of the shit he wrote about our music. But he was definitely wrong in thinking I wouldn't have wanted to know him."

"You would've been a good dad," Atticus said after a moment. "When I need someone to talk to, you're always the first person I go to. When I was going through all that stuff with Nicole, you were a good friend to me. I'll never forget that."

"You're not so bad yourself," I told him. "I appreciate you guys being willing to camp out here while I work through this."

"Are you kidding? I'm having a grand old time corrupting this small town." He winked.

Ronan walked in. "Who are we corrupting now?"

"Not Emily anymore..." Atticus taunted as he hopped off the chair.

I smacked him up the side of his head.

~

The house where my son grew up was as picturesque and reminiscent of a small town as you could imagine. It had a wraparound porch and a big backyard with a lush garden.

Rick and Carol Mahoney were the nicest people, too. It brought me great comfort to know Jacob had such good parents. If I couldn't raise him myself, that was the next best thing. The Mahoneys were twenty years older than me, so technically they were old enough to be my parents, too. And so far, they treated me more like a son than Jacob's father. It brought me some solace to know Jacob had been their first and only child after a long battle with infertility. They'd decided to adopt in their mid-thirties.

After showing me around their property for over an hour, we sat down and had lunch together. Rick had brought in a gigantic bowl of garden tomatoes to send home with me. I wasn't a cook, but I sure as heck could slice up a tomato and drizzle some olive oil on it.

Carol stared at me all throughout the meal, probably because she noticed a lot of Jacob in my face. When she looked at me, I was sure she saw what he might've looked like when he was older, had he not passed away.

As we were finishing up, she turned to Emily. "We're so grateful for you, Em. I'd never planned to read Jacob's journals, because I know how he felt about me butting into his business. I didn't want to upset him even now. But I never imagined they held such meaningful information. I always thought he'd tell me if he was going to find his birth mother. But I suppose he didn't want to upset me. He made up a story about going out of town that weekend with some friends when in reality, he'd gone to see her." She turned to me again. "So, we're very lucky Emily found you. You're a part of our son. And part of our family now, too."

My chest squeezed tight. "That means so much to me. And I can't thank you enough for giving him a better childhood than I ever could've. He was truly blessed."

"We were the blessed ones," Rick said.

Emily smiled sadly over at me. This walk down memory lane couldn't have been easy for her.

"And I have to thank Emily as well," I said. "I don't know how I could've gone through life not knowing I had a son."

"Sometime I've got to show you the photos of Jacob and Emily when they were little. They were so cute together," Carol said.

I turned to Emily. "You never told me how you met him."

She smiled. "I was about seven. Jacob was flying a kite in a park, and the wind took it away. It caught on a branch and wrapped around it. I sort of laughed at him trying to free it, but then I asked if he needed help. We ended up flying the kite together, and I realized he lived down the street. I always kind of felt like that kite getting stuck was meant to be."

It was crazy how one simple thing could change the course of someone's life. If Jacob had never met Emily, who knew if I'd have known about him. Those journals might've gone unread forever.

"I love that story," I said.

"Would you like to spend some time in Jacob's room while you're here?" Rick asked.

"Could I? I would love that."

"Of course." Carol stood. "Follow me."

She led Emily and me to a bedroom at the end of a small hallway.

There was a Chicago Bears poster on the wall. I smiled, satisfied that my son had liked one of my favorite teams. A few pennants were also hung up.

I ran my finger along one of them. "He played baseball? He never mentioned that in the journals."

"Little League and then through high school, yes," Carol answered.

"I played, too." I smiled. "But I stopped before middle school. Kind of dropped sports the more I got into music."

An image of teaching Jacob to play ball as a little boy flashed through my mind. Imagined doing that and getting to see him grow up and play in high school. As much as that made my chest ache, I was happy Rick had gotten to share it with him.

There were a bunch of old textbooks piled on a desk.

This room felt lived in and had clearly remained untouched since his passing.

A navy comforter with a thick orange line down the middle covered his bed. And across from the bed was a closet filled with clothes. There was a pile of shoes on the closet floor.

"Someone had a sneaker addiction," I said.

"He rarely spent his money on anything else," Carol said.

I'd have bought him an entire house full of sneakers if I could. I'd never felt Jacob's presence stronger than in this room. It was different from reading his diary. He felt alive here, like he could walk in at any moment.

I wandered over to the closet and ran my hand along the clothes. The realization that he was never coming back came in waves. And when it did, utter sadness consumed me.

Taking one of his shirts off a hanger, I brought it to my face and smelled it, smelled *him* for the first time. I closed my eyes and let myself get lost in the son I never knew.

Even if you think I'm an overrated buffoon, I'll always love you.

Chapter 29

EMILY

Tristan was quiet as we left the Mahoneys. When we got in his car, he didn't start it, just leaned his head back on the seat and stared out the window.

"Are you okay?" I asked.

"Yeah. That was intense, though." He reached for my hand. "Thank you for holding my hand through this."

The shock of his touch sent ripples of electricity down my spine. "It's my pleasure."

He let go of me. "You were pretty quiet in there. Are you still okay with this process? It must be a lot for you, too—reliving those memories."

"It's actually been nice getting to know him all over again." Sadness about Jacob wasn't the problem. I'd been struggling with my lingering feelings for Tristan.

"How have you been feeling lately?" he asked.

"In what way?"

"In every way. Mentally, I guess. I've been so caught up in learning about Jacob that I haven't checked in with you."

I shrugged. "Coming back to Shady Hills wasn't necessarily good for my mental health at first. I was afraid moving back to my mother's would bring painful memories. But I'm getting used to it. It's been easier than I expected."

"Where would you like to be living?"

"That's the thing." I shrugged. "I don't know. There's no specific place that comes to mind. But strangely, having you here, showing you some of the places that remind me of happier times, has helped me appreciate Shady Hills more."

"Well, I'm glad." He perked up. "Speaking of which, the guys are going to this local bar tonight for karaoke. I was gonna skip out, but I might reconsider if you'd be willing to come with?"

This was the first time he'd suggested we hang out beyond Jacob-related stuff. There was nothing I wanted more than time with him. But I wasn't sure that was the best idea. "I don't know..."

"Come on. We could both use a night out after today. It'll be fun."

The thought of hanging out with Tristan gave me butterflies, and that was exactly the kind of reaction I was trying to avoid. Still, he was right; I could use a night out. Ethan was away, too, working on an out-of-state construction project with his dad. He wouldn't be back until tomorrow.

But the deciding factor? The pout on Tristan's face. That made it impossible to say no. I sighed. You couldn't get much safer than a karaoke bar. It wasn't like he and I would be alone.

"Okay. Why not?"

~

As expected, the guys were mobbed at Tim's Bar, but Atticus and Ronan seemed to soak it up as they always did. Tristan's bandmates had been photographed all over town lately, causing a frenzy at Shady Hills establishments and flirting with the locals.

The bar was soon packed for karaoke night. I wasn't sure if it was always this way in the middle of the week, or if people were calling their friends to come down once they realized Delirious Jones was here.

When it was Tristan's turn to take the stage, the crowd went wild.

He spoke seductively into the mic. "Anything in particular you want me to sing?"

I could practically feel panties melting all over the room as the screams rang out.

"It can't be one of my songs," he said. "Something vintage…"

"Song about robbing the cradle?" a drunk Ronan heckled.

I pretended not to hear that. *Dickhead.*

The crowd's chattering faded as Tristan began crooning Journey's "Don't Stop Believin'."

I wondered if choosing that song was intentional—or maybe subconscious. A small-town girl and boy searching for something more in life; maybe it reminded him of Jacob and all his hopes and dreams that never came to be.

I was certain these patrons had never seen such heart and soul poured into a performance at this little old place.

Imagine going to a karaoke bar and getting a free concert with Tristan Daltrey.

As he belted out the song, I hung on every word, every note. I missed watching him perform live. And maybe it was the break from touring, but his voice didn't crack at all.

As the song ended, Tristan was met with thunderous applause. When he returned to the table, I got the sudden urge to wrap my arms around him, smell his hair... kiss him. I missed touching him. He was so close lately, yet so far away.

Almost immediately after he sat down, another set of arms wrapped around him, though. They seemed to come out of nowhere. Long black hair covered his face as the woman went in for a kiss. "Surprise!" she said.

Nazarene.

His girlfriend.

A look of genuine shock crossed his face. "What are you doing here?"

"I came to surprise you." She had a slight French accent. "Hope it was a good surprise?"

"How did you know I was here?" he asked.

"I texted Ronan. He told me where you would be."

Maybe it was my imagination, but Tristan's rigid body language said he wasn't too thrilled at her sudden appearance. Or maybe that's what I wanted to believe.

"Naz..." He turned to me. "This is Emily."

"Emily. It's so nice to meet you. Tristan has told me all about you."

He has?

Tristan nodded. "I told her about your relationship to Jacob and how you had come on the tour to find me."

Hardly *all* about me, then. Surely she wouldn't be so nice if she knew the truth. "Nice to meet you," I said, holding out my hand.

With Tristan's beautiful, tall girlfriend here, the tone shifted for the rest of the evening. I had to endure her sitting on his lap, basically all over him. His eyes wandered over to me at times, and he wasn't really returning her affection. It continued to seem like he was uncomfortable or holding back for my sake.

The worst part was when Tristan went over to the bar to buy a round of drinks, and I was forced to make conversation with her. Apparently, Nazarene planned to stay in town for two weeks. She asked me all sorts of questions about my life. When I told her I had a boyfriend, she suggested that "the four of us" go out.

When Tristan returned to the table, Nazarene took the drink he'd brought her. "I was just telling Emily we should go to breakfast with her and her boyfriend sometime this week."

Tristan nearly choked on his drink. "Oh yeah?"

Given that I had to endure her in town for two weeks, maybe it was a good idea to embrace reality. It would also be a good reminder of which man I belonged to. Despite my heart continuing to flutter for Tristan, I was with Ethan now. So, I agreed to breakfast, knowing that despite my sense that Tristan was against the idea, he wouldn't say no.

～

Later that night, I was back home in my bed when I got a text around 2 AM. It wasn't unusual for Ethan to text me goodnight, especially when he was out of town.

But when I looked over at my phone, the text was from Tristan.

> **Tristan:** I'm sorry if Nazarene showing up made you uncomfortable tonight. I had no idea she was going to come here.

I deflected.

> **Emily:** She's really beautiful.

> **Tristan:** We don't have to do breakfast. I wasn't sure if you said yes because you felt pressured.

Figured he was trying to get out of it. But I was determined to face the fire. It would be just the wake-up call both he and I needed.

> **Emily:** No, I think it's fine.

> **Tristan:** Only if you want to.

> **Emily:** You don't need to apologize for her being here. It makes sense that your girlfriend would visit you.

The dots moved around as he formed a response. Despite what I'd typed, I seethed with jealousy and hurt. But I'd made my own bed after crossing the line with him in the first place. And I probably shouldn't have gone out with him tonight.

> **Tristan:** I just don't want to upset you. I've disturbed your peace here enough as it is.

I wasn't going to respond, but a minute later he sent another text.

Tristan: You mean a lot to me.

My chest constricted. *You mean a lot to me, too.*

But I wouldn't let myself reciprocate. I typed as simple a text as I could conjure.

Emily: It's all good.

Then I shut off my phone and placed it in my bedside drawer before any further texts from him could keep me up all night.

Chapter 30

EMILY

A couple of days later, Ethan and I met Tristan and Nazarene for breakfast at Sparky's.

After we were seated, Tristan crossed his tattooed arms and aimed some questions at my boyfriend. "So, Ethan, what do you do for a living?"

"I work for my father's construction company, Mills Construction here in town."

"Nice. Family business. Will you take it over someday?"

Ethan played with the wrapper to his straw. "That's the plan." He nudged me with his elbow. "I'm trying to get this one here to work for us, but she doesn't want any handouts."

"Well, I can't blame her for wanting to be her own person. She probably wants to use her degree for something she's, you know, interested in."

"I just meant in the meantime. Instead of waiting tables," Ethan clarified.

"There's nothing wrong with waiting tables," Tristan challenged. "As long as she's happy doing that. It's her choice."

You could cut the tension with a knife. Ethan had never had to endure being questioned by my mother. She wasn't the type to intimidate or interrogate. This inquisition seemed like the closest thing to that, and, yes, the irony of Tristan being the *daddy* figure was not lost on me.

A server came by and set down a carafe of fresh coffee. By some miracle no one had come to bother Tristan for an autograph, but that was probably because he was wearing sunglasses.

You know the awkwardness between Tristan and Ethan had to be bad if I intentionally struck up a conversation with Nazarene. "So...how did you end up working for the band?" I asked.

"Well, I'd worked for them once before. And when Veronica left before the European tour, they called me back since I'm based in France and already had the experience."

So this was Tristan's second go-round with her...

"You live in France full time?" I asked.

"I divide my time between New York and Paris. But I will probably be moving out to L.A. when Tristan's stay in Shady Hills is over."

My stomach tightened. *Of course.* "I see." I swallowed the lump in my throat and looked down at my menu. "We should pick what we want."

Even as I pretended to focus on the menu, I snuck glances at Nazarene's touchy-feely behavior with Tristan. She always had to be touching him, whether it was a hand on his knee or her head on his shoulder. It made me want to jump out of my skin.

Tristan cleared his throat and attempted to lighten the mood. "I'm thinking...literally anything but waffles with pickles and bacon." He flashed me a hesitant smile.

I managed to smile back, but after we ordered, the awkward conversation continued.

"This town is so cute," Nazarene said. "Anywhere in particular I should explore while I'm here?"

"What did you have in mind?" I asked.

"Is there a spa?"

"There is one. It's called Dandelion. I know the owner. It's more of a full-service salon, but it's the closest thing we have."

"Do they do Brazilian blowouts?"

I scrunched my nose. "What's that?"

"It's a keratin treatment to straighten hair. You've never heard of it?"

"No. I don't really get my hair done. I don't think I've cut it in three years."

"No offense, but I was going to say..." She looked down to where my hair fell over my chest. "I can see your split ends. You could probably use a trim."

Tristan's brows furrowed as he flashed her a dirty look. He turned to me. "Don't listen to her. Your hair is beautiful."

The table went silent. I didn't know how to respond to that. I doubted either of our significant others thought much of it, but it rendered me speechless.

Nazarene backtracked. "I didn't mean anything by it. I'm sorry if it came out that way." She switched gears. "What else is there to do here?"

"Not that much, aside from the few bars and restaurants we have," Ethan answered.

"The beauty is in what you *don't* do here," Tristan countered. "It's more of an escape than anything, if you ask me. That's why I like it so much. It reminds me of the small town where I grew up in Iowa. You don't need to go anywhere to enjoy it. That night we went to the karaoke bar, after we came home, I sat on the deck, listened to the trees, and gazed at the stars. Can't remember the last time I did that."

Nazarene looked confused. "I didn't know you went outside that night. What time was that?"

"After you went to sleep, around two in the morning."

I realized that was when he'd texted me. I had to stop myself from analyzing why he'd thought of me while gazing up at those stars.

After we ordered, the food came fairly quickly, and at least then we were able to bury our heads in our plates rather than continue the conversation.

That is, until Ethan let the cat out of the bag.

"What are you two doing the rest of the day?" Nazarene asked as she picked at the sunny-side-up eggs she'd barely touched.

"Well, I'm taking the birthday girl here shopping to pick out a present."

Tristan's eyes went wide. "Birthday girl?"

"Today is my birthday," I admitted.

Nazarene's mouth dropped open. "Oh wow! How old are you?"

"Twenty-three."

"Aw..." She tilted her head. "So young."

Not too young for your boyfriend. I shook that from my thoughts.

"How did I not know it was your birthday?" Tristan frowned.

"Well, I never told you." I shrugged. "Now you know."

Tristan said almost nothing the rest of the time at Sparky's.

Before we parted ways, Nazarene planted a kiss on each of my cheeks, European-style. And Tristan left with a lingering scowl on his face.

~

Ethan took me to a fancy Italian restaurant in St. Louis that night. He did everything in his power to make me feel special, and I felt guilty, because I couldn't stop thinking about Tristan. I felt so guilty, in fact, that I decided not to go home with Ethan, but have him drive me back to my mother's house instead.

After I got home, about eleven thirty, Tristan texted.

Tristan: Are you alone or is he with you?

Emily: I'm alone.

Tristan: Can I call you?

Emily: Sure.

The phone rang a minute later.
I picked up. "Hey."
He spoke softly. "Hi."

"What's up?"

"Did you have a nice birthday?"

"Yeah. It was a great day, actually."

"I'm sorry I didn't know. I feel so dumb."

"How could you know if I never told you?"

"Still not cool. I should've investigated on my own."

"It's not a big deal. I don't understand why you're upset."

"I don't understand it myself, but I felt like shit all day because I couldn't celebrate with you. It made me feel like we were strangers. I couldn't stop thinking about you." He sighed. "I guess old habits die hard. Or maybe..." He paused. "Sometimes they don't die at all."

I didn't know what to say to that, even if I knew exactly what he meant.

"Can I come over?" He exhaled. "I got you something."

"You didn't have to do that."

"I wanted to. Is it okay if I stop by and give it to you?"

"Yeah, of course."

"Okay. I'll be there in about fifteen."

I did nothing but nervously rearrange things until I saw Tristan's car pull up in front of my house.

Opening the front door, I watched as he exited the car and approached holding what looked like a large basket. The moment I saw what it was, I covered my mouth in disbelief. "What the heck?"

"I can explain..." He laughed.

Staring back at me was the biggest rabbit I'd ever laid eyes on. It had long floppy ears and was the size of a large cat. It was sitting on a pile of pink flowers.

Oh my God. Pink peonies.

"Let me preface this by saying my idea was to get you a cute little bunny to mimic the dream you told me you had when you were thirteen."

I continued to look down at the rabbit in shock.

"Anyway, I called a bunch of shelters, and one finally assured me they had a bunny. I told them it had to be little and have floppy ears. Those were my main conditions. They obviously lied about the little part. So I committed to coming to pick it up, not knowing how damn big she was." He sighed. "I felt bad, so I took her anyway."

"*She*? Does she have a name?"

"Bertha."

"Oh my gosh. She looks like a Bertha."

"Pretty sure she's half dog or something."

I snorted as I lifted the rabbit out of the basket. A bunch of the peonies flew around, falling to the ground as Bertha resisted being held. I took her into my arms anyway. "This rabbit is several pounds bigger than the one in my dream."

"I figured that." He sighed. "I can take her back. I—"

"No way! I would never allow you to do that. I will love on this creature for as long as I live. She's staying with me."

"You don't have to keep her."

"How the heck did you remember that dream anyway?"

"I've paid attention to everything you've ever told me. You've opened up in bits and pieces, so when you do, I make sure I'm listening. That dream left an impression on me. It made me feel a little sad but proud of you at the same time. You're right that your dad doesn't deserve the time of day or your tears." Tristan scratched between Bertha's ears. "I always had it in my mind that someday I was gonna get you that damn bunny and the peonies, too. Your birthday seemed like the perfect opportunity. And it would've been really great if the shelter hadn't fucked me over."

I giggled. "Even if she's not the bunny of my dreams, she's the rabbit of my life."

He looked back over at his car. "Well, good. I brought you everything else you need for her. But I couldn't carry it all in because it would've ruined the effect."

"Pretty sure Bertha *herself* ruined the effect."

He nodded. "She *is* bigger than the basket."

"I don't know what to say. This is so sweet, yet so bizarre."

"If it turns out you can't handle her, I'll take her."

"And how are you gonna take care of a rabbit while you're on tour?"

"I'll hire someone to do it."

"I forgot you can just do that. But it shouldn't be necessary." I kissed between her ears. "We should be fine, huh, Bertha?" The rabbit tried to wriggle out of my arms. "But you'd better grab the other stuff so I can take her inside. She's getting a little rambunctious."

"On it," he said, running back to his Range Rover.

After a moment, Tristan carried in a three-foot exercise pen, along with a bunch of food, alfalfa hay, and other supplies. He'd apparently spent the afternoon researching what I'd need.

After we arranged everything in a corner of my bedroom, he asked, "Where's your mom?"

"She's sleeping."

"I'm surprised we didn't wake her up."

"She's a pretty sound sleeper. She uses a white noise machine."

He poured some pellets into a bowl. "Did you ever tell your mom the truth about us?"

I nodded. "Yeah. She knows everything."

"Shit," he muttered.

"She doesn't care."

"She must hate me for messing with you."

"She doesn't."

"Well, then I got really lucky."

"Where does Nazarene think you are right now?" I asked.

"I told her the truth."

My eyes widened. "You told her you were bringing me a rabbit for my birthday?"

"She was with me earlier when I went to pick everything up."

"She doesn't think it's weird that you bought your son's ex-girlfriend a rabbit?"

"Oh, I'm pretty sure she's wondering about a lot of things right now. Especially after the way I reacted at the restaurant earlier. She's not very happy in general. I'm having a hard time with this, and it's showing."

"With what in particular?"

He stared into my eyes, taking a few steps closer. "What am I having a hard time with? Pretending you're just some friend of my son's and nothing more to me. Pretending it doesn't hurt to see you with another guy. Pretending I'm a better person than I am. Pretending I don't practically taste you on my tongue whenever I'm close enough to smell you." He shook his head. "Pretending I can make all of this go away if I just act responsibly."

The space closed between us, and my hand had a mind of its own as I ran my fingers through his silky hair. It felt like forever since I'd touched it.

He closed his eyes and groaned before pulling away. "I should go."

"Yeah..." The air suddenly felt cold. "I'm sorry. I didn't mean to—"

"You're good. It's nothing you did, beautiful. I just don't *want* to leave, and that's exactly why I should."

"Okay. I understand." I walked him to the door.

"Happy birthday, Emily."

"Thank you again for my surprise. I'll cherish her."

He rubbed his hand along my cheek. "I cherish *you*."

Chapter 31

EMILY

The following week, Tristan and I met up a couple of times. We visited the baseball field where Jacob used to play and had coffee with Jacob's best guy friend, Jaden.

Today, though, was the part of the trip Tristan had been putting off. As we stepped through the wrought-iron gate at the entrance, I asked, "Where's Nazarene today? Why isn't she here with you?"

"She made an appointment at a spa in the city. Said she didn't like the one in town."

I nodded.

"What's that look for?" he asked as we walked through the grassy cemetery.

"I'm just surprised she wouldn't want to be here for something so monumental."

"She offered, but I encouraged her not to come. I wanted to do this alone. Well, with you, of course."

We walked quietly toward Jacob's headstone. The air was scented with dirt and flowers. I always found the cemetery to be oddly peaceful, not a sound beyond the melody of chirping birds and the warm massage of a gentle breeze.

I slowed as we approached Jacob's headstone. "He's right here," I said.

Tristan took a deep breath and exhaled as we stopped in front of Jacob's grave. He knelt and traced his fingers along the engraved MAHONEY. Some dying flowers from the last time someone visited lay atop the dirt below it. I regretted not bringing fresh ones with me today and vowed to come back soon to rectify that.

I took a few steps back, giving Tristan space.

Tristan closed his eyes as he continued to kneel before the headstone. Even though he was quiet, I somehow knew he was talking to Jacob. He opened the gift bag he'd been carrying, and tears sprang to my eyes as he placed the worn, gray teddy bear on the dirt in front of Jacob's grave. *Duffy*.

Is he leaving it here? Surely he knew it would blow away and be destroyed by the weather. But maybe the gesture mattered more than anything.

A tear tracked down Tristan's cheek as he looked up at the cloudy sky. Despite many emotional moments, I hadn't seen him cry before.

This trip had thus far been about experiencing Jacob's life, but this part represented the reality of the situation: Jacob *wasn't* alive, and he was never coming back. Tristan had to say goodbye to someone he loved but had never had a chance to meet.

He stood and wiped his red eyes. "We can go."

"Are you sure?"

He nodded. "Yeah." Wiping his eyes one more time, he said, "Thank you for waiting."

"Of course."

My heart was heavy as we walked in silence back to the car. More than anything, I felt so much love for Tristan right now. And having to hold it inside felt suffocating.

"Are you okay?" I asked as he started the car.

"Yeah," he whispered.

The car ride back was quiet, but after a while I had to say something.

"Tristan..."

He looked over from the driver's seat. "Hmm?"

"When the Mahoneys first told Jacob he was adopted, he and I talked about how he was feeling. Even though his parents had never given him any clue about the adoption before, he admitted to feeling like something had been missing in his life, like a part of him. He said he never quite understood it until he found out he was adopted." I reached over and rubbed Tristan's arm. "The missing part was you. I think he's looking down and realizing it all makes sense now."

"I hope he's not disappointed in me."

In my heart, I knew Jacob would've loved Tristan. I just didn't know how to prove that to him. "Remember when you told me you used to study near-death experiences?"

"Yeah?"

"I know you were more removed from the reality of death back then, but you said you felt like there might be a reason for bad things happening, and I keep hoping you still feel that way now that you know about Jacob."

"I'll admit, it's harder to find the good in loss when it's your own flesh and blood."

"Yeah, I can imagine. But you believe there's an afterlife. And if there is, you'll get to see him again."

"I hope that's true. I've never hoped for that more. He'll be the first person I run to." He wiped his eyes. "Maybe by then I'll have written some music he's proud of so I don't have to be embarrassed."

"I think he'd be mortified to know you've read those passages."

"But they're the truth. And honestly? His words have been my biggest kick in the ass to do better, to make him proud."

"I'm certain Jacob is pretty damn proud already. I'm still alive, and my father is nowhere to be found. In the short time you've known about your son, you've been a thousand times the father mine ever was. I know if Jacob were here, you would devote your life to making up for lost time."

He suddenly slowed the car.

"What are you doing?" I asked, gripping the armrest.

"There's something I need to say to you, and I want to pull over to do it. I want to be able to look you in the eyes." He parked the car on a residential side street, turned off the engine, and turned his body toward me. "I've been meaning to tell you something."

My palms felt sweaty. "Okay..."

"I know you say you don't care about your dad anymore. But there's a chance that what he did still affects your view of yourself on a subconscious level. Please don't ever use his insane life decision as a gauge for your value as a person. I need you to understand how special you are and that you're capable of anything you put your mind to."

I nodded after a moment. "I don't undervalue myself consciously, but maybe what he did does impact me in ways I don't realize. Not sure how it couldn't." I sighed. "Lord knows, I don't make the best life decisions."

"Like dating guys you're too good for..." he added.

"Ethan, you mean?"

"I know how you look at someone when you catch feelings. I've been fortunate enough to be a recipient of that. You don't look at him like you used to look at me. And maybe that sounds arrogant as fuck, but if I can't be with you, at the very least, I want you with someone who makes you smile, who rocks your fucking world. You deserve that. And you don't need to stay in Shady Hills your whole life, if it brings back bad memories. You can go anywhere you want...do anything you want."

How can he say that? "Actually, no, I can't. I don't have the means."

"I'll give you whatever you need to live the life you want. I'll buy you a house anywhere you want to live in the world. I'll pay if you want to go back to school."

Whoa. "No, you won't. I would *never* let you do that, Tristan."

"I figured you wouldn't take money from me. So I had to get creative."

I moved back in my seat. "What are you talking about?"

"I went to talk to your mother earlier this week. I asked her for advice on how to help make things easier for you. She agreed that you wouldn't take money. So I asked if I could give it to her, if she'd hold it for you."

Why does this feel like a gut punch? "I wish you hadn't done that."

"I have millions of dollars, Emily. More than I know what to do with. And I have nothing to spend it on. Please let me give you the freedom to do something that truly makes you happy. I could never repay you for what you've done for me." Tristan shook his head. "I won't take it back."

"How much money did you give her?"

"A million."

I nearly lost my lunch. "Are you insane?"

"It's a drop in the bucket for me."

All my blood rushed to my head. "Why didn't my mother tell me about this?"

"I asked her not to until I had a chance to explain it."

Was I crazy for feeling disappointed that someone had given me a million dollars? "I can't believe this."

He put his arm on the back of my seat. "Don't be upset. Just let me do this for you."

He wasn't getting it. My disappointment wasn't about the money. Tristan wanted me to go anywhere I wanted and have adventures. But having the freedom to do that made me realize my heart only wanted to be with him.

Chapter 32

TRISTAN

"Oh look, Emily just got here, and Nazarene left this morning. What a coincidence," Ronan cracked as I ushered Emily in.

"Shut it," I warned him.

Emily waved. "Nice to see you, too, Ronan."

"Don't pay attention to that asshole, Emily," Atticus shouted from the other side of the kitchen.

The guys and I were having an evening barbecue at the house, so I'd invited her. Atticus had just brought in the meat he'd grilled while Ronan handled the sides, which included corn on the cob, pasta salad, grilled vegetables, and cut-up watermelon. I'd somehow gotten out of cooking, although I'd been tasked with running out to buy everything earlier.

Emily and I hadn't seen each other in a few days, since the cemetery visit and my awkward announcement that I'd given her a million dollars. Things had ended on a tense note after I told her I'd transferred the money to her mother's account.

Emily looked adorable in an aqua-colored, sleeveless top and jean shorts. She wore flip-flops that showed off her blue-painted toes. Her hair was up in a ponytail, which I secretly loved because you could see her cute little ears sticking out.

"Thank you for coming," I said, holding back my natural inclination to hug her.

"Well, you said there'd be ribs. I've never been able to turn those down."

"Actually, I think the magic words might have been '*Nazarene left this morning*'. Am I right?"

"That definitely helped." She smiled.

She didn't seem mad at the moment, which brightened my outlook considerably.

"What's your guy doing tonight?" I asked. "You could've brought him."

She looked down at her feet. "Ethan and I broke up, actually."

My eyes widened. "Are you serious?"

Ronan snorted from somewhere behind me. I had no idea he was paying attention.

I touched her shoulder. "Let's go out back and talk."

"What happened?" I asked when we reached the yard and I'd closed the door behind us.

"You were right. I didn't feel about him the way he felt about me. I'd known that for some time, and it wasn't fair to keep things going, as much as I wanted the stability of a relationship in my life. Something about him reminded me of the years I was happiest, back in high school before everything turned sour in my life. Nostalgic. And while I enjoyed his company and felt safe with him, that's not a reason to be with someone. You have to have a stronger connection. I tried. But I'm done lying to myself."

I tried not to seem overly pleased. "Fair enough."

"I take it you're not surprised."

"Can't say I am. I always felt like maybe you rushed into things with him."

"Sort of like you rushed into things with Nazarene?"

More like ran away from my feelings for you right into something I hoped would distract me. I deflected. "Anyway, I'm glad you didn't stay with him if he doesn't make you happy."

She looked back toward the house. "What's the occasion for this dinner?"

"There is none, really. Although, we did finish the album today, so we probably won't be going back to the studio again."

"That must be a good feeling."

"Yes and no."

"Why no?"

"Because now I have this pressure to head back to L.A., and I don't feel ready to leave Shady Hills. Not in the least."

Atticus opened the sliding door. "Food's ready. But no rush if you don't like it hot."

"Let's eat." I gestured toward the house. "We'll talk more later."

The four of us gathered around the rustic, wooden table in the dining room. My stomach growled as the aroma of barbecue wafted through the air. Stacks of ribs were piled high atop a metal tray. There was another plate of chicken breast and flank steak.

"There's enough food here for ten people." I laughed.

Atticus served himself. "Are you forgetting how much Ronan eats? I'm always paranoid we're gonna run out of food."

I turned to Emily. "What can I get you to drink?"

"We'll have to check your ID first," Ronan teased.

She gave him the finger. I *loved* that.

The sun setting outside was a nice backdrop to what turned into a peaceful meal. Emily laughed at Ronan's dumb jokes and devoured an impressive amount of ribs.

Atticus looked over at her in delight. "Here I was thinking I needed to make a lot of ribs for Ronan, but it seems Emily's the one throwing down."

She licked her fingers and shrugged.

"So, Emily..." Ronan said. "Do you know someone named Lilianne Case?"

"I do, actually. She owns the boutique in town."

"Yeah. I ran into her in the coffee shop earlier. Didn't seem fazed by me but really sweet. Put in a good word?"

"You like her?"

"I could get used to this small-town life...for the right person." He pointed his beer in my direction. "This guy's getting up there. It's only a matter of time before we all have to find a Plan B, you know?"

I rolled my eyes. "Thanks a lot."

"Just stating a fact, man."

"She's tough. Not the type of girl who'll settle for being a rockstar's wife, nor would she put up with your road antics," Emily warned.

"I wouldn't respect her if she did..." Ronan threw back some beer. "Anyway, at some point we're all gonna have to settle down and get married."

"You were married once, Atticus, right?" Emily asked.

I cringed. Atticus stopped chewing for a moment, then simply nodded.

"We don't mention Nicole around here," Ronan told her.

Emily squinted in confusion.

"Nicole is his ex," I explained. "We don't talk about her. Except Ronan who occasionally likes to risk getting his ass beat."

Atticus wiped his mouth. "Tough subject," he muttered.

Emily nodded sympathetically. "Well, that must mean you still love her?"

I gave her a warning look.

"Next topic..." Atticus said.

Emily's mouth curved into a sympathetic smile, but she stayed quiet. She seemed surprised to see this side of Atticus, who was always the roughest on the surface.

After we ate, Ronan decided we should make s'mores, something I'd not done since childhood. It seemed like a good idea at first, but I should've known that too much time with the guys was probably not the best, given how much they loved to bust balls.

"S'mores always reminds me of playing Truth or Dare with my cousins when we were younger," Ronan said as we sat around the fire.

"Sounds dangerous," I said, turning my stick to toast my marshmallow evenly.

"Let's do it," he said. "Let's play Truth or Dare."

"Not interested," I countered.

"Why? You have something to hide? Pretty sure all your secrets came out already this year."

"Emily definitely doesn't want to play," I said.

But she just shrugged, seeming not to understand how dirty my friends here liked to play.

Ronan took a bite of his graham cracker sandwich. "I'll start," he said with his mouth full of marshmallow. "Atticus, truth or dare."

Atticus rolled his eyes. "Truth."

"What really happened between you and Nicole's boyfriend the night you nearly got arrested?"

"Fuck you." He glared. "Dare."

"Really? Wow. You'd rather me dare you than answer that? You're fucking crazy."

"You're an asshole, Ronan," I shouted across the fire.

Ronan licked some marshmallow off the corner of his mouth. "You have a choice with this dare, actually..."

Atticus rolled his eyes again. "Oh, lucky me."

"You can kiss Emily here on the lips...or French-kiss Tristan."

Are you fucking kidding me?

"I didn't realize we were in high school." I shot daggers at Ronan and then Atticus. If either one of them so much as looked at Emily, I'd go insane. I was ready to rip both their heads off, if needed. There was no fucking way I was going to sit here and watch anyone other than me put his lips on her. Not that Emily would even allow him to kiss her. But what if she tried to be the good sport? Atticus was an attractive man. I was as heterosexual as they came, but I wasn't blind. Maybe she wouldn't mind kissing him.

Burning up, I marched over to Atticus and placed my hands around his face before going in for the kill, practically swallowing him whole, tongue and all.

Ronan roared with laughter as I made out with my best friend. Atticus tasted like cigarettes with a hint of beer, exactly how I might've imagined.

When I came up for air, Atticus blinked in confusion. He didn't seem to know what hit him. Emily's eyes were like saucers. Ronan was the only one who seemed amused and not in shock.

I wiped my mouth with the back of my hand and addressed Atticus. "What did you think?"

"I'm thinking if I ever decide to swing both ways, you'll be a fine contender, sir."

I laughed and sat back down.

Ronan's stupid game continued for about twenty more minutes, with each of us having one turn in the hotseat. Emily was forced to admit which of our songs she disliked the most. I was relieved that Atticus had gone easy on her with that one. He'd done me a favor by not pulling anything stupid.

~

Later that evening, after we put the fire out, Ronan and Atticus decided to go to a local speakeasy just down the road. It was mostly old men there who didn't give a shit who we were.

Grateful for an opportunity to speak with Emily in private, I hoped she didn't want to flee the moment we were alone. After the guys left to walk to the bar, I smiled at her. "I thought they'd never leave."

"You love them, though."

"I *am* lucky to have them. They're like brothers at this point, even if they drive me nuts. I appreciate them coming to support me down here. We wouldn't have finished the album in time otherwise."

When she shivered, I asked, "Are you cold?"

"A little."

My body yearned to warm her up in several different ways. I tried to ignore that. I stood. "Want to head inside?"

She rubbed her hands along her arms. "Sure."

It had been a while since Emily and I were alone in a private place. The mood shifted now that it was just us. We sat across from each other in the living room.

"That was some kiss between you and Atticus..."

I chuckled. "It was, wasn't it?"

"I was totally prepared to kiss him, you know. You didn't have to do that."

I felt my insides ignite all over again. "You were, were you?"

"Yeah. I always kind of wondered what it would be like..."

My stomach dropped. *Is she kidding?* She kept a straight face, so I had to be sure. "Seriously?"

"No." Emily burst into laughter. "I just like watching your ears turn red."

"I was not about to let either one of those assholes kiss you." *If I can't kiss you, they sure as fuck can't.*

"It was strangely hot, though, you and him. Kind of wish I'd recorded it. Could you imagine how many women would die to see that? Pretty sure you'd break the Internet."

"Maybe I can use that if my voice gets worse and I need a distraction down the line."

She kicked her feet up on the couch. "What *has* been going on with your voice? You haven't really talked about it."

"I know. I've been trying not to think about it while I'm here."

"We don't have to talk about it, then."

"No. I should." I exhaled. "I want to talk about it. With you, anyway. You've always had a way of making me want to talk." I settled myself on the opposite side of the couch, keeping a distance. "Before I came out here, I stopped in to see the specialist in L.A. He told me one of the polyps had actually gotten a lot bigger. I've tried to ignore it, but I found myself struggling a little again in the studio."

Her lips pressed together. "I'm sorry."

"The doctor suggested I do the surgery sooner rather than later. But I'm still really confused about it."

"The risk of permanent damage is small," she said.

"How do you know that?"

"I've been reading up on it ever since you told me."

I sucked in a breath. "You think I should do it?"

"I think you should take some time to think about it once you leave here, and then you should follow your instincts. If you allow yourself enough quiet time, your intuition will tell you what to do. If this is going to continue to plague you, surgery is something you should consider."

"And what if it fucks up my voice, and I can't sing anymore?"

"Don't even think about that. What we focus on becomes more of a reality. Just think positively and believe you're gonna be okay."

"Now you sound like Ronan." I chuckled.

"If you lose your voice, you can always come back to Shady Hills and hide out. There's even a McDonald's you can go to and eat your burger at closing time." She winked.

"Ah, yes." I smiled.

"That's the dream, isn't it?"

"What's *your* dream, Emily? Besides the bunny-in-a-basket one I botched."

"Bertha's the dream I never knew I had." She laughed. "I don't really have a dream right now."

"Sure, you do. You must. If you could do anything you wanted, without anything holding you back, what would you do?"

"You mean, if I had a million dollars sitting in my mother's bank account that some crazy man left for me? Which I still have no intention of spending."

"Doesn't have to cost money. Just something you dream about doing."

She stared up at the ceiling. "I feel like I'm supposed to have an answer to that question, but I don't. What I want isn't tangible. The only thing I really want is a true sense of peace. Jobs and adventures don't matter as much if you have lingering dread or guilt inside you. I don't feel peace here in Shady Hills. But at the same time, I don't know where to go. I feel lost."

"Peace isn't a place," I said. "It's a state of being. You need to live in the present. We all do. Hanging on to the past is as futile as worrying about an imagined future." I patted the couch. "Like here, right now? I'm exactly where I want to be. Sitting here in this quiet house, talking to you. Not on a surgery table like my imagination would have me go. And not in the past, performing on some stage while my son was being rocked to sleep by someone who wasn't me." I paused. *That one's tough to swallow.* "But neither of those situations exists right now. The future is fear, and the past is regret. The only peace we have is now."

"I think *you're* the one turning into Ronan."

"Yeah, maybe he's been rubbing off on me."

"It's true, though. You're right. This right now, here with you...is pretty nice."

"I think that's why I've always liked being around you," I said. "Because my mind never wanders. It doesn't want to."

She rested her chin on her hand and whispered, "I feel the same, Tristan."

"Did your breakup with Ethan have anything to do with me?"

"Cocky, aren't we?" I smiled. "Are you sure you want to know?"

"I wouldn't have asked if I didn't. Regardless of the answer, I never felt he was good enough for you. Then again, I probably wouldn't think anyone was good enough for you." I laughed under my breath. "Least of all me."

"Why *not* you? From everything I can see, you're a pretty damn good person."

"A good person wouldn't covet his dead son's girl-friend."

A tense silence filled the room.

My voice was barely a whisper. "Do you know how hard it is to sit across from you and not touch you?"

She narrowed her eyes. "Don't you have a girlfriend?"

I guess now was the right time to have that conversation. "Yeah, about that..."

Chapter 33

EMILY

"I broke up with Nazarene before she left Shady Hills."

I stiffened, trying not to seem as happy as hearing that made me feel. "You did? Why didn't you say anything when I mentioned I broke up with Ethan?"

"I guess I was using Nazarene as a shield, holding off as long as possible in an attempt to deny my feelings for you."

"I was the reason you broke up with her?"

"You're not the only reason. Our relationship wasn't that serious to begin with, at least from my end. But she kept making all these plans, like moving to L.A., and I knew I had to put a stop to it. She was a desperate attempt to forget about you and everything that happened. But she was never the one. Not even close."

"That's too bad," I mumbled.

"Too bad?" He laughed. "Come on, Emily. You hated every moment she was around. I could read your body language. You couldn't stand her. Just like I wanted to

deck that boyfriend of yours for breathing and chewing."
He gritted his teeth. "God, his chewing was the worst."

I smiled. "You said you still...covet me? I thought
those days were over."

"Just because I said nothing should happen between
us doesn't mean I feel any differently about you. I never
stopped coveting you. In fact, the line I drew makes my
feelings even stronger. There's no more powerful feeling
than wanting something you can't have. If it were just
physical, maybe I could handle it. But it's so much more
than that with us." The light above us reflected in his eyes.
"Don't you feel it, too?"

Do I ever. I felt little else lately. "Even in the midst
of a lie, I never felt more at peace and more like the person I'd always wanted to be than when I was on tour with
you. Every second of every moment we spent together was
real, Tristan. My feelings for you were real. They still are.
You're the reason I had to break up with Ethan. I couldn't
possibly care deeply enough about him if you're all I've
been able to think about since you came into town. Even
if we can't be together, I needed to end things with him
while I'm working through these feelings for you."

He sighed. "Sometimes I wish I didn't care so much
about doing the right thing, about hurting people. I just
want to be happy, you know?"

"I wish you didn't care, either," I said.

Tristan swallowed. "What would be different right
now if I didn't?"

"Pretty sure I'd be sitting over there with you and not
over here."

His eyes darkened. "Fuck, Emily. I'm too damn
tempted around you. What kind of a person does it make

me that I want nothing more than to defile my son's girl-friend right now?"

"*Ex*-girlfriend. And I asked a similar question once, remember? You told me it made me a horny, gap-toothed little minx. I suppose it makes *you* a horny old bastard."

Tristan's body shook as he laughed. "That sounds pretty damn accurate."

His laughter faded into an intense silence. The air felt thick. I squelched the urge to crawl toward him.

"I want to kiss you," he whispered.

My body hummed with need. "I won't stop you."

His voice was hoarse. "Come here…"

Without hesitation, I moved to his side of the couch but stopped inches away from him until the magnetic force between us finally gave way, like a flame igniting after sparking for months. I couldn't tell you who moved first, but when his mouth enveloped mine, there was a feeling of satiety I never thought I'd get to feel again. He'd asked me earlier what my dream was. This was pretty damn close.

With each ravenous stroke of his tongue, my panties grew wetter. The sweet vibration of Tristan's groan down my throat drove me wild as I dug my fingers into his hair. How I'd missed touching it. I couldn't stop the moans es-caping me, even if I didn't want to seem as desperate as I felt. Practically shaking with need, I moved to straddle him. I needed to feel his heat between my legs. His erec-tion was rock hard against my clit. As I grinded over his jeans, our kiss deepened, Tristan's hands searching my body in desperation.

I wasn't sure if the guys had been gone two minutes or two hours. Tristan had only said he wanted to kiss me.

It was wrong to torture him like this, but it felt too good to stop.

He squeezed my ass, pushing me down as he rubbed himself against me, practically fucking me through my panties. His breath hitched as he stopped moving. "You're so fucking beautiful, Emily. You're gonna be the death of me."

Our mouths smashed together again, our tongues colliding as I pulled his hair. Tristan's nails dug into my back as he bucked his hips, sending shockwaves of pleasure through my core.

His breath was shaky. "I feel like I can't stop."

"Don't," I panted.

He lowered his mouth to my neck, sucking at the tender flesh there. My nipples stiffened, yearning to feel his mouth on them, yearning for the way his scruff scratched against my skin. Yearning to know what he'd feel like inside me. My arousal was becoming downright painful, the need to come excruciatingly intense.

"I can feel how fucking wet you are through my pants. You're gonna make me explode right under you."

He was right—I was drenched.

The sound of a turning key registered just before the door burst open. I practically flew off of Tristan before landing on the other side of the couch.

Ronan stumbled in and announced, "The fucking toilet at the bar was out of order. I had to run home! Don't know what the fuck Atticus put in those ribs!"

My heart pounded in my chest. Tristan placed a pillow over his erection, shutting his eyes in frustration as he lay his head back on the couch.

I didn't know whether I wanted to thank Ronan or kill him for what he'd interrupted.

Chapter 34

TRISTAN

A week later, Ronan and Atticus had left Shady Hills for L.A. to get back to their lives. I still had a little time before promoting the new album and other band obligations that would require me to join them. I'd renewed the lease for this house for another month and was putting off leaving Shady Hills. I couldn't figure out if I wasn't ready to leave Jacob or Emily—or both.

I'd arranged things so Emily and I hadn't been alone again since the night of the barbecue. She'd left that evening soon after Ronan had come home from the bar. I'd taken the interruption as a sign that I needed to slow my roll when it came to her. So, we'd met at some of the remaining places she wanted to take me, but we hadn't gone back to my place again. While Emily seemed open to exploring things with me again, I held out. Deep down, I knew I was fighting a losing battle because I'd done nothing but fall harder for her with each passing day. But I hadn't yet figured out how I'd handle the guilt of betraying Jacob, or the worry of not being what she ultimately needed.

Today was the first time in a while I had no plans to see Emily at all. I'd planned to start packing my stuff so that when I felt ready to get back to L.A., I'd be in good shape. But my day was interrupted by a phone call from Carol Mahoney.

"Hey, Carol. What's up?"

"Hi, Tristan. I'm calling because I found something I think you might be interested in."

"Oh? What's that?"

"Well, I'm embarrassed to say this, but I hadn't cleaned under Jacob's bed since he passed away. Today was the first time. I found another journal and peeked inside at the dates. He was writing in this one just before the accident. I figured you'd want to read it."

Holy shit. My heart came alive. This was a gift.

"Wow. Yeah, I'd love to come by and get it, if you don't mind."

"Absolutely. I've just put some coffee on and made a fresh cherry pie, if you'd like to stay a bit."

"That would be awesome. See you soon."

⁓

After I got to the Mahoney's, I sat with Carol in the kitchen, eating pie and drinking coffee as she told me stories about Jacob's childhood. Rick was at work, so it was just the two of us.

Once I left Shady Hills, I knew I'd have to come back here to see them periodically. There were too many things

I'd yet to learn, and I appreciated having Carol and Rick as a connection to Jacob.

"Did you read the journal you found?" I asked her.

She shook her head. "No. I haven't been able to read any of them. Like I said, it's always felt like an invasion of Jacob's privacy. I know that sounds silly since he's not here anymore, but once he turned eighteen, I stopped butting into his business. Or maybe that's just an excuse because it would be too painful to read."

"I hear you." I took my plate to the sink. "Do you mind if I hang out in his room for a while and read it? I feel close to him in there."

"Of course not. Take your time. Our home is your home."

"I really appreciate your hospitality and kindness through all this. I can't imagine if Jacob had parents who didn't support my wanting to learn about him. I'm very grateful to you."

Carol smiled. "We have Emily to thank for finding you."

"That's for sure..."

The mention of her name caused an ache in my chest, a reminder that the end of my time here was looming. I went into Jacob's room, took my shoes off, lay back on the bed, and looked out the window for a moment, taking in the view that was once his.

I finally opened the notebook and skimmed through the pages. It was only halfway full. It hurt my heart to think about why it was left unfinished.

As I started to read, I realized there were some things in this one that Emily didn't know, namely just how much his feelings had grown for Piper, the girl he'd been dating at the time of his death. We'd tried to contact her so I could meet her while I was here, but her mother said she'd just moved away for a new job after graduating college.

My relationship with Piper is making me realize some things when it comes to Emily. I will always love her. But I used to think she was the love of my life, even after she ended things before she went to college. I'm now beginning to see why she broke up with me. We were way too young when we got together. We loved each other but weren't IN love with each other. The fact that I am falling in love so easily with Piper now proves that Emily was right. (Emily usually is.) I was nowhere ready to be with one person for the rest of my life when I wasn't even out of high school. Emily and I weren't meant to be boyfriend and girlfriend forever. But she was always meant to be my best friend. I hope she and I can get back someday to the kind of friendship we had when we were younger. And I hope Emily can find a good guy who cares about her as much as I do and makes her happier than I ever did. She deserves that and has no idea how special she is. Piper is going to have to accept that Emily will always be in my life. The strange thing is, I have this urge to call Emily and tell her all about Piper right now, but that might be a little weird. Yeah, maybe not.

Jacob had been falling in love with Piper when he died. Who knew if that relationship would've lasted, but this was news to me and would be news to Emily, since she'd told me Piper was someone Jacob had just started dating. It seemed he'd been holding back from Emily, maybe because he didn't want to hurt her feelings. I wondered if knowing this would upset her or bring her peace, since she still had some guilt about ending things with him.

The most surprising thing about this new journal was the lyrics he'd written, mixed in with the entries. Jacob had apparently been teaching himself to play guitar, too. I couldn't have been prouder. Many of the songs he was attempting to write focused on love, belonging, and finding yourself. One was about feeling like someone else in your own skin. I got stuck on those pages, trying to imagine a melody to go with his words. The apple didn't fall far from the tree.

Then I came upon a passage that knocked the wind out of me. I had to read the first sentence multiple times to make sure I wasn't hallucinating.

I met my biological father today.

What?
I read it again.

I met my biological father today.

Finally, I garnered the courage to read past that line.

I met my biological father today. It was wild. Delirious Jones played the Eclipse Pavilion in St. Louis, and I scored tickets. It was rare that they played such a small venue. My cousin on my dad's side works there and gave me inside info about when the band would be exiting the club. I didn't tell Eric the truth. I lied and said I wanted a chance for an autograph.

There were only a few of us in the private hall-way outside the band exit. When Tristan came out and walked past me, I yelled his name. I don't think I've ever been that nervous in my en-tire life. It was a miracle the word even came out. I figured maybe he'd keep walking, but he stopped and turned to come over to me. Instead of seeming frustrated, he smiled. He asked me how I liked the show, and I told him it was great. It was. I really like their new music, and Tristan killed it out there. He signed the CD I brought. Then he handed me back my marker and told me to have a good night. I think I said some-thing like, "You, too, man." And then he left. I wanted to scream out, "Wait! You're my dad!" But I couldn't do that to him. It wasn't the right time or place. But meeting him today made me feel like someday I could tell him. He doesn't seem as scary as he once did. So wild.

Tristan fucking Daltrey.

My father.

Wracking my brain, I couldn't for the life of me remember meeting him. I could barely remember that show in St. Louis. Thousands had stopped me for autographs in the past several years, and they all blurred together. I rarely looked anyone in the eye, because that might prompt them to ask questions I didn't have time to answer. It wasn't that I didn't want to talk to my fans, but I only had so much time in a day and would never get from point A to B if I stopped to chat with everyone. So, I'd be cordial, sign what I needed to, and walk away. But boy, was I damn glad I'd taken the time to be friendlier than average to him, even if I hadn't looked closely enough to see myself in his face. Even if I'd somehow noticed a resemblance, I'd have likely thought it a coincidence.

How I wished he'd given into that whim and yelled after me that day. Hearing the words *"you're my dad"* would sure as hell have gotten my attention. But I could understand why he didn't.

The fact that he'd started to come around and liked my music? A huge win. His opinion was everything.

Jacob Mahoney said I killed it.

Jacob fucking Mahoney.

My son.

Chapter 35

EMILY

"I can't believe he was in love with Piper," my friend Leah said. "I never thought they were that serious, but come to think of it, she was really torn up at the funeral."

My friend had come over to visit, and we'd been talking through the revelations from Jacob's lost journal. She, my mother, and I sat around the kitchen table, chatting over tea. I'd filled them in on what I'd learned, though I'd still not told Leah anything about what happened with Tristan and me. She only knew he was Jacob's father and I'd gone on the tour because of that.

Tristan had come by yesterday to drop off the journal. He'd flagged certain passages and stayed with me while I read them. We talked about it some, but he'd been mentally spent after reading it over numerous times and said he needed to be alone for a bit. That was just as well, because I'd wanted to read the entire thing in private.

"How did Tristan take the realization that he'd met Jacob?" my mother asked. "That's so beautiful, yet sad at the same time."

"He has mixed feelings. It upsets him that he doesn't remember it, that he didn't somehow recognize himself in Jacob that day. But it also brings him some peace to know Jacob's feelings about him changed after that encounter."

Leah took a sip of her tea. "Are you okay after learning Jacob was serious about Piper?"

"I am. I've lived with a lot of guilt about breaking up with him. To know that he was falling in love with someone else brings me peace."

"It doesn't make you the least bit jealous, though?" Leah asked.

"Not at all. I prayed he'd meet someone else. It's tragic that he didn't have a chance to see where things went with her, but I feel better than if he'd never experienced love with someone other than me."

"Okay." She took a bite of a sugar cookie my mom had made. "I get that."

"Speaking of love..." my mother interjected. "You do know that man is in love with you, right?"

Leah looked between my mother and me. "Who's in love with her? Are we still talking about Jacob?"

"I haven't explained the situation with Tristan to Leah, Mom," I scolded.

My mother's face reddened. "Shit. I'm sorry."

Leah's jaw dropped. "What's going on with Tristan?"

Up until now, I'd thought the fewer people who knew what I'd done, the better. But Leah was one of my oldest friends, and I knew I could trust her. Plus, there was no way out for me now. So I explained the whole mess—from my lie of omission on the tour that allowed us to get closer, to the money he'd given my mother to hold for me.

"Holy shit. I can't believe you kept this from me. I could never tell Stacia from work. She'd probably jump off a cliff."

"Or burn her jar of hair?" I laughed.

Leah's mouth was still hanging open. "I can't believe he gave you a million dollars. What are you gonna do with it?"

"Nothing." I crossed my arms and leaned back in my seat. "It's gonna stay in the bank."

"That's crazy," she said.

"I'm determined not to use it. I want to earn my own way."

"Can I have it?" she teased. "Kidding."

"When he came to talk to me about holding the money for you, he mentioned wishing he could take away all of your pain from the past," my mother said. "I can tell you one thing: I've never had a man care about me the way he cares about you."

While that warmed my heart, I still felt very much in limbo when it came to Tristan and me. "Where does that leave me, though? Pining for the one living man who truly cares for me but won't allow anything more to happen because of my history with his son?"

"You don't think that the fact that Jacob seemed to move on from his heartbreak regarding you changes anything for Tristan?" my mother asked.

I shook my head. "I'm not sure. But Tristan has to get back to L.A. for work very soon, and I need to start getting used to not having him around."

"Have you actually ever made your feelings clear to him?" Leah asked. "Maybe part of his hesitation is that he

285

doesn't realize how strong your feelings are. Maybe if you told him, that would make a difference."

She was right. Despite Tristan showing me how much he cared, I'd been holding back in reciprocating, mostly out of fear of rejection, and a little out of lingering guilt over Jacob.

I couldn't let Tristan go back to L.A. without telling him how I truly felt, even if he still believed we couldn't be together. It was a risk I'd have to take.

～

I didn't tell Tristan I was coming when I showed up at his rental home late that evening.

He beamed upon answering the door. "Hey. This is a surprise…"

"Is this a bad time?"

"No. Of course not. My door's always open for you."

"I was hoping we could go somewhere and talk, actually. Not here."

"Yeah. Of course. Anywhere you have in mind?"

"There's this restaurant I've been wanting to take you to. They're still open, I think."

"Alright," he said. "Let's jump in my car and go."

Tristan drove as I directed him to the restaurant, and when he saw what it was, he cracked up.

"McDonald's." He laughed. "Good one." Tristan pulled his hood up and put on sunglasses so he wouldn't be recognized.

As we entered the McDonald's, I asked the cashier, "Are you closing soon?"

"Yeah, in fifteen minutes."

I winked at Tristan. "Perfect."

We ordered our food and sat down at a table by the window that offered a view of the dark and nearly desolate parking lot.

"I can't believe this." He chuckled.

"Well, you said you wanted to eat a burger alone at a McDonald's at closing time. Except you're not alone. I'm here. Hope that's okay."

"That's more than okay, beautiful." Tristan grinned.

"Needless to say, we have to eat fast." I popped a fry into my mouth.

A woman mopped the floor around us.

Tristan spoke in a low voice. "Did you arrange for her to be mopping the floor, too? Because that's a really nice touch to the whole closing-time thing."

"Pure luck. Can you believe it?"

He bit into his burger and spoke with his mouth full. "You're adorable."

"Do you feel *normal* right now?"

"You know?" He wiped his mouth. "It's not what it's cracked up to be. The only thing I really love about this moment is the person sitting across from me. I don't think I would've been happy here alone, despite my previous, depressing fantasy."

I smiled.

"I'm glad you came by tonight, Emily. I've been sort of stuck in a rut, not sure what to do. I have to get back to L.A., but I don't want to leave you. It feels like an impossible situation."

"I don't want you to leave, either. That's one of the reasons I came to see you tonight. I need to tell you how I feel before it's too late, Tristan."

Before I could say anything else, the woman who'd been mopping the floor interrupted my pivotal moment.

"I'm sorry, I'm gonna have to ask you guys to leave," she said. "We're closed."

"Sorry..." Tristan said. "We'll go."

We promptly threw our trash away and headed out the door. "Are you satisfied now? You've nearly been kicked out of a McDonald's."

"Not sure anything can top that." He put his arm around me as we walked to his car. "Let's finish this conversation back at the house, though. Okay?"

The ride to Tristan's was quiet as I attempted to gather my thoughts. He took my hand in his and held it the entire way there.

Something shifted between us. He held my hand with confidence. He'd asked me without hesitation to come back to his house. Something told me I wasn't going back home tonight.

After Tristan parked, I followed him inside, but we barely got a few feet into the place before he put his hand at my hip, gently rubbing my side.

"Finish what you were about to tell me at McDonald's."

I took a deep breath. "There's only one thing to say. And that's that I'm crazy about you, Tristan. I don't know where to begin explaining why because there are so many reasons. You make me feel like I'm the most special person in the world. Watching how you've shown your love for Jacob these past weeks has only made my feelings grow. You're a damn good man."

He moved in closer. "A good man wouldn't want to fuck the shit out of you right now, Emily."

"I don't want to go home tonight," I blurted. "In fact, I don't want to leave you ever." I held his stare. "And I don't want to live another day without knowing what it's like to have you inside of me. If that makes me a bad person, I'll have to live with that."

Tristan gritted his teeth. "I've never been so fucking hard for someone in my life."

I took his hand and placed it under my skirt so he could feel how wet I was.

"Fuck..." he muttered before taking my mouth into his.

Goose bumps covered my body as his tongue found mine. His fingers threaded in my hair as he bent my head back to deepen our kiss, practically stealing my breath.

He spoke over my lips. "You think you can do that to me and not make me lose it?"

The next thing I knew, Tristan wrapped my legs around him and carried me over to the wall. My back slammed against it, and he pushed my panties to the side. The vague sound of his zipper lowering registered before I felt the burn of his thick cock entering me. I whimpered at the unexpected surprise—no warning, just intense, instantaneous pleasure. Thankfully, I was more than ready for it. The silky-smooth feel of his hard shaft moving in and out of me, the slick wetness of our mutual arousal was almost too much to take.

He stopped the kiss just long enough to murmur, "I should use something..."

"It's okay. I'm on the pill. You're good."

"I don't normally do this, Emily. I want you to know that. I always use protection. I—"

"It's okay. You feel good like this," I said, moving my hips over him. "I trust you. I'm okay with it if you are."

With that, he groaned and pushed deeper into me. "Do you know how long I've dreamed of fucking you? But bare like this? Nothing has ever felt so damn good."

I pulled his hair as the friction between my legs, the feel of his thick cock pushing in and out, overwhelmed me, nearly bringing me to orgasm several times. It was only the intentional tightening of my muscles that stopped me from losing control.

Tristan spun me around and carried me to his room, somehow managing to stay inside me as we toppled to the bed. "I've dreamed of fucking you from almost the moment I met you, Emily. But over time, I've come to want to make love to you. Make no mistake, that's what I'm about to do."

My body buzzed, so incredibly sensitized and ready for him.

He pulled out just long enough to help me remove my clothes as I ripped off his shirt. His belt buckle clanked as he lowered his pants and kicked them away.

As he pulled down his boxer briefs, I got my first actual glimpse of Tristan's massive cock. Though I'd felt him inside of me moments ago, I'd never had the pleasure of feasting my eyes on it. It was like a thick, veiny rod covered in silk. My mouth watered as I stared, a glistening bead of cum on his tip.

Hovering over me, he ran his calloused fingers down the length of my body. "I just want to look at you for a minute." His fingers landed between my legs as he glided them across my clit. "So damn gorgeous." He positioned himself on top of me. "Open your legs."

I spread for him, digging my nails into his back as he entered me again in one powerful thrust. I gasped.

"Is it too much?"

"No, I love it."

"Good girl."

He went balls deep, and I could feel him throbbing inside me as he gently slid in and out. Then he began to fuck me harder as the bed shook. I squeezed his back, hanging on for dear life as he took my body to places it had never been before. When I felt my orgasm rising to the surface, I continued to will it away, not wanting this to end.

"My cock is drenched from you, Emily. Fucking drenched. You feel so damn good."

My legs wrapped around his back as I lifted my hips to meet his thrusts.

"You feel better than I ever imagined," he hissed. "I'm already addicted. I'm not gonna be able to stop fucking you."

"I hope you never do."

A grunt escaped him with every movement in and out. The heat of our naked bodies molding together felt amazing. Any guilt I might have had was far superseded by the feeling that this man was made for me. And I was made for him. Yes, we'd met under the most salacious of circumstances, but it didn't change the fact that he completed me.

As I pulled his hair, I almost told him I loved him at least a dozen times, but I held back. Still, this was so much more than sex; I loved this man with all my heart and soul.

"You're so freaking tight," he breathed, "even with me stretching the hell out of your beautiful pussy." He tugged my earlobe with his teeth as he pumped harder. "I can't hold back anymore. Can I come inside you?"

"Please." I squeezed his ass.

With that, Tristan gave a guttural growl that echoed through the bedroom as he released his load. I tightened around him, receiving every drop of his hot cum. It was the most amazing feeling. Within seconds, I let myself go as well, releasing the climax that had been building. My vision blurred as every nerve ending in my body rejoiced with the ecstasy of my orgasm.

After he pulled out, he lay behind me, wrapping one hand around my side and placing the other between my legs. "I love feeling my cum drip out of you."

"Me, too," I panted.

He spoke into my ear. "Baby, you totally own me. I hope you know that. I don't want to do anything else for the rest of my life but this."

I turned to face him. "I'm good with that."

"Yeah?" He brushed a piece of hair off my forehead. "You mean that? Because I have a tendency to take things literally when I'm excited."

"Tristan, before you, I'd hardly been excited about anything. When you're around, I look forward to every day. You make me so happy."

"I think what you're trying to say is that...you love me?" He flashed a crooked smile.

Do I ever. "Well, how presumptuous of you. How do you know it's love?" I teased.

"If you look forward to every day now, that mirrors how I feel about you. And I happen to know for a *fact* that I love you, Emily Applewood. I've loved you from the moment you brought me wart remover. I think that was it for me."

"I love you so freaking much, Tristan." I kissed him long and hard. "What does this mean for us?"

"It means you're either coming to L.A. with me or I'm moving to Shady Hills, because I want you in my house, in my bed, and on my face."

Chapter 36

TRISTAN

My morning wood was off the charts. You'd think I'd be tired after last night, but all I wanted to do was bury myself inside of her again. Over and over.

Maybe I should've felt guilty, but for the first time in a long time, I didn't. I hoped that was a sign that wherever Jacob was, he didn't hate me for loving Emily.

He'd said in his journal that he wanted her to meet someone who made her happy. I knew I was that person. When she was with me, she was truly happy; I could see it in her eyes.

This morning, I alternated between wanting to watch her sleep and wanting to wake her up to satisfy my incessant need. Finally, I wrapped my arms around her from behind and pressed my cock against her ass. It took a mere few seconds for it to harden to full mast.

"Is someone trying to wake me up?" she asked groggily.

"He's very wired this morning. Sorry, I can't control him."

She pressed her ass into my throbbing dick.

"Keep doing that and see what you get," I warned.

"If you say so..." She did it again, harder this time.

"Damn, woman, you're gonna drive me insane. I may never perform again because all I want to do is stay in bed and fuck all day."

Emily reached back and cupped my balls. "I'm about to be a raging jealous bitch when all those women throw themselves at you."

"They can throw themselves all they want, but they'll never get me."

She wrapped her hand around my rigid cock. "This is mine."

I nearly came—I freaking loved possessive Emily.

"What do you want right now?" she asked.

"You sure you want to know?"

"I do," she breathed.

I tugged at my eager cock. "I want to fuck your mouth."

Without a second of hesitation, she turned around and lowered her head under the blanket, taking me into her mouth.

Holy shit. I'd fantasized too many times about her going down on me, but nothing felt as good as the moment her sweet, wet mouth wrapped around my cock, her tongue lapping eagerly at my shaft. She sucked gently before swirling her tongue around my crown. When Emily took me all the way down her throat, I tightened my ab muscles like never before to keep from coming.

I moved the bedding aside, because I absolutely needed to see what she looked like doing this to me. *Fuck yeah.*

Emily repositioned herself so I could see better. She pressed one hand to my balls as she used the other to jerk my cock, pumping me into her mouth as she sucked. How the hell had she learned to give a blow job this good? That was one thought I quickly willed away.

When she made a little humming sound that vibrated down my shaft, I nearly lost it. Fisting my hands, I tightened every muscle in my body to prevent myself from exploding in her mouth. Her lips were covered in my precum, her mouth so damn hot.

When she took me all the way down the back of her throat and gagged, my jaw clenched. Then I shrieked as I lost control, my cum shooting out in multiple hot spurts. Emily swallowed every last drop as I watched intently.

Her lashes fluttered as she looked up at me with the most mischievous smile.

"Damn you..." I laughed, nearly out of breath.

Emily and I had always been incredibly compatible. But knowing just how sexually compatible we were? Damn. All prior complications aside, Emily was the first woman I could envision spending my life with. She satisfied me in every way.

But of course, seeing that everything was going so damn perfectly, the first thing that came out of my mouth was, "I'm too damn old for you."

She rubbed her thumb along my chin. "What if I have a thing for older men?"

"You'll never have a normal life dating a rockstar," I added, pulling another warning out of my hat.

"What if I don't want a boring, normal life?" She squinted. "If I didn't know better, Mr. Daltrey, I would think you were trying to push me away right now."

"I just don't want you to have regrets..."

"My only regret is not doing what we started last night sooner."

I leaned my forehead against hers. "You really love me? Like, it's not some weird daddy thing?"

Her breath tickled my face as she laughed. "If you want it to be, it can. We haven't role played yet."

"Don't think I didn't think of that when you called me Mr. Daltrey. Everything sets me off lately."

"Any other excuses you have for why we can't be together, Mr. Daltrey?" she asked.

It wasn't enough to stop me from being with Emily anymore, but it did cast a shadow over my happiness. "Do you think Jacob would hate us right now?"

Her smile faded. "I think it would weird him out at first. But if he understood how much we care for each other, he'd be happy for us." She shrugged. "Maybe he brought me to you somehow. Who knows?"

"Or maybe he hates me even more now that he sees me with you."

She brushed hair off my forehead. "If he's *really* been paying attention, he's seen the way you innocently fell for me when you didn't know who I was. He's seen the way you lift me up and always help me believe I'm a good person who's worthy of peace, despite how I feel. He's seen how much you love him. He could never hate you."

My mouth curved into a smile. "You're good for me, Emily Applewood. You always have been."

"You're good for *me*."

"Is it selfish of me to want you to move to L.A.?"

"I thought you'd never ask."

"You can take your time getting settled. My house is a blank slate, sparse and vastly undecorated. You can have your way with it—as long as you promise to have your way with *me*."

She poked my chest. "I will always partake in that."

"We can come back to Shady Hills whenever you want."

"I'd like that. I didn't visit my mother enough when I lived in Nevada. I want that to change. But I don't need to live here."

I searched her eyes. "When you first met me, you must've thought I was crazy, because as much success as I had, I wasn't happy. I kept wanting to go back to the past, to the time before I was famous. But I realize now, it wasn't the past I needed. I just needed the happiness and peace I had back then. And *you* gave that to me. You brought me back full circle. You brought me home."

Chapter 37

TRISTAN

Since Emily had a job interview this afternoon, I was alone for the first time in a while.

Standing on my balcony, I looked out at the panoramic view of the lush, rolling hills. It had been two months since Emily moved out to L.A. with me. I'd never had anyone to come home to after a long day before. And I never wanted to go back to the way things were before she became my ride or die.

I felt so grateful for the direction my life had taken. Now felt like a good time to do something I'd been putting off.

Taking out my phone, I dialed her number.

She answered on the third ring. "Tristan?"

"How did you know it was me?"

"You gave me your number when you were in Spirit Lake, remember?"

I cleared my throat. "How have you been?"

"Good."

"You must have had your baby by now."

"I did. I had a daughter."

"Congratulations." I smiled. "What's her name?"

"Vivian."

"That's beautiful."

"Thank you."

A long moment passed. Then I heard her sniffle and realized she was crying.

"Don't cry, Cheyenne. It wasn't my intention to upset you."

"I know. I've been trying to block everything out, but hearing your voice brought it all back."

"The reason I'm calling is that a few months back, I spent some weeks in Shady Hills, where Jacob grew up. I wanted to tell you a little about it, if you have some time."

"Please. Yes. I'd love to hear about it."

I then launched into recalling everything I'd learned about our son, from his interest in music to what he liked to eat. Cheyenne alternated between laughing and crying as she listened to the stories I shared.

I finally added, "I also need to let you know that I truly forgive you. When I told you I forgave you when we last saw each other, it wasn't the truth. I just wanted you to feel at peace. You were in a vulnerable state at the time. But after meeting the Mahoneys, I want you to know you *should* be at peace with your decision. Our son had an amazing life, even though it was cut short. And it was better than what we could've given him at that time. I don't want you to live with regret, just as I don't want to live with resentment in my heart."

"I somehow knew you were forcing forgiveness that day. And you're right, I needed to hear it from you at the right time. I'm so happy you found some peace in visiting with his parents." She paused. "Are you happy otherwise, Tristan?"

I didn't have to think about the answer to that question. "Aside from the loss of our son, I'm a very lucky man. I'm healthy, and I'm in love. So, yeah, I'm very happy, Cheyenne. And I really hope you are, too."

～

The heavy front door of my mansion latched closed. I jumped off the couch as I heard her heels clicking against the marble floor.

"How did the interview go?"

Emily looked stunned. "I can't believe I'm saying this, but I got the job."

"Holy shit." I lifted her up and spun her around. "Congratulations."

After I put her down, she narrowed her eyes at me. "You're certain you didn't pull any strings?"

I made a cross over my heart. "I promise I didn't. I wouldn't lie to you."

That was the truth. Since we'd moved to L.A., Emily had gone for a bunch of interviews. None of the positions were right. But then this marketing job for a record label popped up. While I'd heard about the position through word of mouth, I'd done nothing but pass along the info to her.

"The guy who interviewed me didn't seem to know I was your girlfriend. He was very direct and was the type who would've mentioned it if he had."

Emily and I hadn't gone public with our relationship, nor had we been photographed together—to the best of my knowledge—since we left Shady Hills. We'd mostly been hiding out at home as I worked on new music. The album the guys and I had recorded last year in California and had finished in Shady Hills would be dropping soon. That would likely require us to be out and about more.

I kissed her forehead. "I'm so freaking proud of you."

"What apparently gave me the edge over the other candidates was my time working on the Delirious Jones tour. He said there was no comparison to real-world experience in this business. Yet another reason I'm grateful for that."

"God, you and me both." I cupped her cheeks and brought her mouth to mine.

She rubbed her fingers over her lips. "I'm gonna get out of these clothes."

"Music to my ears." I wriggled my brows.

"Gonna go take a shower."

"Let's celebrate. You and me out by the pool tonight. We can order in Middle Eastern."

"That sounds divine."

Once the food was delivered, I arranged a little spread on a table overlooking the pool. Emily emerged wearing a coverup over her bathing suit.

After we finished eating on the patio, I told her about my phone call with Cheyenne.

The sky had turned dark, and Emily sat between my legs on one of the lounge chairs with her back against my chest.

Looking up at the stars, she said, "Now that I have you, I feel like I can face anything, including my past. I finally made that appointment for therapy. It's been a long time coming. I know I can't change anything that happened, but you make me want to be a better person. And that starts with loving myself."

"I'm proud of you," I told her, kissing the top of her head. "And I wish I could love you enough for both of us, but you have your own work to do."

"It's a lot easier navigating life when I feel less alone. That's how you've made me feel from the moment I met you. And that's why I'm finally ready to face the past."

"I'm glad. Last year was all about *my* past. This year is about letting go of those things I can't change and embracing the future." I squeezed her tightly. "See? I'm embracing my future right now."

She turned to look up at me. "I love you."

"Is there anything I could do to make you not love me?"

"I don't think so," she said. "Why do you ask?"

I hadn't yet divulged everything about the new album. "I'm a little worried that you might take issue with one of the songs I wrote. It was a new addition that I completed back in Shady Hills. It's actually my favorite song out of all of the ones we recorded."

"Why would I take issue with it?"

I grabbed my phone and pulled up the album cover, which we'd just gotten the final version of.

Her mouth dropped open. The album title? *Horny, Gap-Toothed Little Minx*

Epilogue

EMILY

Tristan sat next to me as we opened a large manila envelope containing an early copy of the magazine.

On the cover was my beautiful boyfriend, looking deliciously sexy, tousled hair framing his chiseled face in that signature way. Tats peeked out from beneath his sleeves. His fingers, adorned as usual with chunky rings, held the neck of a shiny, electric guitar slung over his shoulder. Neon lights cast a seductive glow behind him. Tristan's eyes smoldered, sure to hold the attention of anyone who happened upon this cover.

"If you weren't my boyfriend, I swear I'd pleasure myself to this cover tonight. I still might."

"I might have to watch while you do." He winked.

Tristan was this month's cover story in one of the biggest music publications in the world. They'd done a feature article on him in honor of Delirious Jones's new album. It had been two years now since the release of *Horny, Gap-Toothed Little Minx*, which had topped the charts.

While the cover of this magazine was stunning, the headline took my breath away. "Oh my God. I just got chills," I said, looking down at the words.

The Rocker's Muse: How the Son Tristan Daltrey Never Knew Inspired Delirious Jones's New Album

Someone in L.A. had overnighted an early copy of the magazine to our house in Shady Hills. Tristan had purchased a home here about a year ago. It was a place for us to stay when we came back and visited my mother and the Mahoneys, but also when we wanted to escape the city. We'd actually driven out here this time, as we planned to stay for several weeks and had brought our new dog and Bertha the rabbit with us. We'd recently adopted an Otterhound named Rusty.

"Let's take this out back," Tristan suggested.

We brought the magazine to our backyard swing, where we sat in the morning sunshine and read the article together.

The piece started out by briefly explaining how Tristan had found out about Jacob—or at least the way he'd led the reporter to believe it happened. The press had not yet gotten wind of the fact that I'd dated Tristan's son. We'd managed to dodge that bullet. They only knew me as Tristan's girlfriend and the inspiration for "Horny, Gap-Toothed Little Minx." The article explained that his son's diaries were found posthumously, and that through them the adoptive family discovered Jacob had found out who his father was.

I looked up at him. "It's pretty amazing that no one's outed my history with Jacob. Not even Nazarene nor Ethan. There are lots of people he and I went to high school with who must've figured out the connection, too."

Tristan shrugged. "If they figure it out, I'll deal with it. I'm not ashamed of anything I've done in this life, least of all loving you. I have nothing to hide."

"You're right. Let them find out. We're strong enough to handle it."

"The only opinion I give a shit about is Jacob's," he said. "And I'll never get that, so..."

I curled into his chest as we continued reading. In the article, Tristan described how Jacob inspired and even contributed to his latest album, with Tristan giving him songwriting credits.

I've spent the past couple of years trying to figure out how best to honor my son's memory. I came to the conclusion that there was no better way than to make his dream of becoming a songwriter come true. His dream became my dream. I've focused all my energy on turning his lyrics into songs. The passion within me has been unprecedented. Jacob has truly been my muse; thus, the title of the album.

The piece went on to point out that critics were calling Delirious Jones's latest album their best work yet.

The Rocker's Muse *showcases the band's evolution while staying true to their modern grunge roots. From beginning to end, the album is a masterpiece of hard-hitting riffs, introspective lyrics, and Tristan Daltrey's signature vocals. The opening track, "Interrupted," draws you in with its bone-chilling melody. Each song is ex-*

pertly crafted, with standout tracks like "Shady Hills" and "Come Back to Me" demonstrating the band's knack for combining catchy hooks with the deeper, emotional themes undoubtedly driven by Daltrey's own loss. The Rocker's Muse *is a powerful reminder of why the band remains a formidable force in modern rock music.*

I couldn't have been prouder. I especially loved that they'd highlighted Tristan's vocal prowess. He'd done everything he could to overcome his vocal challenges. After having surgery shortly after the last album was released a couple of years ago, he'd gone on an anti-inflammatory diet, practiced meditation, and adhered to strict silent periods whenever possible.

About halfway through the article, I noticed my name.

As motivated as I was to write my son's music, it was a difficult and emotional experience. I couldn't have made it through without the most amazing life partner. Having Emily by my side has meant everything. I couldn't do any of this without her.

Placing my hand over my heart, I felt a rush of unexpected emotion. "That's so sweet."

"It's all true."

After we finished the article, I wanted to read it all over again, but we needed to get ready for our backyard barbecue today. Atticus and Ronan were in town, along with some of the band's management who'd flown in for the weekend to celebrate the magazine feature and the release of *The Rocker's Muse* later this week.

"I'm gonna put up those outdoor lights I bought," Tristan said.

"Okay. I'll run to the market and get the remaining items we need."

I grabbed the keys to Tristan's SUV. As I drove, I thought about how much he and I had accomplished in the past couple of years since I'd moved out to L.A. with him. Between his surgery recovery, the completion of another small North American tour, and recording *The Rocker's Muse*, it had been nonstop work for him. And I'd been busy, too. I hadn't been able to join Tristan for most of that tour last year because of the marketing job I continued to hold with Amity Records. The company was currently paying for me to get my master's in marketing while I worked for them, developing campaigns for album promotion.

Now, though, we'd finally have a break in Tristan's schedule to travel. And I'd taken three weeks off of work so he and I could spend some time at a villa we'd rented on Italy's Amalfi coast. We were leaving in a couple of days, which was one of the reasons we'd stopped here in Shady Hills first, so my mother could stay with our dog and rabbit. I didn't trust strangers.

I still struggled with feeling undeserving of this life, but I'd come a long way. I'd likely always be scarred by my past, but I'd gotten enough therapy to start letting go of some of the guilt, even if I wasn't perfect at it. Recovery, I'd learned, doesn't have to be a hundred percent. As long as I was better than before, that was progress.

I arrived at the grocery store and made my way in and out as quickly as possible. Before I knew it, I was back in the car, headed to my man. Whenever I drove one of Tristan's many cars, I felt so freaking fancy and laughed to myself, thinking about the run-down car I'd left behind when I moved to L.A. That old Corolla would likely always be what I felt I belonged in.

I'd recently written Tristan a check for that million dollars he'd given me and insisted he take it back. It was bad enough that I lived with him in that enormous house back in L.A. and he'd bought us a second home here in Shady Hills. He also spoiled me any chance he got. I didn't want to have that money hanging over my head. It made me feel better to give it back, and to my surprise, he'd taken it.

Back at the house, I put away the groceries and went to the backyard to check on Tristan's progress. I stood at the glass door overlooking the pool and watched in amusement as Tristan climbed a wobbly ladder and became entangled in a bunch of lights he was attempting to hang across the greenery in the yard.

"Need some help over there?" I shouted.

"Yeah, I could use a drink."

"Not sure you should add alcohol to whatever you're doing. You're wobbly enough on that ladder."

"And here I was thinking you were the only person in my life who wasn't a ball buster. Guess I was wrong."

I giggled. "You're adorable when you're frustrated, but maybe forget about the lights. They're unnecessary."

"Nah. I'm gonna figure this shit out. They'll look cool at night."

I left him there and returned to the kitchen to arrange plates of appetizers. When I came back to the patio, Tristan had made some progress, but the majority of the lights remained tangled and unhung.

"What the fuck is going on here?" a voice called from behind us.

Tristan and I turned to find Ronan holding a case of beer. He and Atticus had keys to our houses, so they always just let themselves in.

"What are you doing here?" Tristan asked.

"What do you mean? You said there was a party."

"I'm not ready for you yet. It's still morning."

"Never too early to start."

Atticus appeared behind him. "Actually, Emily texted and said to get our asses down here, that you needed help getting things ready."

"I'm fine," Tristan grumbled.

"You don't look fine," Ronan said as he headed over.

Atticus joined in, and I watched gleefully as the three of them messed with the lights, a mix of untangling, bickering, and laughing.

At one point, Atticus suddenly climbed down the ladder to answer his phone. He rushed off to take a call inside.

Ronan took Atticus's place and turned to Tristan. "What was up with that?"

Tristan shrugged. "I dunno. Seemed weird."

A few minutes later, Atticus returned, looking a bit frazzled.

Ronan stepped down off the ladder. "What's going on?"

"That was Nicole…"

His ex.

Ronan and Tristan looked at each other.

"Nicole? What's up with her?" Tristan asked.

"She needs to talk to me about something. Asked if I'd have some time to chat in like an hour. She's at work right now."

Ronan blinked. "What does she want?"

"She says she has a favor to ask. I have no fucking idea what it could be. My head is spinning."

Tristan put down the lights. "When was the last time you talked to her?"

Atticus still seemed dazed and confused. "Huh?"

Ronan repeated Tristan's question. "When was the last time you talked to Nicole?"

"Like a year ago." He shook his head. "I'm gonna go back to the hotel. I don't want to have the phone call here."

Tristan patted his shoulder. "Yeah, man. It's no big deal. Just come back whenever you're done. You bastards are early anyway."

"Cool. Thanks," he said before taking off.

When Atticus was out of earshot, I asked, "What actually happened between him and Nicole? No one has ever told me."

"We *could* tell you, but we'd have to kill you," Ronan joked. "Or rather, *he'd* kill me for telling you."

"What's the big secret?" I looked between them. "I don't get it."

Tristan whispered in my ear, "I'll tell you later."

"One thing I will say..." Ronan added. "My guy has been searching for his heart since the day things ended with them."

Tristan rubbed my back. "Let's put it this way. She's his Emily. And I couldn't imagine losing you or what I'd be like if that ever happened."

⁓

Several hours later, our backyard was still filled with people drinking and chatting around the pool. It had been the perfect Shady Hills afternoon, comfortably breezy and sunny, but it was starting to get dark now. Tristan had just turned on those outdoor lights he'd worked so hard to get up earlier. And they were honestly beautiful.

My mother and the Mahoneys—who'd given us their blessing when we'd told them about our relationship before moving to L.A.—had just left. However, most of Delirious Jones's crew and their significant others were still here. We hadn't set an end time for this shindig, but I was sort of hoping the remaining guests would leave so Tristan and I could unwind alone.

Interestingly, Atticus hadn't returned after going back to his hotel for that phone call with Nicole. He'd texted Tristan that he wasn't in the mood for a party and apologized. Ronan had left a short time ago to go check on him.

Everyone seemed to be talking Tristan's ear off tonight about the article. He finally managed to break away from them and found me. He nuzzled my neck. "How's my baby?"

"Incredibly happy. So proud of you and how hard you've worked in Jacob's honor on this album. And really looking forward to our vacation. I'm feeling grateful for this life."

He lowered his voice. "I kind of can't wait for every-one to leave tonight. I just want to be alone with you."

"Oh my gosh, I was just thinking the same thing. Want me to start singing? That'll scare them away."

He pinched my side playfully. "You're lucky I love you with that voice."

"Actually, I have a better idea if you really want to give them a hint," I said.

"What?"

"It's time for Rusty's swim." I winked.

Tristan flashed a mischievous grin.

We'd had to keep our dog, Rusty, inside all night be-cause he had a tendency to get a little too excited around the pool.

I went inside to get him. The moment he spotted me, Rusty wagged his tail. I led him out to the patio. "Rusty has been dying for a swim," I announced to our guests. "Hope you guys don't mind!"

Everyone basically ignored my warning until our dog did what he did best, jumping into the pool with a huge splash, sending a deluge of water everywhere.

Tristan cracked up as he winked at me. Rusty contin-ued to splash around for a while and then managed to get himself out of the pool, proceeding to shake on the deck, sending water flying. Doug and his girlfriend were the first to start gathering their things, and the other people left followed suit.

"So sorry about that," I told everyone. "He has a little too much fun sometimes."

"No worries," Doug's girlfriend, Jane, said. "We need to get going anyway."

After everyone finally left, Tristan collapsed on one of the lounge chairs and patted his chest, prompting me to sit on top of him. With my back against him, he cradled me in his arms.

"Your Rusty idea was freaking brilliant. It's only eight PM, and we've cleared them all out."

"Thank you. But Rusty did all the work."

He rested his chin on my head. "The lights are cool, huh?"

"I'm glad you pushed forward with that task. They turned out really pretty, and I especially like them now that it's just the two of us."

"Well, that was my hope. I didn't do it for everyone else. I did this for us. That's why I was so adamant about it. For this moment."

"Hmmm…" I hummed, feeling so relaxed.

He began to massage my head. I bent my neck back and closed my eyes, relishing this feeling of being loved.

"I need you to stand up for a minute," he said. "I need you to see me."

We both stood, and I turned to find Tristan reaching into his pocket. My heart raced as he took out a box.

Is he doing what I think he is?

He opened it and inside was…

I tilted my head.

Inside was my scrunchie. The one he'd stolen from me back on the tour.

"I can't believe you still have that."

"Are you kidding? It's my most prized possession. What did you think, I lost it?"

"I hadn't thought about it, but yeah, I would've assumed it was long gone."

Planning to place it in my hair, I took it out of the box, but stopped when I felt the weight of something dangling from it.

That's when I noticed it, a massive, rectangular-shaped diamond.

Tristan took it from me before getting down on one knee.

"Emily, when I first met you, I liked you because you didn't know who I was. But I *love* you for the opposite reason. You're the one person who knows exactly who I am, knows every part of me, every vulnerability, every fear. The day I met you was the most important day of my life." He paused. "And today is the second most important day... if you say yes." He held the ring out. "Will you marry me?"

Too stunned for words, I simply cried, wrapping myself around him, feeling the way his heart beat against mine. "Yes," I whispered against his neck. I held my hand out as he placed the heavy rock on my ring finger. I looked down at it. "This is too much."

Tristan winked. "I had to get that million dollars back to you somehow."

My mouth dropped. "Oh my God. I would ask if you're serious, but sadly, I know you are." I wrapped my arms around him. "I can't even be mad, because I'm too damn happy right now."

"Me, too, baby. The only thing that could make this moment better would be knowing we have Jacob's blessing."

"You have to believe we do," I whispered.

Tristan went inside for a bottle of champagne. As he brought it back out, I thought I heard someone at the door.

"Is that the doorbell?"

"Yeah."

"Maybe it's Atticus?"

We checked the security camera to find a man standing next to a police officer. A cop car was parked behind them.

Tristan immediately headed to the door and opened it. "Can I help you?"

"Hi, sir. You don't know me—obviously, and I swear, I'm not a crazy fan or anything. My name is Bob Shields. My brother Ed here is a cop in town and let me know where you reside." The police officer nodded as the man continued. "You always give the police department a heads up when you're coming to Shady Hills so they can be on alert, and I asked him to let me know the next time you were here. When he told me you were back, I had him come with me, so your security didn't kick me out."

"Wise decision." Tristan nodded. "I don't actually have security here, although I probably should. But I checked the camera, and you're right. I wouldn't have opened if you weren't with a cop. Anyway, how can I help you?"

"I've been holding something I think might belong to you, unless there are two Tristan Daltreys in town, which I doubt."

He reached into his bag. To my utter shock, he took out Tristan's weathered, gray bear, Duffy.

Tristan's jaw dropped as he took the bear. "Where did you get this?"

"My son—he's ten—found it on the side of the road. I noticed it in his room. Asked him what the hell it was and read the tag that said to return to you if found. I told him we'd better do what it said, that someone out there might be missing this thing, as ugly as it is. No offense."

"None taken. And thank you. I appreciate this. I left it at my son's grave. Not sure if someone stole it, or if it blew away or what." Tristan stared at the bear. "Or maybe he wanted me to have it back."

"Anything's possible, I suppose," Bob said. "Anyway, I'm really sorry about your son."

"Thank you. I appreciate that." Tristan reached into his wallet and took out two crisp, one-hundred-dollar bills. "I'd like to give your son something for his kindness. I appreciate him not just leaving this on the side of the road." He held the money out. "Will you please take this?"

The man held his palms up. "That's not necessary."

"Please," Tristan urged. "It's the least I can do."

"If you insist, I'll take it. He's saving for a new bike, so this will really help."

"Well, good." Tristan returned his wallet to his back pocket. "What's your son's name?"

The man smiled proudly. "Jacob."

Don't miss Atticus and Nicole's angsty, earth-shatteringly passionate love story, *The Drummer's Heart,*
coming February 24, 2025.
Preorder now!
https://penelopewardauthor.com/books/
the-drummers-heart/

Other Books by
PENELOPE WARD

Acknowledgements

I always say the acknowledgements are the hardest part of the book to write. There are simply too many people that contribute to the success of a book, and it's impossible to properly thank each and every one.

First and foremost, I need to thank the readers all over the world who continue to support and promote my books. Your support and encouragement are my reasons for continuing this journey. And to all of the book bloggers/bookstagrammers/influencers who work tirelessly to support me book after book, please know how much I appreciate you.

To Vi – You're the best friend and partner in crime I could ask for. Here's to the next ten years of friendship and magical stories.

To Julie – Cheers to a decade of friendship, Rebel cheese, and Fire Island memories.

To Luna –When you read my books for the first time, it's one of the most exciting things for me. Thank you for your love and support every day and for your cherished friendship. See you at Christmas!

To Erika – It will always be an E thing. Thank you for your love, friendship, summer visit, and Great Wolf Lodge bar time—one of my favorite moments of the year.

To Cheri – It's always a good year when I get to see you, my dear friend! Thanks for being part of my tribe and for always looking out and never forgetting a Wednesday.

To Darlene – What can I say? You spoil me. I am very lucky to have you as a friend—and sometimes signing assistant. Thanks for making my life sweeter, both literally and figuratively.

To my Facebook reader group, Penelope's Peeps – I adore you all. You are my home and favorite place to be.

To my agent Kimberly Brower –Thank you for working hard to get my books into the hands of readers around the world.

To my editor Jessica Royer Ocken – It's always a pleasure working with you. I look forward to many more experiences to come.

To Elaine of Allusion Publishing – Thank you for being the best proofreader, formatter, and friend a girl could ask for.

To Julia Griffis of The Romance Bibliophile – Your eagle eye is amazing. Thank you for being so wonderful to work with.

To my assistant Brooke – Thank you for hard work in handling all of the things Vi and I can't seem to ever get to. We appreciate you so much!

To Kylie and Jo at Give Me Books – You guys are truly the best out there! Thank you for your tireless promotional work. I would be lost without you.

To Letitia Hasser of RBA Designs – My awesome cover designer. Thank you for always working with me until the finished product exactly perfect.

To my husband – Thank you for always taking on so much more than you should have to so that I am able to write. I love you so much.

To the best parents in the world – I'm so lucky to have you! Thank you for everything you have ever done for me and for always being there.

Last but not least, to my daughter and son – Mommy loves you. You are my motivation and inspiration!

About the Author

Penelope Ward is a *New York Times, USA Today* and *#1 Wall Street Journal* bestselling author.

She grew up in Boston with five older brothers and spent most of her twenties as a television news anchor. Penelope resides in Rhode Island with her husband, son and beautiful daughter with autism.

With millions of books sold, she is a 21-time *New York Times* bestseller and the author of over forty novels.

Penelope's books have been translated into over a dozen languages and can be found in bookstores around the world.

Subscribe to Penelope's newsletter here.
http://bit.ly/1X725rj

SOCIAL MEDIA LINKS:

Facebook
www.facebook.com/penelopewardauthor

Facebook Private Fan Group
www.facebook.com/groups/PenelopesPeeps/

Instagram
@penelopewardauthor

TikTok
www.tiktok.com/@penelopewardofficial

Twitter
twitter.com/PenelopeAuthor